JULIANE MAIBACH

ENTWINED FATES

Book 2
Goddess of Destiny

Chapter 1

D arkness. I perceive nothing but darkness and cold. Am I dead? I must be. I was engulfed by that endless sea of flames. Merciless and consuming.

"Hey, wake up, come on!" commands a familiar voice in an equally familiar unfriendly tone. It takes me a moment to realize I must be alive. Or did Ayden follow me to hell to haunt me there?

I open my eyes, feeling a little dazed. I'm still lying on the ground in the alley. Noah's gone. Only Ayden and Snow remain, and Yoru, who's sitting beside me and nudging me affectionately with his snout.

"Come on, get up," Ayden growls at me. "Noah's gone, the coward." His voice is full of hate.

I'm just relieved that the fight seems to be over for now. I pick myself up and stand on my shaky legs. I can still picture the flames that swept over me and engulfed me only moments ago. But my body shows no signs of this.

"Stop searching yourself for burns," Ayden snaps. "I can control my fire, so it won't harm you. Anyway, your key spirit also commands fire. Key carriers are generally more resistant to their own spirit's element."

I narrow my eyes and glare at him. "It's not fun watching a massive wall of flames rushing at you. How was I supposed to know it wouldn't kill me?!"

"You annoy the hell out of me, but you should know I wouldn't hurt you," he adds in a calmer tone.

"Go figure," I mutter, taking another look around me. Fortunately, Noah actually has vanished. And I really hope it stays that way.

"We should get out of here in case more Noctu show up," I suggest.

Ayden nods. "My bike's parked near here."

We leave the alley in silence. My knees are still quaking, and the memory of the fight is still vivid in my mind. Noah's a Noctu. I went on a date with him, thinking he was a normal human – even worse: a friend, who I liked a lot, and who I even imagined may become more than a friend someday. Is everyone I meet only interested in pumping me for information and using me?!

"Do you have anything to say about all this?" Ayden snarls. Again, I see the anger and impatience like a raging fire in his eyes. "I'm waiting!"

I sigh and wonder whether this guy is even capable of being tactful. "Why?" I reply, feigning innocence, which only provokes his anger more.

"Where the hell did you meet the guy? How did he even find you, and how could you be such a sucker? I mean, did you really have no clue? Can a person actually be that stupid?!"

I fold my arms across my chest. I don't even want to respond to these insults. What's wrong with the guy?

"How was I supposed to have a clue? I don't know any Noctu personally. Until today, I'd only seen those hideous monsters. I hadn't seen any that were still human. Or looked human. Apparently, you've already run into Noah a bunch of times. To me he was just a nice boy who I met now and then. I couldn't..."

Ayden stops in his tracks. He looks horrified. "Now and then?!" he parrots, drawing the correct conclusion. "You're saying you went out with him more than once?" He can't believe it. And somehow neither can I.

"Today was the first time I went out with him," I correct him. "Before that, I randomly ran into him three times. The first time was on a bus. He accidentally spilled his coffee on me."

Ayden sighs and rolls his eyes. "That was no accident. He knew for sure that you were a key carrier, and he wanted to make contact with you. He was probably keeping tabs on you for a while before that."

I swallow hard. That's a distressing thought. Did Noah really spy on me? For how long? In what situations? What does he know about me? I feel dirty and used. And I also feel a deep sense of unease, because if Noah's been watching me without my knowledge, then he can do it again.

"Didn't your fox ever notice that you were being followed?"

"He didn't *say* anything," I retort, feeling attacked. "And do you think I would have gone out with him if I knew he was a Noctu?"

He looks at me suspiciously, which leaves me speechless. But then, he finally draws the right conclusion. "No, not even you are that dumb."

"You're too kind," I snarl quietly.

We keep walking in silence, each preoccupied with our own thoughts.

"He was just trying to find out if I was actually a key carrier. Wanted to know if it was worth killing me," I muse aloud, feeling a pang inside. I was so stupid. This is the second time I fell for a guy who was only toying with me. But this time, it almost cost me my life.

Ayden shakes his head. "It wasn't just that. Noah kept saying he had plans for you. He probably wanted you to help him find out more about us, about our school, training, and abilities. You were supposed to be his inadvertent spy."

I swallow hard. Ayden's probably right. I immediately start running through everything I said to Noah and what conclusions he may have drawn. Luckily, I was careful. I picture his smiling face again, but his normally warm, cheerful eyes are scornful and cold. That makes me think of something else. I look at Ayden. The words are hard to say. But I know without a doubt that I have to say them.

"Thanks for your help. Without you, I probably wouldn't have survived that fight."

Ayden says nothing for a while, just stares at me, and then, after what feels like an eternity, he nods.

"Yeah, you're probably right."

Those words feel like another dagger in my heart. I was so happy when I learned how to send my odeon to Yoru. I believed I finally belonged in the world of the key carriers. And now I realize I still don't know anything, and I'm basically a complete beginner.

"My heart skipped a beat when I saw you with him on the other side of the street," says Ayden. His voice is amazingly calm, almost gentle. "I couldn't see him clearly from that distance, so I wasn't sure it was him, but I had a suspicion. And it turns out I was right. He singled out our weakest link and risked an attack. He's not stupid. He knew exactly what he needed to do."

"You say I'm the weakest link, but that's mainly because I don't know enough about your world. What has anyone ever told me about the Noctu and their intentions? How could I have guessed he was one of them?"

He gives me another one of those penetrating stares that makes me simultaneously hot and cold.

"They don't normally behave like that. It must have been all Noah's idea. That guy's capable of anything."

"If none of you saw it coming, how do you expect me to?"

Ayden sighs and shakes his head. We continue

along the street. The world around me seems surreal. Less than a half hour ago, I was staring death in the face, fighting with my key spirit against a Noctu, and now we're walking along a busy street, pedestrians who have no idea of what's really going on in their city casually passing by us.

"You're right," Ayden admits, and I can't believe my ears. "You had no way of knowing. And Noah's pretty smart."

I'm happy to hear these words, and I feel slightly relieved. It gives me the confidence to probe a little.

"You seem to know Noah pretty well."

He laughs and shakes his head. "No. I just had the dubious privilege of facing off against him in a few fights. But I'm not the only one. There are some other hunters whose encounters with Noah didn't go so well. But I know from those fights that he shouldn't be underestimated. He's really dangerous. Which makes it even worse that you got involved with him. I really hope you didn't give him any sensitive information about us."

I meet his gaze and refuse to be intimidated. I say in a steady voice, "I didn't tell him anything about our school. All he knows is that I'm at a school for gifted students and that I'm finding it hard. We really only talked about harmless stuff."

Ayden looks a bit doubtful, but he finally nods.

"If you say so."

We reach the parking lot, and I climb on the motorcycle behind Ayden. I was actually hoping I'd never have to sit on this hellish machine again. Ayden pulls out and turns onto the street. Our key spirits have long since left our sides. They're now hiding behind buildings, trees, or hedges. But they're nearby, and they'll keep following us, I'm sure of that.

"We need to report the incident to Mr. Collins," he says.

It's a strange feeling, being this close to him again, wrapping my arms around him and feeling his body under my hands. But right now, there's other things on my mind.

"You mean your father?"

He nods. It doesn't surprise me that he doesn't call him Dad when he's talking to me. Ayden's way too focused on his job and can only think about the school and the task at hand. His father's also his boss. If he referred to him as dad, it would make his father seem more human. And I guess there's not a lot of room for humanity in the world of the key carriers.

My stomach clenches at his suggestion. What will Mr. Collins say about all this? Will he believe

I didn't tell Noah anything about the school? Will he assume I willingly allowed myself to be used? Or will he just think I'm weak? Will he finally agree with Ayden's assessment of me and decide I'm unsuitable? Will I be kicked out of the school? For a moment, I wonder what that would mean for me. Could I just go back to my old life? And what would happen to Yoru? I really hope I never have to find out.

We stop in front of my house, and I climb off the bike.

"Try to get some sleep and don't think too much about earlier. We'll have a few things to explain tomorrow, so get some rest. You're going to need it."

"I don't suppose you have any reassuring words up your sleeve?"

That earns me a faint smirk. "I guess even thoughtful types like me can't brood all the time."

I know he's referring to something I said when we first met, which has become a kind of inside joke.

"Sweet dreams," he adds, then roars off.

I unlock the door, go up to my room, and flop on my bed, feeling perplexed. Before I close my eyes, there's one thought going through my head: hopefully, I'll wake up tomorrow morning and discover that this was all just a terrible nightmare.

Chapter 2

I hardly sleep all night. I keep thinking about Noah. His kind words, his smile, his friendship. And then the bitter truth. That arrogant grin, the contempt in his eyes. And then, I hear the cracking hexes that rained down on us during the fight. This can never happen again! I can't allow myself to be used like that again. But does this mean I have to expect the worst from everyone I meet? Am I prepared to go through life like that?

What weighs on me even more is the knowledge that Noah wormed his way into my life. How much does he really know about me? Only what I told him? What will he do with that knowledge?

Then, a sudden realization makes my blood run cold. When Max baited the Noctu and got us into that fight, I fled and ran into Noah. Another encounter that was definitely no coincidence. Noah took care of me and even escorted me home. I didn't think about it at the time, but now I realize what a grave mistake that was. He could show up here anytime and do something to me or – even worse – my mom. But wait – he's known for a while where I live and has never shown up here. Then again, he didn't show his true colors until now. I know I need to tell Mr. Collins about it today. But it won't be easy.

I sigh and get up. It's still way too early, but I can't go back to sleep anyway. I shower, dress, and go downstairs to the kitchen, where I make myself a coffee, then sit down drowsily with my hands wrapped around the mug.

When someone appears beside me, I flinch so violently that the coffee spills on the table.

"Sorry, I didn't mean to scare you," says Mom, scrutinizing me. "Why are you up so early?"

I'm really not a morning person and normally stay in bed and savor every last minute. So, Mom's surprise is totally justified.

"I couldn't really sleep last night."

She pulls up a chair and sits beside me.

"Is something wrong? Did something happen at school?"

I shake my head and attempt a smile. I'd love to tell someone about everything I'm going through right now, but my mom's the wrong person. I would have to tell her the truth about my school, tell her about Yoru, and then about the fight. Would she let me stay at the Siena Hartford Academy? I doubt it. She'd be so shocked that she'd pull me out immediately. And that's not what I want. As weird as it sounds, I can't and don't want to leave the world of the key carriers.

"I just slept badly. I probably drank too much coffee yesterday," I say, but I can see the doubt in Mom's eyes.

"Alright, well, I hope you feel better soon."

I nod and try to change the subject.

"How was work? You must be tired."

She nods and suppresses a yawn.

"You know how I move between the different wards depending on where I'm needed? Well, this week I'm in orthopedics. Thankfully, it's way more relaxed there than in emergency surgery. At the moment, it's mostly older patients in the ward for hip replacements, or recovering from broken bones."

I know from what Mom's told me in the past that it's not always easy dealing with elderly patients. They often come from care homes and have dementia, so they're sometimes hard to handle.

"Are they still mentally fit?" I ask.

"Most of them aren't, unfortunately. Tonight, an elderly man climbed out of his bed again, even though we had the bars up. He wouldn't let me take him back. Luckily, Chloe helped me. She's currently doing shifts in orthopedics too. We finally managed to calm him down."

"Sounds like an exhausting night."

She stretches and yawns.

"Yeah, but don't get me wrong – I wouldn't trade it for anything. It's a great feeling at the end of the day when you know you've helped people. And they often express their gratitude – even if it's just with a warm smile. Chloe told me again today how happy she is with her job at the General Hospital. There are clinics where the atmosphere is nowhere near as collegial and where the working conditions are really tough."

"I'm glad you're happy there."

"Yeah, I get along especially well with Chloe. She wants to come visit us sometime. Maybe I'll make my carrot cake."

"If you let me know when she's coming, I can do that," I offer. Partly out of self-interest, although I love my mom more than anything, she's not a gifted cook or baker.

"That's sweet of you, honey. But you have enough going on right now, and I can manage a cake," she says with a wink.

"If not, just say it's a brownie. That will explain the dark color," I tease, and Mom elbows me gently on the side.

"I'm going to bed. Have a great day."

She kisses the top of my head and goes upstairs. I empty my coffee mug and brace myself for the conversation with Mr. Collins that I'm sure is coming.

I sit at my desk, watching the classroom door. Our math teacher Mr. Klein will show up any minute, but I'm expecting to be called to the principal's office before that. Part of me hopes so because I want to put the conversation behind me as soon as possible.

"I was expecting a lot more from that party," Lucia says at the desk beside me.

Max is sitting on her other side, and she nods in agreement. "The music was shit; the food was a joke; there wasn't enough alcohol, and everyone there was totally boring," Max summarizes. She turns to me. "You didn't miss anything. How was your date, by the way?"

I should have known the question would come, but I've been too busy thinking about Noah to come up with a cover story.

"It was nice," I say, trying to casually play it down.

"Hmm," says Max, then she comes to sit beside me so she can look me straight in the eye. "Doesn't sound great. Did it go that badly? I thought you were just friends. Or did he want more?" Her eyes widen. "Or did you want more? Did he brush you off?!"

All I manage is a loud snort. She's my friend, but there's no way I'm telling her the truth. I doubt anyone at this school would have much sympathy if they knew I went on a date with a Noctu.

"We decided not to see each other again, at least for now." That's what I hope, anyway. I get that uneasy feeling in the pit of my stomach again. What if Noah ambushes me again – maybe in front of my house?

"Aw, that sucks. That bad, huh? If he turned out to be a total asshole, I hope you let him know and told him what you thought of him."

Hmm, with all the fighting key spirits and flying

hexes, it was hard to find the right moment. But I guess even he must realize I wasn't thrilled about his murderous intentions toward me.

Lucia tries to make light of the situation. "Men," she says, rolling her eyes. "Who can make sense of them?"

"Tell me about it!" groans Max. "Most of the ones I meet are total idiots. Like at that party."

The fact that she's bringing it up again means the evening must have been a really low point in her party life. I feel sorry for her.

"Ayden wasn't even there. He said he was coming. And I haven't seen him today either," Max continues.

"His bike's in the parking lot. He must be in the residence," says Lucia.

Apparently, someone's keeping a record of Ayden's presence and absences.

"Maybe he just had another late night and he's sleeping it off," Max muses. She looks at me. "It's not like it's the first time he's come late or not shown up at all."

I wouldn't put it past him to stay out clubbing all night, even after a serious fight. Maybe that's exactly the distraction he needs to clear his head. I just can't get the images out of mine – but there's no way I'd throw myself into the nightlife or the arms of some guy because of that. I instantly picture Ayden with some girl. Disgusted, I roll my eyes and try thinking about something else.

To my relief, Mr. Klein arrives, and the class begins. But I struggle to focus on the work. Maybe it's a good idea to speak to Mr. Collins alone first. I'm pretty sure Ayden won't back me up if his father decides to throw me out. And there's no getting around the fact that I'll have to talk to him at some point. I mean, I made a huge mistake, and I'm already under close scrutiny...

I'm relieved when the class ends. I decide it's best to go face the music. I can't concentrate in this state. I need to clear this up. I take a deep breath and brace myself – I won't give up easily. I want to stay in this school.

I tell Max and Lucia I have something to take care of. They look doubtful, then they shrug and disappear down the corridor. I square my shoulders and try to order my chaotic thoughts. Then, I head to the principal's office.

Just at that moment, there's an announcement over the loudspeaker that makes my stomach churn.

"Teresa Franklin, please come to the principal's office. Miss Franklin, if you could please come to the principal's office."

I can guess what this means. Ayden must have gone to him already and told him everything. I was anxious before, but now my instincts tell me to expect the worst. I should have gone to him sooner myself.

Chapter 3

The school secretary waves me straight through to his office. I knock briefly and then go inside with a hollow feeling in the pit of my stomach. Once again, I mobilize all my strength for this battle.

"Mr. Collins," I begin as soon as I enter. "I don't know what Ayden's already told you, but please believe me when I say that I never would have let Noah..."

"...get away, if there was any way you could stop him," a voice interrupts.

Bewildered, I look to my left. Leaning against the wall with his arms folded, not far from the principal's desk, is Ayden.

"I already told Dad all about the fight. I explained that you were out with a friend from your old school and were on your way home when Noah attacked you out of nowhere. Snow sensed the release of odeon, and we followed the trail. We fought Noah, but he managed to get away."

He shoots me a warning look, then turns to his father.

"You know how good he is at using his key to open the doors in the Odyss during a fight. In the end, he escaped through one of them."

I can hardly believe what I'm hearing, and I just stare at Ayden dumbfounded. Why is he helping me? Why did he protect me by telling his father this story instead of the truth?

"Noah's a very skilled fighter," Mr. Collins says, interrupting my train of thought. "He's one of the best, but unfortunately there are others like him among the Noctu."

Ayden snorts with contempt. "They're not stronger than we are. They just have the advantage of being able to use the doors in the Odyss in a fight. They've been occupying and defending the Odyss for a long time. If we got control of it, we could..."

His father shakes his head. "Ayden, we've discussed this so many times. The Council and the other hunters and I have racked our brains over that often enough. It's just too dangerous, a total suicide mission. We need to find other ways of defeating the Noctu. Trying to invade their territory, their home, is no solution."

Ayden growls quietly to himself. He makes no secret of the fact that he disagrees with his father on this point.

"Can I ask a question?" I chime in. As usual, I understand hardly any of this conversation, and it's making me uncomfortable. "Who's the Council?"

It takes Mr. Collins a moment to realize I'm serious.

"Sorry, I keep forgetting this is all new for you." He clears his throat. "Well, we have a Council that meets regularly to discuss new developments. That includes reviewing fights and attacks involving Noctu. There are also discussions about counter-measures and tactics that can be used to ultimately stop our enemy. But also, about deaths, newly discovered keys, and new candidates. The Council is made up of hunters and members of prominent families who have been fighting on our side for a long time. Obviously, I'll be informing them of the attack on you and Ayden, and we'll consider appropriate action."

"Which means you'll send out a few of us hunters again to release some odeon and bait a couple of low-ranking Noctu." Ayden pushes himself off the wall and takes a couple of steps toward his father, who's still sitting behind his desk. "Just admit it already – we'll never draw out their best fighters that way. It's only the fallen that wind up in those traps. And they'll die anyway, sooner or later."

"You know as well as I do that they keep themselves alive with the breath of a dying person. That's why the Noctu hunt so voraciously."

"It's irrelevant," Ayden interrupts him. "The fallen are insignificant."

"Would you say that if one of them killed you or someone you care about? Wouldn't that make you want to destroy these creatures? Don't underestimate them. You know how many of us they've already taken out."

Ayden snorts again. I can see the anger bubbling up in him. He's about to say something else, then shakes his head and heads for the door.

"I guess that covers everything." He opens the door and looks at me expectantly. "Are you coming?"

For a moment, I'm stunned, indecisive about whether to say more to Mr. Collins. Wouldn't it be better to tell him the truth? Noah knows where I live. But then I'd be forced to tell him the whole truth, and I'm pretty sure that would mean being expelled from the school. It wouldn't be Mr. Collins' decision alone. The Council would decide, and I doubt they'd tolerate such carelessness – especially not from someone who's totally new to this world.

I turn and follow Ayden as he storms out of the office.

"How can anyone be so stubborn and dogmatic?!" he rages, and I'm pretty sure he's not pissed at me for a change. "Nothing but caution and inaction. We'll never achieve our goals that way. And I don't want to keep watching our people get taken out."

"Have you ever lost someone close to you?"

Ayden stops abruptly. Apparently, he's already put me out of his mind. He looks at me and nods. "Hunters who were friends of mine."

"That must be really hard." I leave it at that because the pain of losing someone can't be put into words, and it's no use trying to sugarcoat it. "Thanks for not telling your father the truth."

"He'd kick you out of school if I did. The

Council would insist on it. I mean, you got involved with a Noctu, who pumped you for information and probably had you under surveillance."

"I never thought you'd change your mind and actually do something to help me stay in this school." I give him a wry smile and lean against the wall. "I figured you couldn't wait to see the end of me."

Ayden sticking up for me and preventing me from being expelled is a pretty unexpected development.

"It wasn't your fault," he says, leaning against the wall beside me. I get a whiff of his wonderful scent, and when he turns his face toward me, I look into his deep green eyes, which are like windows to another world: simultaneously exciting, mesmerizing, and dangerous. "Noah manipulated you and took advantage of the fact that you still don't know much about our world. You thought he was a friend, and you were bitterly disappointed. That must have been really hard."

I swallow. Is this some kind of apology for his own behavior? He did something similar to me. Can he finally see how painful that kind of deception can be?

Ayden's standing so close to me that I can feel his body heat. And whether I like it or not, it feels good. So do his words.

I want to say something, but my head's empty. My heart is beating fast though, and it reminds me of the moments when Ayden manipulated me. It still really hurts. I can't forget that. But maybe someday I'll be able to forgive him, even if that moment still hasn't come.

"Noah's one of their best fighters," Ayden continues. He gazes into the distance, lost in thought. "Even if we opened the door to the Odyss with our keys, it would be crazy to attack them there without a solid plan. But if we had more information about the place and about the Noctu stationed there... It would be a valuable opportunity for the hunters. And that's why we need Noah. He knows his way around the Odyss better than anyone. He knows all the doors and probably also where the Noctu live in there. We just need to get our hands on him."

I frown as the significance of Ayden's words slowly sinks in. He pushes himself away from the wall abruptly and stands directly in front of me. His green eyes sparkle with zeal. Fire and ice shoot through me.

"You're the key to that. Noah made contact with you and tried to pump you for information. But to gain your trust, I'm guessing he told you things about himself. Maybe something that could be useful to us, or something that could help us locate him or lure him out."

I stare at him incredulously. So that's why he wants me to stick around. He's hoping I can give information on Noah so he can track him down and overpower him. He just wants to find a way for him and his people to enter the Odyss safely. Bile rises in my throat, and I try to control the nausea. None of this was about me!

His incredible eyes are still gazing at me. I can see something like hope in them. I shove Ayden aside roughly and snap at him, "I don't know anything about Noah. And if you think you can use me, or my mom, as bait to lure him out so you can catch him, you can think again. I'll never ask for your help."

With that, I storm off down the corridor and leave him standing there.

Chapter 4

It's been a few hours, but my emotions are still bubbling over. Ayden was trying to take advantage of me again for his own selfish purposes. When will I learn? Every time I think I see even the smallest spark of kindness in him, it always turns out to be a big mistake. Furious, I go get my books from my locker for the next period.

What makes Ayden think I have information about Noah that could help him? And he's willing to put me and my mom at risk. Then again, I never told Ayden that Noah knows exactly where

I live. If I did, he'd probably camp out in front of our house and wait for his archenemy to show his face. I doubt Noah would be that dumb. He's smart enough to anticipate that tactic. Even so, I can't dismiss the fact that Noah still poses a threat to me. But I'll deal with that myself. I'll never ask Ayden for help. Especially not after he tried to manipulate me again.

My phone vibrates, signaling an incoming message. I pull it out of my jeans pocket and see that it's from Leah, one of my best friends from Tucson. She still sounds sad about having to cancel her visit with Sue and Tonya.

"How are you? I hope the pressure at school eases off soon and that things are going okay for you. It sounds tough. But just because we don't live in the same city anymore doesn't mean we're not here for you. We all miss you so much! We're going shopping this afternoon, so we'll be thinking of you. Hugs, Leah."

I feel really bad having to shut my old friends out of my life. But everything's so complicated right now I don't even know where my head is at. How would I keep it all secret if they visited me? And more importantly, how could I keep them out of harm's way? It's just too big a risk.

I write a short reply, full of empty words, then

put my phone away and head to training. I try not to think about the fact that I'll see Ayden there.

I catch up with Max and Lucia in the locker room. "You've been in a really bad mood since you went to see the principal," Lucia observes. "Is it really that stressful, having to fill out some forms?"

That was the best excuse I could come up with at the time.

Max cocks her head and says, "No, I think it's more about the guy she had the bad date with."

I hate to admit it, but she's hit the nail on the head, even if the circumstances are nothing like what she thinks.

"Trust me, I'm not wasting a single thought on him," I reply, wishing that were the truth. Max seems to sense this, but she just nods and keeps her opinions to herself.

We enter the gym together. We're the last to arrive. The others are already gathered around Mr. Laydon and Ms. Rupert.

"Today, I want you to focus on rationing your odeon so that your key spirits can hold out as long as possible. We'll come around and discuss with each of you what you can improve on and what needs attention."

The students nod and get to work. I glance at Ayden, who's walking to the other end of the hall.

Snow slinks out of the shadows and pads up to his master's side. Ayden doesn't even acknowledge me with a glance, but that's typical. He's only interested in me if I'm useful to him. I sigh. I'm about to go use the fitness equipment when Ms. Rupert says "Ms. Franklin, wait a moment please."

It can't be anything good. I wonder what the two teachers have in store for me. I bet it's nothing helpful.

"We said we'd think about assigning you a training partner."

My brow creases, and I don't let the teacher finish speaking. "Yeah, I remember. But you said you'd only do that if I didn't make any progress. And I've learned how to send odeon to Yoru now."

The two teachers exchange a meaningful glance, from which I can clearly read that they consider that insufficient.

"See, the thing is," begins Mr. Laydon, searching for the right words, "that's a big step, and it shows that you're making progress..."

"But not fast enough," I say, to put an end to his pussyfooting.

I've realized by now that my late start here at this high school and my lack of family heritage makes me a rarity, which means that half the time they don't know what to do with me. Both of them have been trying to provide assistance, like they're doing now, but it only makes me feel like more of a pariah.

"You can be really proud of what you've achieved so far. Just look at this as additional assistance that will help you progress even further," says Ms. Rupert.

Yeah, but will my training partner see it that way? I quickly scan the room and wonder whether the student they've selected is already aware of their good fortune.

Who would I even want to train with? Preferably Lucia or Max, I guess. At least they're my friends. Anyone but Ayden, although I have to admit it's thanks to him that I learned how to send my odeon to Yoru.

"Ms. Mitchell?" Mr. Laydon calls across the room. A girl turns around. She minces her way over to us, and I roll my eyes in dismay. Actually, can I please have Ayden as a partner?

"You wanted to talk to me?" asks Amber. She looks me up and down. Amber's a friend of Lucia and Max. I had the dubious pleasure of meeting her once when we all went to a club, along with Kate. Both Kate and I arrived at the conclusion that it was best to stay out of Amber's way.

"Ms. Mitchell, we'd like you to supervise Ms.

Franklin for a while. We want you to train together as a team, and you can take her under your wing, give her tips, and help her progress."

Could this be any more humiliating? Where did these guys do their teacher training? Guantanamo?

Amber gives me a sugary smile and says, "Sure, I'm happy to help."

Yeah right. Her fake smile doesn't convince me.

"Great. Good luck you two. We'll come by occasionally to see how you're doing."

"Oh, I'm sure we'll be fine," purrs Amber.

"Yeah, totally," I say, aping her sickly, sweet tone. I follow her to a corner that's a little less crowded, and she turns her head. A bird instantly flies down, presumably from one of the rafters, and sits on her shoulder. A small kestrel if I'm not mistaken.

"This is Lancelot," she says.

I bite my lip to stop myself from laughing out loud. I guess it's unfortunate that most of the students name their key spirits when they're small children. Some of the names they come up with are really corny.

"Okay, tell me what you can do. I mean, other than attacking unsuspecting people out of nowhere," she adds with a scornful smirk.

Great, she has to remind me of my first training

session, when I let Ayden provoke me so Yoru transformed and attacked him.

"Well, I figured out how to find my odeon and send it to Yoru," I say, ignoring her provocation.

Amber raises her eyebrows. "And?" She gestures with her hand as if she's waiting for more.

"Uh, we can create a few fireballs. But why are you asking me this? The whole class trains in this hall. You must know what I can and can't do."

"I was hoping there was more and those disappointing performances weren't all you have to show for yourself." She looks at Yoru and sighs loudly. "What a waste. You of all people having a fire spirit, and you can't even make use of its power. Such a tragedy."

"That's why I have you," I retort. "I'm sure I'll make fast progress training with you, and then my poor key spirit won't be so underutilized."

"Uh, that depends on you. It's not up to me." She turns around and scans the room. "Monica, can you come here for a minute?"

"What's the plan?" I ask. "You're bringing Percival into it? Then the round table will be almost complete."

Amber responds to my comment with an icy glare. But I'm already distracted by the tall girl walking toward us. Her stature reminds me of

Ms. Rupert. She has impressive biceps, and her leg muscles are well defined under her leggings. She looks me up and down casually, but she also radiates this hard-ass attitude that makes me wonder if she even knows how to smile. A small monkey is dancing around at her side. It can't keep still, and its bright, playful nature is in total contrast to her.

"Monica's one of the best in class," says Amber. She turns to the tall girl. "Can you help us out? I want to see how Teresa conducts herself in a fight and then give her some tips to help her improve."

I spin around and hiss furiously at her, "What is this? Are you trying to offload me?! You know I'm supposed to train with you."

"And that's what we'll do," she says. "My job is to give you tips, and that's easier if I can watch you and figure out what your weaknesses are."

"You know you're not a teacher, right?"

She shrugs. "I'm supposed to help you, and that's exactly what I intend to do. I guess you'll just have to accept my way of doing things. Or should we go straight to the teachers and tell them you want to stop? I wonder what they'll say about that."

She strikes a mock-thoughtful pose with a finger on her chin, and I force myself to swallow the words that stick in my throat.

"Let's get started," suggests Monica. Her little monkey is now hopping around and shrieking as if it can't wait for the fight to begin.

I nod because I obviously have no choice. It's not like she's going to kill me.

The monkey transforms immediately. It grows, and its fur takes on a silvery hue, glittering strangely. I can see glowing red symbols all over the monkey's face. But its eyes are the worst part. They look huge and somehow... crazed.

I look at Yoru and try to send him some odeon, but the monkey has already reached us and shoots a huge stinking fountain of water out of its mouth, trying to drown us.

Yoru jumps out of the way, and so do I. But the water has a life of its own. It turns into a column that bends and chases after me.

"You're way to slow," Amber remarks. "That's never going to work. You need to get Yoru to transform."

"Oh really?! I never thought of that."

"See? That's what I'm here for."

I could strangle Amber right now, but unfortunately, I have my hands full. I leap aside as the water thunders down toward me, escaping it by a hair's breadth. I'm really struggling to concentrate on anything, or even settle on an emotion. But then Amber proves helpful in that regard: I only need to glance in her direction and my rage almost boils over. I hold on to that feeling and let it spread through my body until fills me up. It shoots through my veins, then it leaves me abruptly. I don't even need to look – I know Yoru received the odeon and has already transformed.

The monkey flies through the air with a blood-curdling howl. It's holding two blue spheres in its hands. The moment they hit the floor, they turn into huge waves and surge toward us.

"Don't just stand there. You need to do something," Amber commentates.

"What can she do?" Monica scoffs. "You can see just by looking at her that she's no fighter. Look at her stance. She's never even held a dumbbell in her hand."

"Don't need to. I just hold my can of Coke and lift it when I want a drink," I yell at her as I'm running. I really have better things to do than talk smack, but this woman is getting under my skin.

"And she has a big mouth," Monica observes. "How did she even wind up here?"

"I don't know, she must have something going for her," says Amber. "But I'm afraid it's just her powerful fire spirit, which is basically useless as long as she has it."

The waves tower over us. I get the impression they're actually swallowing all the light. I'm speechless, experiencing firsthand what it's like to face a tsunami. Another experience I could really do without.

"You're still too slow," says Amber. "You really need to pick up the pace."

"Great tip, really helpful," I snarl. I turn my head as Monica lets out a loud cry. She claps her hands together and stamps her feet as if she's trying to do a New Zealand war dance. Her monkey grows even bigger and wilder. He hurtles toward us at such incredible speed that I can hardly keep track of his movements. Then, the waves break over us. I rush to Yoru and try to summon all my strength and send it to him.

"Yoru, now!" I cry. He opens his mouth, and a big stream of fire shoots out of it. It's aimed directly at the waves, hits them, and generates such enormous heat that the water turns to steam.

"Great! Keep it up," I shout to my key spirit, but I can feel myself becoming empty, tired, drained. I try to sustain it.

The waves evaporate in front of us. I jump excitedly in the air, and at that moment, something hits me from below. I forgot about the damn monkey

– a mistake that will stick in my memory for a long time. My opponent's key spirit just spat a massive fountain of water at me, which is now surrounding me. I'm knocked to the floor, swept along by the water, and I can't breathe. It's not until I slam against the wall that the water finally disappears.

I open my mouth to gasp for air. A big mistake. "Eww," I groan, shaking my arms so that the sticky liquid flies off me in streams. "Gross! That's disgusting!"

Monica shoots me a nasty look. "Yeah, water comes in many forms."

I gradually become aware of the stench that's clinging to me. It smells so bad I almost throw up.

"So, that wasn't exactly glorious," Amber remarks. She's standing in front of me with her arms folded, looking down her nose at me. "There were so many mistakes in there that we need to go through. I don't even know where to start." She wrinkles her nose. "That stuff smells especially bad on you. I wonder why."

She giggles, turns around, and high fives Monica.

The first thing I need to do is get under a shower. I can't stand this a second longer. I walk across the hall, dripping, with all eyes on me. I notice one face in particular: Ayden's eyes look as stormy as a wild ocean or a volcano that's about to erupt.

Apparently, I've failed again and made him wonder if maybe it was a mistake to cover for me in front of his father. Because I'm still good for nothing when it comes to sparring.

Chapter 5

I stand under the shower for what feels like an eternity, repeatedly reaching for the shower gel and lathering myself. I feel so disgusting and humiliated. I have no idea how I'm supposed to work with Amber as my training partner. After today, it's clear to me that it's not going to be a walk in the park. Every part of me dreads going back out there and facing Monica and her spitting monkey again. I admit it, nobody's going to do me any favors in a real fight. But at least I'll be spared the moronic comments.

I close my eyes and enjoy the feeling of hot water on my skin a while longer. Then, I dry off and get dressed. I'm still wondering how this is going to play out. Do I really want to subject myself to Amber in the long-term? Can I handle it, stay strong, and actually get something of value out of this scenario? I'm not so sure. I'm about to put my phone in my pocket when I notice I have a message. Maybe Leah replied.

I open it and can't believe my eyes.

"Hey Tess, how you doing? Recovered from the fight? Noah."

I hold my breath and stare at the letters, which don't seem to make any sense. My first thought is so trivial that I almost laugh at myself: I forgot to delete Noah's number and block him. I read the short message again, and its meaning slowly sinks in.

"What the hell is this?" I whisper to myself. Why is Noah messaging me? And why these lame questions? There's only one explanation: he's trying to scare me. But I can't figure out why. I delete the message. I'm about to block his number, but I pause with my finger over the screen. Is that a good idea? He could just use a different phone and keep harassing me. I need to get myself a new number. But then what? There's a risk that he'd just find another way to contact me. He could wind up at my front door, or worse – harass Mom at the hospital.

That idea is worse than anything. Even if I could somehow protect our house, there's no way I can do that at the hospital. Noah knows where my mom works, and he can find her there any time. For now, I need to play along and find out what he wants from me. I quickly type a reply.

"You must be insane messaging me like this as if nothing happened! You tried to kill me. How do you think I'm doing? Stay out of my life and don't go near my mom!"

I'm not about to take any risks, but I want to give him a piece of my mind. It never pays to let people think you're intimidated by them. He needs to know who he's messing with and that I won't let him ruin my life.

I flinch when a reply comes in a few seconds later.

"Nice to see you're back to your old self. I'm glad. And don't worry, I don't plan to involve your mother or harm her in any way. So you can relax. Have a nice day, catch you later."

I'm staring at my phone again. If the others could see me, they'd think I'd lost my mind. But I can't help it. I scan the message over and over and try to read between the lines. At first glance, his reply seems bland, harmless, but I suspect there's a lot more to it. What am I supposed to make of it?

He says he won't do anything to my mother, but can I believe him? And by saying he doesn't want to hurt her, is he implying that he wants to hurt me? And then the last part: "Have a nice day, catch you later." It sounds like a threat. That I should make the most of what time I have left, because Noah's going to come for me again soon. An icy shiver runs down my spine, and for a moment, I can't breathe.

I feel like I should tell someone, and the first person I think of is Ayden. But then I remember our last encounter. He'd be happy to learn that Noah's still interested in me. Ayden would try to use me to get to his nemesis. And I'm tired of being their punching bag. I delete the message and make my way home.

Noah could have ambushed and attacked me anytime. But for some reason, he prefers tormenting me via text. I want to know what his intentions are, and I won't let him scare me.

When I arrive home and open the door, I hear laughter and two voices talking. A little surprised, I go to the kitchen, where I find Mom drinking coffee with another woman. At first, all I see is a slim figure from behind, with dark hair drawn up into a bun.

"Oh, Teresa, you're home early." My mother glances at the clock and raises her eyebrows. "It's that late already?! Wow, I totally lost track of time."

The stranger now turns around and greets me in a friendly tone. "Hello Teresa. Nice to see you again."

I realize it's Chloe, Mom's colleague.

"Would you like some cake?" Mom asks, nodding at a plate on the table containing various delicacies. "Chloe's visit was totally spontaneous, so we just bought a few things. Help yourself and don't worry, none of it's burned."

"You know I don't have a sensitive stomach," I say with a wink. I fetch myself a plate and select a mini chocolate cake that looks incredibly tasty. I sit with them at the table, pour myself a cup of coffee, and savor the first bite. After a difficult day, this is just what I need.

"How was school?" Mom asks as she watches me devour my cake.

I wave my hand dismissively and roll my eyes. "Don't ask."

"Sounds like you had a hard day," Chloe guesses. "Your mother told me you go to a school for gifted students."

I nod. "But that doesn't really apply to me. They just took me because of my writing talent."

"Don't be so modest," says Mom. "You're perfectly capable of keeping up with those overachievers; otherwise, they wouldn't have taken you. You should be proud of what you've achieved."

"Do you like it there?" Chloe asks.

"A lot of things still aren't easy. But the school is actually really cool and I'm glad to be there."

"But it's problematic for society to think along such lines and create the kinds of institutions that only serve to increase inequality in the world, don't you think? I mean, for one thing, it creates the impression that the students at this school are somehow superior. But at the same time, there's a lot of pressure on them. They have certain standards to live up to just so they don't fall through the cracks in the system."

I raise my eyebrows in astonishment. Chloe's right, in a way. But I'm attending this school now, and I'm not about to let out of some sense of social justice. And anyway, is this really a topic I want to discuss when I'm trying to calm my nerves with cake?!

Mom just laughs and shakes her head. "That's typical Chloe. She always wants to change the world."

Chloe shrugs. "Only in areas where the fight isn't hopeless. I'd never champion a lost cause."

"If you're referring to the patients again..." Mom begins, but Chloe shakes her head.

"Don't worry, I know that's just the way you are, and you can't help it. But I'm telling you, if you put your heart and soul into every case, you'll burn out one of these days. Sometimes we have to accept that it's best to just get the job done and not become personally involved with the patients."

Mom shakes her head and puts down her coffee mug.

"I could never do that. When someone needs help – and sometimes it's just a few kind words of encouragement – then I'm there. And I can't help thinking about my patients outside of work now and then. That's totally normal." She glances at me and explains, "We're both float pool nurses, and we were recently in the maternity ward together. It's generally lovely working there, but last time we were there, one of the babies suddenly fell very ill."

This is news to me, but I can understand why Mom didn't tell me about it. It must be so hard when the really little ones are suddenly in a life-threatening situation, and you have no choice but to watch them lose the battle. I can't bear thinking about it.

Chloe gives her a warm smile that softens her harsh words.

"I know that's just how you are, and that's one of the things I like about you. But I want you to take care of yourself. You can't always be there for everyone."

I can see that Chloe's words are gnawing at Mom.

"In any case, we see life's ups and downs, day in and day out, and that should make us enjoy the time we have, don't you agree?" Chloe reaches for another cake and takes a bite. She rolls her eyes with pleasure. "It doesn't get any better than this, right?"

"No," laughs Mom. "Coffee, cake, and great company. What more could a girl want?"

She helps herself to another piece of cake too.

"Well, maybe Dr. Carter's smile. Have you seen his dimples?" Chloe raises her eyebrows, and Mom bursts out laughing.

I stand up.

"I think I'll go now, before it gets too risqué. Then you can discuss all the dimples, teeth, eyes, and whatever men's body parts you like."

I give my mother a kiss and leave the kitchen. I

hear them both laughing again behind me. Some of the stuff Chloe says is a little weird, but she seems nice. And the main thing is that Mom likes her. I'm happy that she's found a good friend.

Chapter 6

Just try it. It's not like you have anything to lose," Amber says with a condescending smile that I'd really like to wipe off her face. I've been training with her for two weeks now, and my aversion to her increases every day.

I'm supposed to get Yoru to conjure and throw some kind of ring of fire – I have no idea how – and all the while Max, Lucia, and Monica are sitting around me on the floor, watching.

"Shouldn't you guys get back to your own training?" I hiss.

"We're taking a break to help you," Max reminds me.

I know they mean well, but it's not very helpful.

"You need all the help you can get," Monica chimes in. "If I were you, I'd be asking myself if I even belong here. You still can't do much of anything."

"Thanks for the exceptionally motivating appraisal," I snap. "Most of you started from a totally different place. You grew up in families who prepared you for the challenges at this school, in this world. I didn't have that, and I don't mind saying I'm proud of what I've achieved in the last few weeks."

"Pretty low standards," Monica mutters.

I open my mouth to say something, but Mr. Laydon interrupts.

"Okay, break's over. It's great that you want to help your friend, but that's enough for now. Ms. Franklin has an excellent training partner, and she'll be fine."

Lucia and Max comply. But Monica doesn't seem ready to give up.

"What do you say? Should I spar with her again? That was fun."

"Don't get too cocky. I learn quickly, even if you don't think so," I growl.

But Amber waves her away.

"We need to keep working on Yoru." She regards my fox with an icy stare. "I still don't understand why you got a fire spirit." She shakes her head as if to banish the thought, and then claps her hands. "Give him some odeon and get him to produce a ring of fire. Come on!"

"I have no idea how to do that," I say again.

"You need to teach him by sending him various odeon pulses. They're basically silent commands."

I roll my eyes but try to follow her instructions.

"This is hopeless!" she exclaims after a while. "Is your fox retarded? I mean, he did choose you after all. Maybe there's something wrong with him." She goes up to him, tugs at his ear, and looks into his face. "He looks kind of demented to me. Hey, is he cross-eyed?"

Yoru closes his eyes and whimpers. I go straight over and grab her hand, forcing her to release him.

"You indulge him too much," Amber lectures. "Either you're doing it all wrong, or he's refusing to obey you. You need to show him who's boss. Otherwise, you'll never stand a chance at this school."

"I'm not going to hurt Yoru no matter what you or your freakish friend say."

"You know what?" Amber snaps at me. "You're

a failure, just like your retarded fox. You're both pathetic."

"Coming from you, that's something I'll definitely take to heart."

Our altercation doesn't go unnoticed. Mr. Laydon comes over and asks, "What's going on here? Are you two arguing?"

Amber pastes on a sugary smile and says, "Yoru's being difficult and won't obey certain commands. I was trying to tell Teresa that she shouldn't let him behave like that. But she won't listen."

"Ms. Franklin, what Ms. Mitchell says is true. Now and then, key spirits can be a bit uncooperative, but it's at those times in particular that you can't afford to show any weakness."

"Let's get one thing straight – I'm not going to punish him!"

The bell rings, signaling the end of the period.

"That's enough for today," I mutter and walk away, leaving them both standing there.

"Ms. Franklin, I'm talking to you!" the teacher calls after me.

But I just keep walking. I'll probably be in trouble, but right now I couldn't care less.

I take my sweet time in the locker room, take a long shower, and then get dressed. By the time I'm finished, everyone else is gone. I leave the locker room and flinch when I see a figure leaning against the wall opposite of me. I'm really not in the right frame of mind to deal with Ayden right now. My mood reaches a new low. I walk past him without a word, but I stop when I hear his voice behind me, speaking in a surprisingly gentle tone.

"How are you?"

"Since when do you care?"

He rolls his eyes and pushes himself away from the wall. "You're doing really well in there."

This statement is unexpected, especially coming from Ayden.

"You think?" I ask sarcastically. "Considering the fact that Amber and Monica humiliate me every day, and the teachers see nothing wrong with that, then I guess you're right. But unfortunately, that doesn't change anything."

"Yeah, you're not learning too much from them," he observes.

At least we can agree on that. But I can't help making another cutting remark.

"You should be happy. There's a good chance I'll be kicked out of school."

So far, I've managed to avoid looking at Ayden in the eye, but I'm so angry right now that I figure I can resist the effect of his deep green eyes and their magical magnetism. Just for a moment, I think about how beautiful they are and how they remind me of glittering emeralds. His face is flawless too and could belong to a really well-paid model. But I know what kind of person is hiding behind that alluring façade.

"I've come to accept that I'm not going to get rid of you so easily, and that you have a pretty combative spirit."

"If that's meant to be praise, you could really use some practice. Why are you saying all this, anyway?" But I already know the answer. "Oh, I get it. You're still thinking about Noah, right? You want me on your side in case I can reveal something useful about him." I look at him again and see his eyes widen, and I know I've hit the nail on the head. "You're repulsive," I say.

Then, I turn and leave him standing there. But he catches up to me with a couple of strides, grabs my arm, and spins me around. I'm so surprised that for a moment, I'm speechless.

Suddenly his arm is around me, his eyes flash, and I can feel the tension in his body.

"You got me all wrong. I'd never put you in danger, don't you know that by now? And I've given up on the whole Noah idea. You don't want to do it? That's fine by me."

I can't believe what I'm hearing, and it takes me

a while to process his words. It doesn't help that Ayden's right hand is on my arm and his left is around my waist. It's as if I can feel his fingers burning my skin through my clothes. And that gaze, which unfortunately still hasn't lost its power over me. Those deep green, fathomless eyes... the power in them – like a violent storm buffeting me. We're so close, too close, and I can't deal with it right now.

"I just wanted you to know," he says, and his tantalizing breath caresses my skin. Then he lets go of me.

I stare at him incredulously. "Was... that some kind of apology?"

He smiles and shakes his head, amused. "Call it whatever you like. I just wanted to tell you that."

"Would it be so terrible if you had to admit you made a mistake?"

"You're so obstinate," he says, but without any sharpness in his voice. "Anyway, now you know I'm not trying to use you for anything, so hopefully that clears the air. And I won't tell my father about the thing with Noah. You can trust me to keep it to myself."

I nod, but I'm not sure what to make of this conversation. My heart leaps because his words mean so much to me.

"Don't tell me you're suddenly okay with me staying in school."

"I wouldn't go that far," he teases, but the twinkle in his eyes softens his words. "You're pretty hard to get rid of."

With that, he turns and walks away from me. Before he goes through to the residence, he calls out, "Don't let them get you down!"

I stare after him, speechless. A peace offering from Ayden? I can't believe it. But my heart flutters with relief. It would be nice to have at least one fewer person against me.

Chapter 7

On the way home, I can't stop thinking about what Ayden said. Is this another one of his games? I don't really believe that because he sounded genuine. Then again, he still hasn't apologized to me. And I don't want to be too gullible when it comes to him, despite everything.

I picture his face again. His features looked much softer, not as harsh as usual, and I got to see that incredible smile again. But I now know that he's acutely aware of his good looks and the effect he has on people. And he has no scruples about exploiting those traits. So, I try to push him out of my mind.

I turn into my street and look around for Yoru. He normally shows up at this point to come inside with me. But I can't see him anywhere. I'm almost at the door, and as I turn around again, I notice movement. I walk a few steps toward it, quietly calling his name. But to my surprise, it's not my little fox that appears. A figure stands up. He must have been sitting near the door, concealed by a shrub.

The grin on his face is cold as ice, and for a moment, I'm so stunned that I can't move. I forget to breathe, and my heart skips a beat as I look into those bronze-colored eyes watching me with amusement.

"Finally. I was starting to worry you were at a friend's place and would never show up."

Noah's words slowly penetrate the dense fog of thoughts flooding through my mind. What is this? What's he doing here? This is the guy who tried to kill me last time we met.

I finally regain control of my body. I step back and call out to Yoru, who has also recognized the danger and is now rushing to my side.

I'm fully aware that Noah's too strong an opponent for me. Even Ayden can't easily defeat him.

So I should do everything I can to avoid a fight. But if there's no alternative, I want to be ready. I assume a defensive stance and try to concentrate on my emotions and latch on to one in particular. That's not difficult in this situation because I'm incredibly angry. I focus on this feeling to help me transfer enough odeon to Yoru so he can transform and fight.

This doesn't escape Noah's attention. He cocks his head and keeps grinning at me in that way he does, which until recently I found kind of sexy. Now, all I see in it is malice and callousness.

"Hmm, I was afraid you might be a little upset about what happened."

Most of my fear fades into the background to be replaced by a sense of disbelief. I raise my eyebrows and glare at him, full of hate.

"Upset?! I'm upset?! I'm out of my mind with rage, hatred, and disappointment. And not just because you lied to me this whole time. You also tried to squeeze supposedly sensitive information out of me to pass on to your people. And as if that weren't bad enough, you then tried to kill me. So the word 'upset' doesn't really cover it."

"Let me set the record straight: I was trying to kill Ayden, not you."

"Oh really? That's not how it looked."

He shrugs. "If I really wanted to kill you, I had so many opportunities before that night. Why would I wait so long?"

I shake my head helplessly. "How am I supposed to know what goes through your sick brain?! The fact is, you attacked us and almost defeated us. And believe me, even if it's true that you only wanted to kill Ayden, that doesn't make it any better."

"Really? I thought you couldn't stand him and he was making your life difficult. That's how it sounded in your messages. Even before you mentioned his name, I could guess who it was. Trust me, I've had the dubious pleasure of encountering Ayden a number of times. The world would be a better place without him. And by the way, every time we meet, he tries to end me."

"We're not in preschool. I don't give a shit which one of you had the toy first and tried to hit the other one over the head with it. This is no game. This is about life and death."

Noah laughs, and all I can do is stare at him, totally dumbfounded. He just stands there, bent double with laughter. Finally, he wipes a tear from the corner of his eye.

"You really have a way with words and so much energy. It's just fun being around you. That's what I like about you."

"If this is how you show your affection, you really need therapy," I snap. I stare at him again. He's just standing there in front of my door. Luckily, Mom's at work, but he's already shown up there under the pretext of reading to patients. His real reason for being at the hospital... I don't even want to think about that. Anyway, he knows too much about my life.

"Just tell me why you're here? Are you trying to threaten me? Are you going to hurt my mom if I don't feed you information about our school?"

He shakes his head and slowly takes a couple of steps toward me. I instinctively retreat, and Yoru protectively positions himself in front of me and makes growling noises. I can't see Noah's black wolf Rain anywhere, but I'm sure he's just well hidden.

I cling to the knowledge that Noctu only risk attacks in empty streets and areas where there's nobody around to see. If there's a chance they could be seen by other people, they don't dare pick a fight.

Because if humanity found out about them, some kind of war would break out. And that definitely wouldn't make it any easier to capture people's dying breath, which they so desperately need to survive.

"Tess," Noah says in a cool tone. When he realizes I'm still retreating from him, he stops advancing. "I'd never do anything to your mother."

He gives me that strange grin and cocks his head.

Okay, not my mom, but what about me?

"You still haven't told me what you want from me."

"I basically just wanted to see how you're doing after that fight, and make sure you didn't draw the wrong conclusions."

"Don't worry, I didn't," I snarl.

He smiles with relief. "Good, I was really worried about that. Obviously, I realize I've lost some of your trust, but it feels like we've taken a step in the right direction today."

He tries to come closer, and I step back again. When he sees this, he just nods and doesn't seem particularly concerned.

"It was nice to see you again, and I'm glad we could clear a few things up."

He raises his hand with a mischievous smile, and I prepare myself for a counterattack. But he just waves.

"See you next time."

He takes out his key, inserts it in an invisible lock, opens a door that wasn't there a moment ago, and disappears through it. I stand rooted to my spot, staring at the place where he vanished, not daring to breathe. When nothing else happens, my tension melts and I slump, exhausted and agitated.

Chapter 8

What the hell was that? I lean against the door after closing it behind me and try to organize my thoughts, with my heart in my mouth. Noah must have lost his mind, I keep thinking. He can't be serious. Not after everything that's happened, everything he's done. The guy's insane.

"The question is, what am I going to do about it?" I whisper to myself. Yoru looks up at me, and I see something in his expression that looks like a readiness to fight. "No, we're not ready. Not yet.

We can't get involved in any fights. First, we need to find out what Noah really wants because there's no way I'll accept his bizarre apology."

I go up to my room and can't help but glance over my shoulder again. Noah's appearance scared me, as much as I resent that. He established that he can show up anytime and threaten me.

I throw my school bag in a corner and sit by the window. I automatically scan the street, but he's nowhere to be seen. I seem to be safe from him now. Still, that can change at any moment. Maybe that's what Noah was trying to tell me. He calls the shots.

But if he really wanted to kill me or Mom, he's had plenty of opportunities to do that already. So what's his game? In my mind I hear him saying, "I never wanted to kill you, only Ayden." As if that's any better. But a small part of me believes he's telling the truth. He doesn't want to kill me. At least not yet. But why?

Yoru springs into my lap and nestles up to me.

"I wish I didn't have to wreck my head over this guy now too."

I ruffle Yoru's fur and try to come up with a solution. I know I could ask for help. I could go to Ayden – he's dealt with Noah several times, if only in combat. But something holds me back from trusting him. Yeah, maybe that's just it: trust. I just can't trust him anymore. If Ayden knew, he would immediately come up with some plan without consulting me, and I don't want that. This is about me, my mom, and my home. I want to be the one to decide, or at least be involved in the decisions.

"Noah will show up again," I say to Yoru. He looks at me with what I interpret as a serious expression. "And I'm pretty sure he won't do anything to me. So we'll just stick to our plan and try to find out what he really wants from us."

I'm so lost in thought that I jump in fright when my phone vibrates in my pocket. A message. I have a bad feeling as I take it out and look at the display with bated breath. But it's not from Noah, it's from Kate. Relieved, I breathe again and read it.

"Hey, I was wondering if you're free? Mom's at a friend's so I could come round to your place. Maybe we could go see a movie later."

I reply immediately and invite over. It's exactly the distraction I need.

I brew coffee while I'm waiting. Before long, the doorbell rings. I open it and give Kate a big hug.

"I'm so glad it worked out," she says cheerfully.

"Yeah, and it's great that we have so much time."

She hangs her jacket, and we go through to the kitchen.

"Mom's at a friend's party. So hopefully she'll be out late."

"And instead of using the time to study, you'd rather meet up with me? I'm really not a good influence on you," I joke, using the words her mother said to me the first – and only – time I met her.

"That's a matter of opinion," she says, sitting down at the table as I place a steaming cup of coffee in front of her.

"How's school?" I ask.

She shrugs. "Okay, I guess. Seeing Maria's sad face has been cheering me up lately." She giggles. "I know I shouldn't indulge in schadenfreude, but Maria deserves it. She's still in a funk because Ayden disappeared again so quickly. I heard it had something to do with his father getting a job on the other side of town, but I guess you know better than me." She looks me in the eye. "Or maybe not, because hopefully you don't have a lot to do with him and he's leaving you alone."

"We don't talk much and try to stay out of each other's way. But he was as shocked as I was about us winding up at the same high school again."

Kate sighs loudly and puts a sympathetic hand on my shoulder. "That's really bad luck. I was hoping you'd finally be free from him."

"I can handle it. We have a few classes together, but the school is big enough that we don't run into each other constantly."

We go up to my room. Yoru's curled up in his favorite spot by my bed. He lifts his head as we enter.

"Hello, Yoru," Kate says, crouching down beside him. He goes straight to her and nestles his head in her hand. "He's so unbelievably sweet," she says, sitting on the floor beside him. Yoru accepts the invitation and curls up in her lap. "Does your mom know about him now?"

I shake my head. That's another thing I really need to take care of. But I've just had so many other things on my mind.

"I'm still waiting for the right moment."

Kate strokes his fur.

"When she sees him, she won't be able to say no. He's so cute." She looks at him fondly, then suddenly frowns. Her fingers stop moving through his fur and she says, "That's weird. Are his spots getting lighter? Is he molting? Does an animal's fur change color when they molt?"

I swallow hard and don't know what to say. Kate's supposed to see him as a cat with red fur and black spots. That alternate appearance is the natural protection that all key spirits have to allow them to move around among ordinary people without attracting attention. And until now, it's always worked on Kate. I have no idea why she's starting to see changes. Maybe she's just imagining it. But she still sees Yoru as a cat, and that's the main thing.

"Yeah, maybe he's molting," I say. "There's a lot of his hair around the place."

"It suits him, anyway. Foxy red without spots – that would look great on him too."

The way she describes his color makes my heart race. I stand up and pick up my math homework.

"I know it's not fun, but since you're here, could you take a quick look at these math problems?"

She stands up, and Yoru leaps off her lap and returns to his spot by the bed. Good, now he's out of her line of sight, and hopefully out of her mind too. As she explains the math problems to me, I keep glancing at Yoru, who's now asleep. Why can Kate see his real fur color coming through? Does my key spirit need energy from my odeon for this illusion? It sounds plausible, so I guess I need to release more odeon for him to maintain his camouflage. I look at Kate, who's started writing calculations on the paper. Would she tell me if she noticed other changes in Yoru?

Chapter 9

"You'll love the movie," Kate promises as we step out of the bus and walk the rest of the way to the movie theater. We're early, so we have plenty of time. "At least, I've heard it's hilarious."

I shake my head in amusement. "You're a walking film guide."

"I love movies," she admits. "I don't often get the chance to go see them, thanks to Mom."

I put my arm around her shoulder. "We're going to have fun."

She nods and smiles, and we continue down the street.

Thanks to all the training I've done lately, the steep streets don't tire me out anywhere nearly as much as they used to, although my heart's still pounding in my chest.

"This is nothing," says Kate, slightly out of breath. "Filbert Street is the steepest in the city, with an incline of 31.5 percent. You get super puffed walking up there. And driving down it, you need to really step on the brakes. But as you know, there are loads of streets like that. Another thing I love about this city. There's always something interesting to see. And all the stories."

We cross a quiet street and pass a narrow side alley. It's badly lit, and I start to get a bad feeling. I shudder and feel like I'm being watched again. Is that just Yoru? Or are we in danger? I want to get out of here as fast as possible, to a bigger, brighter street, with other people. But Kate stops and doesn't seem to notice my anxiety. She's still in tour guide mode.

"But there are a few places that aren't so nice, where horrible things have happened." She nods toward the empty alley and looks at it with a somber expression. "In 2011, Phil Kennwood was attacked here. Based on the evidence, the attacker must have come out of nowhere. They took his valuables and mangled his body pretty badly. The killer was never found." She's silent for a moment, still looking into the alley. "I wonder what his last thoughts were. He had just left work, probably thinking about the evening ahead, maybe planning dinner and looking forward to a quiet evening. And then something like this happens. He's attacked and torn apart in this alley. He screams and fights back, but he doesn't stand a chance. The attacker strikes, the victim curls up into a ball to protect himself. It all happens so fast. One heavy blow and Phil Kennwood breathes his last, his empty eyes staring up at his murderer as they riffle through his clothes without remorse and take all his valuable possessions. It amazes me how anyone can be so vicious."

I'm still staring into the alley, and it's almost as if I can see the dead man lying there. An icy chill creeps up my spine, and the urge to get out of here as quickly as possible becomes even stronger.

"Sounds like you know all the San Francisco stories – even the really macabre ones," I observe.

"Sorry." She glances at me, aghast, then avoids my eye. "I got a little carried away."

"All good," I say, trying to play it down, and we continue on our way, which instantly helps me relax. We turn a corner, and my sense of humor returns.

"You should design a sightseeing tour. I'll bet there are tourists who'd love all that stuff. The sinister side of San Francisco."

She grins. "That would be a great way to drive my mom crazy."

"I can just imagine. You should really think about it -- just seeing her face would be priceless."

She laughs and shakes her head. We arrive at the movie theater and buy tickets. Kate has picked out a comedy for us that I know nothing about. We treat ourselves to jumbo popcorn with butter and sink into our seats. But as soon as the movie starts, my thoughts begin to wander. I'm reminded of the feeling I had when I peered into that dark alley. I'm probably just on edge because the place reminded me of the alley where Noah attacked us. My nerves are a little raw these days.

Noah. The name ghosts through my mind, and I instinctively glance around the dark movie theater. The light from the screen flickers across the room, casting spooky shadows on the walls. I scan the faces of the moviegoers and breathe a sigh of relief. He's not here. But the fact that I can't feel safe anywhere, and keep looking out for him whe- rever I go, makes it clear I'm still in shock after his sudden appearance at my house. I try my best to concentrate on the screen again. I really don't want to give him that much power over me.

"Boy did that make me laugh," says Kate as we leave the theater. "What do you say we grab a burger? There's a place not far from here that has the best burgers in town."

I'm still full from the popcorn, but I really feel like something savory. So I shrug. "Sure, why not?"

We walk to the burger joint, and Kate's in high spirits, relaxed and babbling happily about everything under the sun. All the anxiety she usually carries around seems to have vanished. A little freedom from her mom obviously does her good.

"I'm having such a great night," she says.

I have to agree, and I slowly start to relax too.

We buy burgers and stroll down the street with them. Kate wasn't exaggerating – the food is incredible. I only wish I weren't already so full.

"What did I tell you? Delicious, right?"

I nod and take another bite, then it happens again. My vision starts to flicker. I curse silently. Not again. But I can't do anything to stop it. My field of view narrows, darkens, with flashes of light shooting across it. I squeeze my eyes shut and take a deep breath. Keep calm, I tell myself.

Kate's beside me. Naturally, she doesn't fail

to notice that something's up with me. She says something, but I don't really hear her. When I open my eyes, I pray that the attack has passed, but it's even worse. I can see it totally clearly: a dazzling light dancing through the air. For a moment, I'm stunned, unable to believe what my vitreous opacity is making me see. The golden light is stuck to a person, a man walking down the street. Without thinking twice, I start moving. In a matter of seconds, I'm running, pushing past pedestrians as I try to get to that light. It's so clear, so real, so bright and piercing that it can't just be my vision impairment. It must be real; it must mean something.

A group of tourists is standing in my way, and it takes me a few seconds to fight my way past them. I burst through the group, my heart pounding, stagger, then keep running. I finally reach the guy, grab his arm, and turn him around. He stares at me in astonishment. He's an elderly man with thinning gray hair. He's wearing glasses. His eyes are pale blue, and they look at me mistrustfully. I frantically look him up and down, but there's nothing – no light, no glow, just an irritated stranger.

"Can I help you?" He sounds really annoyed.

I gradually become aware of my surroundings and realize a few passersby are staring at me. A group of young people are talking loudly, apparently in party mode.

"I'm sorry, I thought you were someone else."

"Tess?"

I turn around, astonished and a little embarrassed.

"James," I say.

He goes to my school and was one of the first people I met there. Like me, he also found his key by chance and wasn't prepared by his family for the bizarre world of the key carriers in which we live. I slowly notice the rest of the group. There are two other boys and a few girls, but I've never seen any of them before. And I doubt they go to our school. I notice another young man standing a short distance behind the others, and my stomach clenches instantly. Ayden. He's looking at me again with that piercing glare that I can feel in every cell of my body. The feeling's not pleasant, nor is the expression on his face.

"Are you okay?" James asks. "You look like you saw a ghost."

"I'm... I'm okay," I stammer. Fortunately, the old man has already left. But the others must have seen what just happened.

"We're on our way to a party," says James, glancing at the others. "Friends of ours. They're not from our school, but that often makes it more fun," he says with a mischievous smile. "Want to come? Judging by your face, you could use a diversion."

I'm about to shake my head when Ayden interjects.

"I doubt she'd be into this party. And she looks like she really needs to go home and get some rest." He looks at me again. "Is everything okay?"

The question seems like an afterthought, and he could have saved his breath.

"Thanks for your concern," I growl. "Everything's great. I just thought I saw someone I knew."

"Yeah, sure, the guy had one of those totally ubiquitous faces," he says ironically. "I can't help wondering who you thought he was."

"Let's go," one of the girls says quietly. She's tall and slim with thick dark curls. She hangs off Ayden's arm and bats her brown eyes at him. "We're missing all the fun."

"I already told you I won't stay long. I have things to do."

"Oh, don't be like that," she says, pressing up against him. I feel sick. "Come on, give yourself a break. Can't you take care of it another time? The party will be lame without you."

I roll my eyes, raise a hand in farewell, and turn

on my heels. "Have a great time."

Why does his behavior irk me so much? He can do what he wants. But every time I see him, he drives me nuts. I hurry back to Kate, who's keeping a safe distance from Ayden.

Chapter 10

I still haven't decided which subjects I want to take. It's obviously important that I graduate with a high school diploma, so some classes are unavoidable. And there are others I'm still trying out. I'm interested in biology, and I need two science subjects for my diploma, so I've already settled on that. But the teacher, Ms. Warren, moves at a really fast pace.

I try to follow her explanation of how odeon transforms into key spirit energy. In a nutshell, I would just call it nourishment. Again, my pen flies across the paper as I jot down various words and phrases that I hope I can make sense of later.

"To control the precise amount of odeon and guarantee a targeted supply," she continues, adding more figures to her comprehensive diagram, "you take the number of effective hexes per day, times the elemental power, and divide that by the spirit's weight. Please take into account the varying strengths of the elements. We know that fire spirits are the strongest, so we apply a factor of three there. Wind is a little more economical, so we use the lower value of 2.65."

Lucia is sitting beside me and doesn't even try to write anything down. Either she's a total biology whizz or she's thrown in the towel.

"My brother's done all this stuff, and he was really good in school. He studies medicine now. He often helps me study for exams," she explains quietly as I try desperately to scrawl down what Ms. Warren is saying. "Save yourself the trouble. If you like, we can study together. That's way more useful than scratching out confused sentences on paper."

Ms. Warren turns back to the whiteboard and starts drawing obscure symbols on it, and I finally put down my pen. "I give up," I say in a huff and lean back in my chair. It's probably a better use of my time just to listen attentively, then maybe I'll understand more of it. But after a few minutes, I realize that's not the case.

"Odeon is pure energy, and it's directly absorbed by the nerves and sent to the muscles. Pay attention to your key spirit's eyes. Are they dull? What does the fur or skin or scales look like?"

"This is biology, right? Not some class for aspiring key spirit veterinarians?"

Lucia grins. "Yeah, but when you see the exam, you'll keep asking yourself that. Don't worry, we'll prepare ourselves. Ms. Warren always announces the topics that are going to be in the exams and recommends a few reading texts. You'll be fine."

I really hope so; otherwise, I'll be forced to choose a different science subject. My eyes wander to the seat ahead and to my right. It's empty. Ayden and I only have a few of the same classes, but this is usually one of them. I don't even want him in my life or in my thoughts. I don't want any guy to take up this much of my headspace. But all I can think about is where Ayden might be. I guess he had a late night. It kind of seems out of character because he's given me the impression that the school and his role as a hunter are his top priorities. The only thing he seems to care about is fighting the Noctu.

At that moment, the door opens, and someone enters. I can't help snorting irritably. When you think of the devil...

Ayden mutters, "Sorry, I overslept," and takes a seat.

Ms. Warren shoots him a warning look.

"It's not the first time you've come late to my class. If it happens again, I'll have to take it up with the principal."

I wonder how much that will achieve since the principal is Ayden's father, but maybe that makes it even worse. Who knows how strict Mr. Collins is with his own son?

Ayden says nothing, just takes out his things and throws them on the desk but makes no move to start writing. He seems to think note-taking is futile too.

Ms. Warren continues drawing her diagram, and I tilt my head a little in the hope that I might understand it better from a different perspective. This jumble of lines and circles could basically mean anything. I hope I get to study with Lucia and her brother otherwise, I'll flunk this course.

I glance at Ayden. How can anyone follow this stuff so attentively? I have to keep stretching or at least shuffling my feet so I don't nod off. Suddenly, his head lolls forward, and his right arm slides limply off his lap. My eyes widen, and I take a closer look. He doesn't move at all, and his breathing is slow and even. There's no doubt about it – Ayden's asleep. I guess someone partied hard last night, judging by his late arrival and then falling asleep in class.

Apparently, I'm not the only one who's noticed. A boy behind him leans forward and gives him a gentle shove.

"Hey, Ayden."

Ayden flinches and slowly turns around, drowsily running his hand through his hair.

"You were asleep," says the boy.

Ayden mumbles something, then props his head on his right hand and looks down at his open book – or pretends to. When the bell rings shrilly at the end of class, he nearly jumps out of his skin.

"Looks like he had another hard night," Lucia observes, gathering up her books.

"Does it happen a lot?"

She shrugs. "Now and then. Ayden sure knows how to have fun. And as long as his grades are good – which they are – the teachers generally just give him warnings."

Lucia leaves the room, and I gather up my things. Just as I'm about to head out, Ayden blocks my way. I guess he didn't see me because he looks at me in surprise. "Sorry," he says and steps aside. He looks pale, and there are shadows under his eyes. It really does look like he had a hard night.

"You probably should have stuck to your plan and gone home early. You look wrecked," I say.

There it is again, that smug, arrogant smile bearing down on me.

"Don't worry about me. It would take several long nights to really knock me off my feet," he says, quoting something I said the first time we met. He walks past me without another word and leaves me standing here. I really need to stop thinking about him.

Before I head out of the locker room, I take a deep breath. The training sessions have never been my favorite periods. But since I've been forced to work with Amber, I've developed a real aversion.

Amber's already waiting for me in the center of the hall. As soon as she sees me, her expression darkens. Apparently, she doesn't enjoy our time together either. At least we have one thing in common.

"I'd really like to do some endurance training today," I say, hoping to escape her prescribed assistance.

"Suit yourself," she says with a smirk that

couldn't be creepier if she tried. I don't need to be told twice, and I start jogging. Yoru runs at my side, matching my pace.

"You should push your key spirit harder. You're not challenging him."

I respond to her tip with a withering glance and just ignore her.

"That won't achieve anything. At least get him to double back now and then or try sending him odeon while you're running. That would be a useful exercise."

"I'll try that some other time," I retort.

Amber rolls her eyes and huffs loudly. "How am I supposed to help you if you won't listen to me?"

"Maybe I don't need your help," I snarl, unsure if she even heard me.

"What's going on here?" Mr. Layden butts in, approaching Amber.

"Teresa seems to be in a bad mood today. She won't even listen to my suggestions."

"Ms. Franklin, what's this I'm hearing?" the teacher asks me.

I go to him, try to catch my breath, and say "I just want to run a few laps with Yoru and work on my endurance. Why do I always have to do a thousand things at once?"

"Because you need to be able to do that in a

fight. You need to run, evade, summon your odeon, send it to your spirit, and guide him. The sooner you learn that the better. Ms. Mitchell is absolutely right."

"I never said I was fundamentally against it, it's just that right now I want to do what I feel like for once."

"And waste time," says Amber.

I take a deep breath and try to stay calm, which is really hard. I bite back my anger and turn to Yoru.

"Come on little guy, let's practice a few things while we're running."

This time I act as if I'm sending Yoru commands. I keep changing my pace, so he's not constantly at my side, in the hope that Mr. Laydon finds nothing to object to. But Amber, who doesn't take her eyes off me, sees through my tactic.

For the remainder of the class, I try to take her instructions on board and comply with them. But since the two of us don't get along, the results are negligible. At the end of the class, I'm frustrated and out of breath.

I stay under the shower long enough to be sure Amber's left the locker room when I come out. Max and Lucia are still in front of the mirrors, blow-drying their hair.

"What a horrible training session," I say as I join them.

Lucia pulls a sympathetic face. "Amber drives you pretty hard."

"Parades me around more like."

"She doesn't mean it that way," says Lucia. "She's just a little overzealous, and really stubborn. Once she's decided on a course of action, she sticks to it mercilessly. And now you're on the receiving end of that."

"And she's obviously determined to drive me crazy."

Lucia smiles and shakes her head. "No way."

"Try paying more attention to what she says," suggests Max. "Amber's not a bad fighter and Lancelot's pretty powerful. You could learn a thing or two from them."

"I have my doubts that she even wants me to," I say. "To me it seems more like she's trying to hold me back and make me look stupid."

"Everyone's responsible for themselves in the end," says Max coolly. "See it as a challenge. Or do you think you're not up to it?"

I say nothing for a while, not sure what to make of that. On one hand, she's right, but on the other hand, it sounded pretty harsh.

Lucia puts a soothing hand on my shoulder.

"We could train with you sometime too. Maybe that would help so that Amber doesn't torment you so much. We're here for you, anyway."

Max nods and hugs me.

"We're friends, and nothing's going to change that."

"Thanks guys," I say with a sigh.

Maybe they're both right, and I just need to try harder. I decide to bite the bullet and train a while longer today.

Chapter 11

To my amazement, Ayden wasn't in the gym, and I wonder if he's so tired from his long night that he's actually skipping his afternoon training.

I shower a second time, and my stomach growls loudly. I have no desire to cook, so I decide to get takeout and visit Mom at work again. That instantly makes me think of Noah. Hopefully I won't see him there. Then again, maybe it wouldn't be such a bad thing because then I could find out if he's hanging around my mom.

I order Chinese on the way and grab a few spring rolls for Mom, which she loves. The closer I get to the hospital, the more anxious I become. I glance around, but there's no sign of Noah. Yoru follows me, sneaking through the bushes on the other side of the street to remain unseen. He seems to sense that I'm looking out for something. In any case, he keeps an eye on me and the passersby and tries to stay as close to me as possible.

We arrive at the hospital without encountering any trouble. Yoru and I separate at the entrance – I don't feel great about this, but I can't take a cat into the building. Anyway, I'm sure Yoru could find a way inside without being noticed. I know him pretty well by now; nothing and no one can hold him back – he'll always be nearby. With this sense of certainty, I enter the foyer and ride the elevator up to the maternity ward where Mom's currently working.

Visiting hours are over, and the new mothers are taking the opportunity to rest. The corridor is totally empty. Behind some of the doors I hear women's voices in conversation, and behind others I hear crying babies.

After all that time, and the exertion of childbirth, they can finally hold their children in their arms. It must be an indescribable feeling. Although, this joy is sometimes short-lived as I know from my mom. It doesn't happen often, but sometimes a baby has to go into intensive care. I can't imagine what the parents must go through.

I've never been in this ward before, so I need to find the nurses' station first. I'm walking down a corridor when one of the doors suddenly opens and a nurse comes out pushing a buggy with a newborn wrapped in warm blankets.

He's crying, his head is bright red, and he's being returned to his mother. I guess it's just been taken for an examination, and the poor little thing isn't impressed.

The nurse doesn't notice me because I'm walking diagonally behind her. She only has eyes for the screaming newborn, whose little fists are clenched and shaking with outrage. But I recognize the nurse. It's Chloe. I'm about to go up to her and say hi.

"Hey, hey, hey," she says to the little one, "what's with all the screaming?" She bends over the child and places a finger on his forehead. The baby tries to look at it and suddenly becomes very quiet. I can't tell why. Was it Chloe's voice, the strange gesture, or the fact that they stopped moving? Anyway, I just stop and watch Chloe, who still only has eyes for the child.

"That's better," she says, and continues on her way. The newborn seems to be staring intently at her, even though I'm pretty sure babies that small aren't capable of that.

"Don't look at me like that," she says, and her voice sounds weird. Am I just imagining it or does she suddenly sound distant, aloof, cold even?

She bends over the child again and murmurs, "It won't help. I've made my decision, and you can't change my mind."

Even though I'm sure I didn't make a sound, Chloe turns around. There's a grotesque smile on her lips that makes her look almost lunatic, and I take a step back. I feel dizzy. I glance around, see a handrail, and grab it to find my balance. When I look back at Chloe, she's still smiling, but the crazed expression is gone. She looks just as friendly and open as always.

"Teresa?" she says in a totally normal voice.

What did I just witness? Was it my imagination? Was I mistaken? I'm not sure what to think.

"Are you here to see your mom?" she asks. Is that a hint of nervousness in her voice? I have the feeling she's speaking slightly faster than usual. As if trying to... distract me from something?

"Uh, yeah," I say, unable to take my eyes off the newborn, who is still staring at Chloe.

"Oh, I'm just taking little..." She seems to realize mid-sentence that she's forgotten the baby's name and has to check the nametag on the buggy. "...Connor to his mother. She's waiting. I tested his hearing. Everything looks good." That strange smile again. "Your mom's in the lunch room. Things are a little quieter right now so she's on a break."

I just nod, and Chloe waves goodbye.

"Have fun you two," she says.

Then, she opens a door and takes the child in to his mother.

I shake my head, baffled. I noticed last time we met that Chloe can be a little strange at times. In that moment, she seems to lack compassion and warmth. But maybe that's just her way of protecting herself from all the suffering she sees every day at her job. Maybe Chloe's lost patients in the past – maybe even a baby like this one.

I find my mother sitting at a table with another nurse. She's drinking coffee, which isn't unusual for my mom at this hour. She has to stay awake somehow during her long shifts.

"Tess," she says happily, coming to greet me with a hug. "So good to see you." She nods at her colleague. "This is Holly. She works permanently in this ward, not in the float pool like me."

Holly is tall, slim, with a roundish face and friendly brown eyes.

"Nice to meet you. Your mom's told me so much about you. It's so nice of you to visit her at work. And you even brought something to eat! I hope my children will do that if I ever have any. I haven't found the right man yet. But who knows what the future holds?" She gives Mom a knowing look and stands up. "I should get back. See you later, Maggie."

She leaves the room, and I sit at the table with Mom. I take her spring rolls out of the bag.

"Oh, those look delicious. And I'm starving. We were so busy today. It was like working on a production line. One birth after another. We had to prepare the rooms and then take care of the women and the little ones. But I really like it here. The work is so different in this ward." She bites into a spring roll and looks at me enquiringly. "How was school?" She glances at the clock on the wall. "It's late. Did you have classes until now?"

"No, I stayed after to do some more training. You know I'm a little behind."

"Please don't overdo it. Working out is good, but don't exhaust yourself. You shouldn't have to stay so late after classes every day."

"I'm taking care of myself," I say with a reassuring smile. "Hey, have you seen Noah lately?"

I just had to ask. She looks a little confused.

"You went out with him a few nights ago. Did something happen? Why do you ask? I mean, aren't you two communicating anymore?"

I hold up my hands in a placatory gesture. "No, no, it's all good. I was just trying to remember when he comes here to read to the patients."

Mom frowns thoughtfully. I'm not sure if she buys it.

"I haven't seen him lately. But the Read and Dream program is mainly for patients who can't read to themselves anymore. So the volunteers don't usually come to this ward."

I nod slowly. I should have thought of that. Still, Noah could have found some flimsy excuse to come looking for her, so I'm relieved she hasn't seen him.

Maybe he was actually telling the truth: he's not interested in my mom and has no intention of using her to advance his own agenda.

"And you're sure everything's okay? You two didn't have a fight? You look kind of anxious."

"I'm just tired. It was a long day."

I can see the concern in her face, but she knows me well enough to know there's no use pressing the issue. I try to change the subject.

"Will you work late tonight?"

She nods. "I want to stay late. We're so busy and need all the help we can get, and I want to relieve Chloe. She's worked so many extra shifts lately."

"Chloe," I say slowly, trying to choose my words carefully. "Does she enjoy working on this ward?"

I poke around pensively in my chop suey carton.

"She's doing great work, and she's always at hand when she's needed," she says. "Why do you ask?" Then she answers her own question. "Oh right, you saw her. Did she seem a little frosty with one of the mothers? She sometimes sounds brusque, as if she doesn't care about the patients. But that's just her manner. She's actually way too compassionate, so she has to be careful that the work doesn't get to her. Otherwise, she wouldn't last long in this job."

"But you're different," I say.

My mother waves her hand dismissively.

"Everyone has their own way of dealing with things. Neither is better or worse. We all just need to figure out what works best for us."

I nod, picturing Chloe and little Connor again. Now, I'm not so sure about what I saw. I push my food carton aside. Mom's done eating too.

"I'll head home then, I guess you have a lot to do."

"Thanks so much for stopping by," she says, hugging me goodbye.

I leave the break room and automatically keep an eye out for Chloe, but I don't see her anywhere.

Chapter 12

The cool night envelops me. I inhale deeply and feel a little more awake. It's been a long day, and I still have the bus ride home. I wish I could just crawl under my duvet and sleep.

I pause briefly and look around for Yoru. I'm pretty sure he was in the hospital with me, although I didn't see him. I just hope he knows about surveillance cameras and that it's best to avoid them.

But right now it doesn't feel as if he's nearby. I take a few steps, peering behind shrubs and under parked cars. Hopefully nobody sees me because I must look pretty suspicious.

"Yoru," I hiss. "Come on, I want to go home."

I stick to the milky light of the streetlamps. I'm getting cold, and my impatience is growing. I'm suddenly aware of how dark it is. Where are all the people I just saw getting out of their cars or walking toward the hospital?

I glance around again and open my mouth to call out to Yoru one last time before making my way home. If I don't find him, I'll just have to trust him to follow me. But before I utter a sound, something grabs me from behind. Two arms encircle me and press me against a body. A scent wafts over me that I instantly recognize. Sweet, subtle, and alluring – or that's how it once seemed. Now, all I smell is danger and death, and it makes me hold my breath. When I hear the voice close to my ear, I feel sick, and my mind races.

"So nice to see you again. I was hoping we'd run into each other here. Fate seems to keep bringing us together."

I hear the words, but their meaning doesn't really register. All I feel are his strong arms crushing me. I kick out behind me as hard as I can and catch Noah's leg. To my surprise, he lets go of me, and I don't give him the chance to grab me again.

"Yoru!" I yell at the top of my voice, and my fox

finally appears. I summon all my odeon and send it to him in a hot surge. Yoru uses it immediately and assumes his alternate form. He stands protectively in front of me, his nine tails fanned out, waiting for my command.

"Oh, come on," Noah complains, rolling his eyes. "Do we really have to do this? I'm too tired."

"Now! Attack!" I silently command my fox, and his tails wag excitedly in the air. I know I have no chance against Noah. But I have to try. If nothing else, to show him I'm not some defenseless victim he can overpower without a fight. He has no business being here!

Yoru opens his mouth and spits out a big fireball. It flies at Noah so fast I can hardly keep track of it. Noah just stands there, expressionless. Then, he's completely engulfed by the flames. When the fire dissipates, Noah's gone too.

"Shit," I growl, looking around for him. He must have used his key again to open a door and escape into the Odyss.

"Nice try, but way too predictable," murmurs a voice beside me. I spin around in fright. Noah's standing to my right, his arms folded across his chest, and an arrogant smile on his face. "You need to direct the attack more precisely. Any idiot can evade a straight shot like that."

"Thanks for the tip," I grumble, calling for another attack. As Yoru throws another fireball, I glance around for Rain, but I can't see the black wolf anywhere. I'm certain he must be around here somewhere. There's no way he'd let Noah out of his sight.

Before the fireball hits Noah, I command Yoru to send another one, but this time, I get him to shoot it up in the air. Noah has no problem evading the first one – he just leans to the left, and the flames shoot past him.

"You're not listening to me."

That's what he thinks. I can't help grinning, and he seems to notice this. He turns around, then looks up and sees the fireball hurtling toward him. He jumps sideways to save himself.

"Not bad," he says appreciatively, studying my face. "But still not enough."

He runs at me and raises his arm.

I have no time to issue another command to Yoru. I hold my breath, squeeze my eyes shut and throw myself to the right. But I stumble and land hard on the pavement. When I open my eyes, Noah's disappeared again.

"What an ass– "I'm cut off mid-word as he grabs me and lifts me off my feet. His arms are wrapped tightly around me again.

"You shouldn't rely on your eyes so much. Switch on your other senses. They'll reveal more."

I kick and wriggle like an eel, and when his grip loosens, I slam my elbow into his ribs. I hear an amused laugh as I tear myself free, run a few steps, and turn to face him. He's holding his hand over the spot where I elbowed him.

"You're ruthless, my poor ribs."

It can't have hurt that much. But Noah exagge-rates and pulls a face.

"So cold-blooded."

"I've been called worse. And coming from you..." I shrug.

He shakes his head and laughs. "That's what I like about you. Never a dull moment, it's always fun."

"You call this fun?!"

The guy's insane! But he's not the only person I know who loves to spar.

"Well, I'm having a great time," he says, charging at us again. This time, I manage to send odeon to Yoru in time, and he spits out another fireball. Noah just ducks under it and then disappears again.

"I'm not going to make it easy for you," I whi-sper to myself, trying to gauge where he'll show up next. My eyes dart from side to side, but I see nothing. Maybe... I close my eyes and try to focus on my other senses.

I feel the cool wind brushing my skin. I hear a whooshing sound... which is interrupted by a vibration. I open my eyes and throw myself to my right. And sure enough, Noah's hand grasps at the air. But he quickly corrects his mistake and grabs hold of me again.

He pulls me close, and I can feel his firm torso against my back, his muscles moving in and out in time with his fast breathing.

"Not bad for a first try. You learn fast."

"Let go of me!" I hiss at him, trying to free myself again, but his grip is like iron.

"That was really entertaining. I look forward to our next encounter. Can't wait," he breathes into my ear. A shiver runs down my spine. "See you later," he whispers, then he lets go of me abruptly.

I spin around, but he's already gone. I'm breathing hard. The fight was short-lived, but those few minutes really drained me. I slump to the ground, exhausted, and try to understand what just happened. Is Noah just having fun and toying with me? Was he trying to test me? Or was that actually an attempt to help me? Was that some kind of training? But why would he do that?

Yoru has resumed his usual form and comes up

to me. He nuzzles me, and I stand up.

He's right – all the odeon I just sprayed everywhere will surely lure other Noctu. We need to get
out of here.

Chapter 13

Thankfully, Noah doesn't show up again over the next few days, but I admit he's still taking up an unreasonable amount of my headspace. I can't even go to school without expecting to see him around every corner. I really need to figure out how to get him out of my life for good. But to do that, I need to find out what he wants from me.

"I know you have him!" Paul snaps at his class-mate Isaac.

They're both in my history class, but that's pretty

much all I know about them.

"What have you done with Blizzard? Where are you hiding him?"

Paul puffs himself up threateningly, which is particularly effective due to his height and his striking appearance. He must be well over six foot, and although the era when his haircut was fashionable is long gone, he has a green mohawk and a little green goatee.

Isaac looks at him totally calmly, but the cool smile on his lips suggests he knows more than he's letting on.

"I have no idea what you're talking about. Why would I do anything with your key spirit?"

"Don't play dumb. I know this is some kind of moronic revenge. But this time you went too far."

Paul's anger is building, and he's struggling to control himself. He reaches for Isaac and is about to grab him when Mr. Brian shows up. The teacher merely glances at the two boys, and they quickly move apart and follow him into the classroom along with the rest of us. But the looks they give each other speak volumes.

"I wish they'd finally sort out their stupid tiff," Max mutters beside me. "It's been going on for weeks. They can't even remember who started it. But apparently, it started with some prank that got out of hand. Since then, they've been having this feud and harassing each other the whole time. Like children."

She rolls her eyes.

Paul and Isaac sit as far apart as possible and keep glaring darkly at each other over the heads of the other students.

I take out my things and try to focus on Mr. Brian, who's begun his class.

"In the coming weeks, we're going to delve more into San Francisco. It's a city rich in history and an important location for us key carriers. I want you to choose an aspect of it and write an essay. The info sheet I'm about to give you outlines the expected word count and formatting. It's due in four weeks. The essay will make up 20 percent of your grade for the year. What's most important to me is that you focus on an event and explore it in detail. Since this is a critical piece of work for your overall grade, I'll give you some leeway in selecting your topic. You can either choose a historical event in the city that relates to the key carriers or focus on San Francisco as a whole. It could be a positive aspect of the city or something about its darker side. Remember, we have Alcatraz in the bay, which once housed a high security prison. As you all know, there was a significant battle against the Noctu there. I imagine that would make a great essay topic. Give it some thought – I'm interested in hearing your ideas."

He hands out the instruction sheet, and I skim read it. I have so much going on right now that an in-depth essay like this is the last thing I need. But I'm already clear on one thing: I don't want to make it even harder for myself, so I won't choose an event that involves key carriers. But the assignment itself seems interesting. Among the suggestions on the sheet, I read the key words "darker side" again. That immediately brings up the image of me and Kate on our way to the movies. That little alley. I recall her description of the heinous crime that happened there. Maybe that's an idea: a murder that remains unsolved to this day. I could try to find out how the police dealt with it back in the day. That's certainly one idea I can follow up.

Mr. Brian has launched into his lesson and is telling us about the founding of San Francisco and how the city developed over time. As dry as history may seem at first glance, Mr. Brian manages to capture our attention with well-chosen subject matter and anecdotes.

At the end of class, I gather up my things, still wondering how best to approach the assignment. I know the school has a comprehensive library.

Maybe I'll take a look there.

I wait for Max and Lucia, whose spirits seem dampened.

"As if we don't already have enough to do," Max complains. "And a history essay! I'm really starting to wonder if I should drop this class. Mr. Brian's constantly making us write essays."

"I actually like his classes," Lucia admits. "They're usually not too taxing. But you're right about the workload. This essay on top of our upcoming exams." She shakes her head. "It's a lot."

"For the last time," a voice echoes along the corridor, "where's Blizzard?"

We stop and spot Paul a few meters ahead of us, holding Isaac by the collar and glaring furiously at him.

"Maybe you should stop following me around and actually go look for him. I bet your key spirit's closer than you think."

At that moment, a girl opens the door to the toilets and screams in fright as a creature bursts out, bleating loudly. For a moment, I don't know what to think. In the middle of the corridor stands a goat, and someone has given it a makeover: the fur on its head is green and spiked up in a mohawk, and its little beard is also green. It has white cotton balls stuck all over its body. There are also cotton balls dangling from its long ears like large earrings, and they wobble when the goat utters a plaintive "mahhh," which it's doing plenty right now. It must have been locked in the bathroom for the entire period.

"Hmm, the resemblance is unmistakable," Isaac observes. "That has to be your key spirit. And he's finally living up to his name: a real blizzard."

For a moment, Paul is lost for words. It takes him a few seconds to gather his wits. Then, he lunges at his antagonist. A white cat instantly appears at Isaac's side, increasing in size and growing long fangs that remind me of a saber tooth tiger. Blizzard, the defaced goat, also goes to its companion's side and changes his form. He grows larger, bulkier, and his horns grow into impressive spirals.

"Those guys are nuts," says Lucia. "They're going to be in so much trouble."

"But you gotta hand it to Isaac – he did a great job. Blizzard looks phenomenal," Max laughs.

"I expect he had help," says Lucia. "Paul's not too popular."

The first hexes fly through the air and crack against the walls, which tremble alarmingly.

"We should get out of here. One of the teachers will probably show up soon, and then there'll be real trouble," says Max.

We turn around and walk back along the corridor. In that moment, I hear a soft hum. It's almost too subtle to perceive, but the faint rush of air that accompanies it tells me everything. I immediately leap sideways as far as I can and smash into the wall. I feel a sharp pain in my shoulder, and I know I'll have an impressive bruise there. I look up and see the hole in the floor – right where I was standing a moment ago.

"Damn," I mutter, looking over at Lucia and Max, who are standing a short distance from the hole, also staring at it. Then, they look at me in disbelief.

"I'm... so sorry," Paul calls out to me. "I didn't mean to do that. The hex wasn't meant for you, it..."

Paul swallows hard, and I can see in his eyes how horrified he is at his error. An error that almost cost me my life. But I was able to evade it because I was paying attention to my other senses. I'm reminded of my fight with Noah. I'm acutely aware that he was the one who gave me the tip. But it can't be true... he can't have been actually trying to help me.

Two teachers storm around the corner and immediately start yelling at the two adversaries.

"Are you alright?" one of them asks me, bending over me with a concerned expression.

I nod and stand up. "Nothing happened," I say, rubbing my aching shoulder. If things had gone a little differently, I wouldn't even have a shoulder.

"And you two!" the other teacher snaps at Paul and Isaac. "Come with me! Fighting with your key spirits in the school corridors! Are you out of your minds?!"

The teachers escort the boys and their spirits down the corridor. I stare after them. My thoughts are swirling. Thoughts of Paul, of Blizzard, but mostly Noah.

Chapter 14

I'd prefer to take it slow in afternoon training because my shoulder's still pretty sore. But Amber doesn't let up.

"I'm your sparring partner today," she says, assuming an intimidating stance in front of me.

I still don't find these skirmishes all that useful, but there's no way I'm going to make it easy for her. Who knows, maybe I'll actually manage to hit Amber. Yoru and I have improved a lot recently. I ruffle the fur on my key spirit's head, and he looks at me trustingly.

"Get ready, little guy," I whisper to him, sending him a large dose of odeon. I instantly feel the strength leave my body, and for a moment I feel cold, but that passes quickly.

Yoru transforms, gets much bigger, and his fur turns blood red. His nine tails wag excitedly in the air, and he emits aggressive sparks. Amber isn't intimidated by him. Lancelot transforms too. The large bird immediately flies up in the air and launches an attack. We evade his gust of wind effortlessly, and I try communicating silently with Yoru.

"Throw a fireball, try and distract Lancelot with it, and then attack Amber straight after."

I send him more odeon, and he makes use of it. A fireball forms and shoots forward but misses Lancelot by a few meters. I guess I should have expressed that more precisely. But the bird cranes its neck and glances after the fireball. Meanwhile, Yoru spits a hot flame at Amber. Her bird quickly blocks it with a kind of whirlwind. Now, the wind is raining our fire down on us, and I have to throw myself out of the way again. As I do this, I try to rely less on my eyes and instead feel the heat and listen to the sounds – the way I learned when I was fighting Noah. The burning projectiles fall hissing to the floor and glow there like hot coal. I'm relieved to see that the floor of the gym is protected; otherwise, it would have large scorch marks on it by now.

Three fireballs hurtle down at me, and I try to take advantage of this.

"Be ready, Yoru," I say mentally, then I tell him what he needs to do.

I throw myself forward awkwardly and slam hard into the floor. I peer at Amber out of the corner of my eye and see a smile appear on her lips. I curl up a little and my face contorts with pain as I touch my aching arm. My ruse seems to have worked because Amber takes her eyes off her bird, figuring she's won the fight.

"Now, Yoru," I call to him as she comes a few steps closer. Yoru immediately produces a huge flame, which twists and turns above the floor, then spirals into a kind of eddy that sucks up all the little glowing projectiles still lying on the floor.

Amber shouts and holds up her arms to shield herself. Lancelot tries to protect her with gusts of wind. Exactly in that moment, I command my spirit again.

"Yoru, attack!"

A single stream of fire shoots out of his mouth directly at Amber. Lancelot throws himself in front of her and counters with a gust of wind. I can see the hexes colliding, but both spirits hold their ground. Yoru intensifies his attack, and I watch his stream of fire gradually move closer to Lancelot. But the bird immediately tries to increase his power too.

"Try harder," Amber hisses at him. "Take the odeon and don't give in to them. You can't let someone like her defeat you!"

She has an expression of sheer determination. Her bird squawks and tries to obey her command. His body trembles as he intensifies his magic. Yoru doesn't let up but focuses his energy too.

"Damn it, Lancelot! Attack harder! Are you listening to me?!"

Her bird briefly wobbles in the air then does as he's told. His breast heaves, and he utters a hideous cry as the hex leaves his body. I'm horrified when I realize Amber's demanding way too much of her key spirit, and I tell Yoru to abort his attack before the bird gets seriously injured.

But it's too late.

"Yes, good, and again. We almost have her," Amber cries.

I can tell she's just given her spirit a pulse of odeon because the convulsions that go through him are unmistakable. He gives it everything he has – and then drops to the floor like a stone. The remainder of Yoru's attack shoots forward and misses Amber by a hair's breadth – fortunately because it probably would have seriously injured her. For a moment, she just stares straight ahead, wide-eyed, clearly unable to grasp what just happened. Then, she clenches her jaw and her fists and goes to Lancelot, who's lying motionless on the floor in his everyday form.

Ms. Rupert and Mr. Laydon rush to her aid and examine her key spirit.

"He's completely exhausted. That was too much for him," says Mr. Laydon with a reprimanding glance at Amber. "While it's true that we need to be firm with our key spirits, we should always remember that they're our friends and companions. We're responsible for them, and they should be treated well. That includes accepting their limitations. Your behavior was wrong, and I hope you realize that. It's a shame your bird has to pay the price." He picks up the animal, which rests limply in his arms. "I'll take him to the infirmary."

Amber looks guiltily at Lancelot, and her eyes fill with concern. "Will he be alright?"

"Let's hope so," says Mr. Laydon. Then, he leaves.

Amber glances at me, and I see rage flash in her eyes before she turns and follows her key spirit.

I ruffle Yoru's fur. I can't understand how

anyone can treat their spirit animal like that. She seems to regret what she's done to him, at least. I hope she'll respect his limits in future.

At the end of the period, I decide to stay a while. My shoulder still hurts, but I want to train on the fitness equipment and run, hoping that will clear my head.

After 20 laps of the hall, I wipe the sweat from my brow and glance at the door. Ayden has skipped his after-hours training again today. I stretch and force myself to take deep, even breaths. I feel the exhaustion deep in my bones and decide to call it a day. I quickly shower and dress. It's already dark when I leave the gym complex. I come to a corridor. One way leads to the main entrance and the other to the residential wing. I'm about to turn left when I detect movement. I instinctively pull back behind the wall and peer around the corner.

Ayden steps into the corridor. He's dressed in dark clothing – a long black coat that makes him look kind of intimidating. Snow follows hot on his heels, but they're not alone. With him are a young man, who looks about twenty, and a woman of a similar age. They have key spirits too: a huge gray snake and a raven.

"It's about time we got out and saw some action," the young man says gleefully, winking at the big snake beside him. "You're excited too, right Gray?"

The snake lifts its head and hisses quietly. The guy is tall and muscular, judging by his bare arms sticking out of his vest. Not only can I see the well-defined muscles in his arms but also the tattoos covering them. His hair is short and blond, almost silver in the dim lighting. He has several piercings in his ears, nose, and lip.

"Sure, but no messing around. Let's just get this done fast and do it right," says the woman, who comes across as very serious. Her dark eyes linger on the pierced guy and shoot him a warning look, but he doesn't seem to care.

"Stop taking everything so seriously, Vicky. There's nothing wrong with a little fun – we don't often get the chance."

"I'm warning you," she hisses. "Don't you dare get me mixed up in any of your shit."

Even with that angry expression I have to admit she's exceptionally good looking. Long, slightly wavy hair tumbles down her back, making her look like she's just stepped out of a salon. Her figure basically epitomizes the modern-day beauty ideal. Long legs encased in tight black pants. A wonderfully narrow waist and a flat belly clearly defined under her tight top.

The raven at her side squawks loudly, as if it too is trying to talk sense into the guy with the tattoos, but he dismisses it.

"Not you too, Raven, give it a rest. I heard her the first time."

Raven. I roll my eyes. Someone didn't put much effort into coming up with a name.

"Are you going to lecture me too? Or are we on the same page?" he asks Ayden, who's been silent up to this point.

Ayden glances sideways at him and sighs. "What do you want me to say? You always just do whatever pops into your head anyway."

The other guy nods. "That's always worked out pretty well for me so far."

"Oh man," Vicky sighs, shaking her head. "Ty, one day your attitude's going to land you in deep trouble."

Ty just laughs and puts his arm around her shoulders. "That's why I have you guys."

She quickly shrugs him off and shakes her head. "Don't get any ideas. We're not your babysitters."

They reach the end of the corridor and exit the school building. I hang back for a moment, my heart pounding, and think about what I've just heard. Who are those two and why are they going out with Ayden? And my most pressing question:

what's their plan?

It doesn't take me long to reach a decision, and I hurry after them. Their key spirits disappear once they're outside. Snow and the snake hug the shadows, and the raven seeks out a perch in a nearby tree. I glance around for Yoru and instinctively know where to find him. He's sitting under a VW Bus, watching me intently. He seems to sense that we're on a mission. We follow the others. It's not easy, because I need to stay a reasonable distance behind them to be sure they don't see me. I almost lose sight of them several times, but fortunately I manage to find them again.

First, they follow the main road, then they make a few turns and disappear down smaller side streets. The farther we go, the fewer people there are, which makes it harder for me to remain unseen. I have to fall back even more, taking cover behind buildings, cars, and dumpsters. Yoru's a master of concealment, and he helps me by quickly finding good spots for me to hide.

At some point, I lose sight of them and curse furiously under my breath. I continue cautiously with Yoru in tow and try to figure out where they went. But all I see are two deserted alleys and a few unlit courtyards. A chill runs up my spine. I try to avoid dark corners, knowing that deserted places like this are where Noctu tend to hang around. But I'm already in too deep. I should turn back right now and head home instead of straying even farther from the busy streets. But I can't. Something spurs me on. I'm curious. I want to find out what those three are up to.

So, I keep walking. I peer into a lonely courtyard, where stagnant water has collected in the cracked pavement. A rusted fire escape hangs askew from the building closest to me. There are a few foul-smelling trash cans. That's all I find. There's no one here. I look at Yoru, who suddenly seems alert, and in that moment, I hear the hissing of hexes. I spin around but see nothing. I hear shouts, the sounds of combat, and my heart pounds in my chest. The noise is coming from somewhere very close. I hurry back out to the street, and it doesn't take me long to find them. Two buildings along is another narrow alley leading into a rear courtyard, and that's where the light is coming from.

I sneak up to the corner and peer down the alley. Several Noctu are there, attacking Ayden, Ty, and Vicky. Unlike the Noctu I've seen before, these ones don't all look like animals. Some of them have human features: hunched bodies, bald skulls with dark sunken eyes staring out of them. Their skin looks leathery, and their movements are jerky but fast.

Black hexes flash then hurtle at the three of them like an impenetrable wall. Vicky's black raven has transformed into a huge bird of prey, its wings giving off a shimmering blue light. He opens his beak and ice-blue waves shoot out of it, hitting two Noctu, which are instantly encased in a block of ice.

Ty commands his snake to attack, and it digs itself into the ground before shooting forward and tearing large chunks out of the pavement. Together, they smash the frozen Noctu, who shatter into thousands of pieces.

Ayden's wolf Snow has also transformed. He's shrouded in dark smoke that emits sparks. Little tongues of flames keep shooting out of it, revealing how tense the wolf is. His red eyes glimmer as he spits out a fireball, and the front line of Noctu are engulfed in flames. A few of them drop to the ground, and others try to shield themselves with hexes, surrounding themselves with a dark substance that smothers the flames.

I watch the fight with bated breath and don't know what to do. Part of me wants to help them, but another part urges me to keep a low profile and not show myself under any circumstances.

The group's position slowly changes, and I realize I'm no longer safe in my current hiding place. So I dash out and creep behind a large dumpster for cover. I'm now much closer to the action, but nobody can see me here.

Ayden runs at two of the Noctu with Snow. He clenches his fists and flames shoot out from between his fingers. Snow dodges attacks from a couple of Noctu as Ayden runs undaunted toward his opponent. The Noctu raises its arm, which elongates into a dark smoky column and whips out at Ayden. He dives under it, then he's on his feet again and rams his burning fist into the Noctu's gut. When he pulls back his hand, there's a gaping hole with smoldering flames inside it, which spread out. The Noctu opens its mouth and cries out, launching a last desperate attack. But Snow quickly throws himself in the way, countering the attack with a fireball. The Noctu melts into a sticky dark mass until there's nothing left of it but a black puddle on the ground.

Ty and Vicky attack again too, but the remaining Noctu now throw everything into neutralizing their enemies. Hexes fly in all directions, cracking through the air and making the ground quake.

"Finally, a chance to really let off some steam," Ty rejoices, flinging up his arms. A towering column of dust shoots up from the ground and impales a Noctu. The sight of it makes me shudder and close my eyes for a moment.

When I open them again, Ayden is running at the next attacker, who fires a dark quivering orb at him, which Ayden catches in his hand and flings aside. It hurtles through the air, straight at me. I throw myself flat on the ground, and I let out a horrified scream. That's enough to draw everyone's attention. The Noctu look in my direction and begin to growl. Ty, Ayden, and Vicky also have registered my presence.

"Oh, who do we have here?" Ty asks gleefully. "An audience. That makes it even more fun."

"Are you out of your mind?" Vicky retorts as she kills another Noctu by commanding her raven to blast it with another huge wave, which knocks it off its feet and then shreds it with a shower of ice crystals.

Ayden just glares at me with a withering look that says more than a thousand words. I'm not wanted here; I'm in the way, and I'm making him pretty angry by being here.

He wipes out the last Noctu with a fireball, causing it to collapse into another sticky black puddle. All eyes turn to me as their key spirits assume their usual forms once more. I see a wide range of emotions reflected in each of their faces. Ayden's still incredibly pissed; Vicky looks mostly irritated, and Ty... He walks up to me with a grin and studies me as if I'm some rare animal.

"Hey, you have a key spirit too," he comments when he sees Yoru. "Then you're one of us. Good; otherwise, I'd have to kill you."

My eyes widen in surprise, but Ty just laughs and slaps his thigh.

"That was a joke. I was kidding. Do you really think we kill people?"

He offers his hand to help me up because I'm still lying on the ground.

"You're still in school, right? So I guess you're from the Siena Hartford."

I take his hand and let him help me up.

"Uh, yeah," I say and can't stop my eyes from wandering to Ayden. Wow, he looks like he's about to explode.

"What are you doing here?" he asks. "Why do you always show up where you're not wanted?!"

"I happened to see you guys, and you looked like you had a plan. Turns out I was right."

"So you like sticking your nose into things that don't concern you," Vicky says, looking at me with her arms folded across her chest.

"I think she's cute," says Ty, giving me that look again, as if I'm some adorable little pet and he's not sure if I belong outside or if I need a cat toilet.

"What are you doing here?" I ask. "Why did you lure out the Noctu?"

I'm sure those creatures didn't show up for no reason.

"We were acting on the instructions of the school principal and the Council. That's all you need to know," Ayden growls.

I raise my eyebrows. I wasn't expecting that. It can only mean one thing.

"So you two are hunters too."

Ty grins. "Tylor Waydon. I've been a hunter for two years. Before Ayden joined us, I was the youngest to be inducted into our elite circle." He nods at Vicky. "And this is Victoria Smith. She's been a hunter a while longer."

I nod at her, but her expression is still dark, never mind Ayden's. I have so many questions, but this definitely doesn't feel like the right time.

"Uh, okay, nice to meet you. I guess I'll head home then."

I've barely taken three steps before Ayden catches up to me, grabs my arm, and drags me away from the others.

"Hey, do you know her? Is she a friend of yours?" Ty calls after us.

"No way," Ayden snarls. I feel a slight pang

at these words even though I know they're true. "She's just a girl who shouldn't be here."

"Aha!" I hear Ty yell after us. "Is this Teresa, the one your dad accepted against your recommendation? Pretty cute, I gotta say. I would have reconsidered if I were you."

I can hear the smile in his voice. Ayden doesn't reply. He drags me farther away from the others and shoves me roughly against a wall. It's damp and unpleasantly cold. He fixes me with a piercing gaze and plants his hands on either side of my head so I can't just walk away. His eyes flash with rage, like a hurricane that's about to sweep over me and tear up everything in its path. Merciless and unstoppable.

"What the hell were you thinking? Did you use your brain at all? Do you even realize what kind of danger you put yourself in?" He doesn't give me time to reply. "No, of course not. You just wanted to satisfy your own stupid curiosity and didn't think for a second about what you were doing. And that's exactly why you don't belong in our school. When you're not attracting danger, you're blindly throwing yourself into it."

"I thought you revised your opinion of me. I mean, I wouldn't even be at the school anymore if it weren't for your help."

"You'd be dead without my help."

"Thanks for your undying confidence in me," I mutter.

He's so close that I can feel his body heat. And I can't stand the fact that it feels good, familiar, tantalizing even. And those incredible green eyes have so much power over me – even now, they're bringing me to the brink of emotional collapse. And provoking my rage!

"I'm not as weak as you think," I retort. "I've learned a lot lately. And I've proved that I'm not so easy to kill."

Ayden breathes a sigh of contempt. "Sure, and you've shown that you're a magnet for danger and an easy target for our enemies. Do I need to remind you about Noah? I can't believe how close he got to you."

His right hand moves closer to my face. My heart feels like it might explode.

"That could have happened to anyone," I hiss. "If your father or the teachers or you made sure I was better informed... No one explains anything to me!"

The rest of what I want to say gets stuck in my throat. I can't think straight anymore. All I can see are those deep green eyes in front of my face and those incomparable lips drawn into a thin, scornful line. His breath on my face makes my skin prickle.

"Just stay out of our way," he says, tearing himself away from me. He turns and stalks off. For a moment, I watch him go, then my trembling legs give way, and I slump to the ground. What have I gotten myself into, again?

Chapter 15

M y classes crawl by at a snail's pace. I keep checking the time and expecting to be called to the principal's office. Surely the hunters had to debrief him on their mission, and I doubt they kept quiet about the fact that I showed up. Why do I keep sticking my nose into everything? I should have just let Ayden go. Oh well, it's too late to worry about that now.

I rest my head on my palm and draw circles on my writing block instead of taking notes. Right now I have math, which is a subject I need to focus on if I don't want my grade to drop. But I have more important things on my mind just now.

My phone vibrates in my pocket. At least that'll distract me from my gloomy thoughts. I hold it below my desk and open the message. I'm suddenly wide awake, as if I've just had an electric shock.

"How's school and how's your training? Any progress to report? I'm always available for another lesson. So if you need help, let me know. I look forward to it. Noah."

What the hell?! I stare at the message, reread it several times. How can he pretend we're friends, as if our encounters are pleasant experiences that I'd want to repeat?! The guy must have a loose screw. Or am I supposed to read between the lines? I have a feeling he's trying to remind me with these messages that he's still out there somewhere. That he knows everything about my life and all because I let him get too close to me. I opened a door that can't be closed, and he's making sure I know that.

"Leave me the hell alone or tell me what you want from me so we can put an end to this stupid game. I've had enough of you and your threats."

I get a reply less than a minute later. "Tess, do you really think I'm threatening you? Trust me, that would look very different. And deep down you know how important it is for you to maintain contact with me. Why else haven't you told anyone about me?"

What's he trying to say? And how does he know that? I guess if I had told someone, there'd be some kind of reaction, and he'd know about it for sure. My heart races as I run his words through my head. Yeah, why can't I bring myself to tell someone about Noah and ask for help? Because my place at this school is precarious, and I'd have to admit how much trouble I'm already in. If Mr. Collins found out that Noah knows way more about my life than I've let on... Even if he did nothing, once the Council learned of it, I'd have to leave the school. And then, what would become of me? I'd be forced to give up my key. I'd lose Yoru. But at least the Noctu would lose interest in me. Or they'd kill me without consequence, to take my last breath. No way, I can't let any of that happen.

"If you figure you're doing me a favor with all this attention, then forget it. Just say what you want to say. Or disappear from my life. You've done enough damage already."

I stare at the screen, waiting for a reply. It takes a lot longer than expected. I stare at my phone for several minutes. Then, finally: "Not yet. All in good time."

Such a cryptic reply! But those two short sentences freak me out. I try to breathe evenly and stay calm. Because now my suspicion is confirmed. Noah has something in store for me.

"You were texting pretty hard there," Max observes at the end of class. "Is there someone new? If so, I'm happy for you." She smiles and puts a friendly hand on my shoulder. "Your luck's gotta change sometime."

"No, it was just a friend from my old school."

I feel bad lying to her, but what choice do I have?

Max raises her eyebrows doubtfully. "Then I guess you had something to clear up with her, the way you were pounding at your phone."

"A minor disagreement," I say, and Max just nods. I'm not sure she believes me.

"Ayden!" she suddenly shouts happily, raising her hand in greeting. "Are you free after training? Lucia, James, and I wanted..."

Without looking at her, he snaps, "Not now." He stops in front of me. "Tess, can you come with me? I need to talk to you."

I raise my eyebrows in astonishment, and I'm not the only one with surprise written all over my face. Max seems taken aback too.

She mouths at me, "What's up?"

I just shrug and follow Ayden down a quiet corridor. Two students pass us and disappear around a corner, then we're alone.

"What's with the dramatic entrance?" I ask. "If it's about yesterday, I'm really sorry I..."

"Just keep out of our way in future. You seem to have no clue about how much danger you put yourself and us in."

His words are like a slap in the face, and they don't miss their mark. Obviously, I've caused a shitstorm again, and he can't resist rubbing my nose in it. I endangered their mission and their lives with my reckless behavior.

"Don't worry, I never intended to get mixed up in any hunter business. I'm not interested in your weird club, and I'm happy to stay out of your fights. I'm only at this school to learn to defend myself in emergencies and strengthen my bond with Yoru. That's all I care about."

His gaze is so formidable that it takes all my resolve to meet it. Why can't he just leave me alone?! I'm so angry I want to scream at him. But I hold myself back because it's true: I made a mistake, and I shouldn't have interfered.

"I hope you can stick to that plan. You have a real talent for showing up at the wrong place at the wrong time."

"Thanks. Do you have any other kind words that you urgently need to express?" I blurt. So much for my plan to stay calm. "I already apologized and said I'll stay out of your way. What more do you want?!"

He grinds his jaw, and his expression is a mixture of bubbling rage and the struggle to keep it in check.

But I'm fuming too.

"I told you how sorry I am. But you can't just leave it alone. You always have to have the last word. I think it's best if we just try to steer clear of each other and get on with our lives."

My words seem to hit home. I can see his mind working; several times, he seems to be on the verge of saying something, then thinks better about it. But his expression says it all. He simultaneously comes across like a block of ice and a volcano that's about to erupt. Then he just nods.

"I agree."

"Good!"

I turn around and leave him standing there. But then I hear his voice again.

"I just came to say that you don't need to worry about my father. I assume you've been wrecking your head about that since last night. We decided not to tell him, so you can relax and get on with your life."

I hear scorn in his words, and I instinctively turn around, but Ayden's already disappearing down another corridor. I briefly wonder why they didn't want to report me but then decide to forget about it. It's pointless dwelling on it. Just like it's pointless wrecking my head over Noah or Ayden. I need to try to keep my word and finally get my life under control.

At afternoon training, Amber mostly leaves me alone. Apparently, Lancelot still hasn't fully recovered – he's nowhere to be seen, anyway. I use the time to work on my communication with Yoru. Amber can't resist making a few comments, but she's way more restrained than usual. I continue sending him silent commands, which he carries out more or less correctly. I practice sending him odeon too. It's not easy gauging the right amount.

At the end of the period, I notice that Ayden's staying back, so I decide to go home. I've trained so much over the last few weeks that I figure I've earned a break.

I take a long shower, then get dressed, and I'm one of the last to leave the locker room. Two girls walk out ahead of me. They glance to their right, looking a little startled, whisper to one another, then hurry on. I don't think anything of it until I hear a voice to my right.

"There you are. I was starting to think you'd skipped class."

A young man is leaning against the wall beside me. His short silvery-blond hair is conspicuous enough, but his numerous tattoos and piercings really make him stand out from the crowd. I must look totally dumbfounded because his face breaks into a wry grin. But I honestly don't understand. What's Ty doing here? He must be in his early twenties. So unless he's had to repeat a grade several times, he should have graduated years ago.

"You were waiting for me? Can I ask why?" I sigh. Then, I answer my own question. "If it's about me following you guys and watching you fight – yeah, I shouldn't have done that, I get it. Ayden already gave me a dressing down, so you can spare me the lecture. Don't worry, I'll stay out of your hair in future."

I'm about to turn and leave, but he grabs my arm and holds me back. As he turns me around, I hear his bright laugh.

"I'm starting to understand how you manage to get Ayden so worked up." He cocks his head, and his brown eyes look me up and down with interest, apparently taking in every detail. "I figured

I should take a closer look at the young girl who creeps out at night after a group of hunters and gets mixed up in fights."

I shake my head and pull out of his grasp. "Ty, right?"

He nods, grins, and bows. "At your service."

"Very funny," I retort. "For one thing, it was late afternoon, not the middle of the night, when I followed you. And I didn't get mixed up in your fight. It didn't even cross my mind. And third, as I said, I get it, and I'm more than happy to keep my nose out of your business."

Again, I turn to go, but I hear his voice again. "That's a shame. I thought maybe I could tell you a little about us and our work. Aren't you interested in that? I heard you only found out about the existence of the key spirits, the school, our work, and the Noctu a few weeks ago. I imagine you still have a few questions. Am I right?"

I frown and try to read his expression. "And you want to answer them? Why?"

That laugh again. "To be honest, because I find you incredibly refreshing. Most of the students here know I'm a hunter, and we don't have a lot to do with each other. They treat us with this weird kind of reverence. Unlike you. The way you talk to Ayden – that was awesome."

"I guess you can't stand him either if you want my help to wind him up."

He looks shocked. "Oh, no way. Ayden's one of my best buddies."

Okay, that comes as a surprise.

"That's why I think it's great when someone can shake him up a little now and then. He's always so composed, knows exactly what to say and how to act to keep people at arm's length. But that means he never really gets out of his comfort zone."

I know what he means because I've experienced it myself.

"You're saying he's a good actor, and he knows how to manipulate people. I totally agree." Before he can respond, I continue, "Fine, if you can answer my questions and tell me about your world, I'll take you up on the offer." I'd be pretty stupid not to. "So, you're a hunter. So far nobody's really explained to me how someone becomes a hunter."

"Well, basically, we were all at this school at some point. The ones who really distinguish themselves over the years are usually taken on as hunters. But that also means specialized training and obviously a more intensive education program. Many of us live here in a separate area of the school, but there are also plenty of hunters who live elsewhere in the city and have families. There are even some who have retired and live totally normal lives, except that they're members of the Council and get consulted on important decisions."

"So Ayden lives in this separate area too?" I can't help asking.

"No, he's still in school, so he lives in the residential wing. Not so long ago, I lived there too, and that's how I met Ayden."

I scrutinize him again, and I guess he can read in my face the question that's going through my head right now.

"I'm no grandpa. I'm only 22." He pushes himself away from the wall and jerks his head for me to follow him. "Come on, I'll show you something."

I hesitate just for a moment, then I follow him.

Chapter 16

He walks down the corridor and stops outside the residential wing. I don't know why, but suddenly I get a bad feeling, as though I'm not allowed to enter this place. I know it's not off-limits and that students are allowed here. But it feels like I'm about to overstep some line, and again, I see Ayden's face in my mind's eye. I certainly don't want to run into him here.

I quickly push that thought out of my mind. This was Ty's idea after all. We enter a large foyer with several corridors and a staircase leading off it. I read signs that point to common rooms, students' rooms, the laundry, storage rooms, a roof terrace. The school is really well equipped.

Ty heads for the stairs, and we go up to the next floor. There are two corridors, one leading to the students' private rooms, but we continue upstairs until we come to a bridging passage made entirely of glass. A quick glance tells me how high up we are, and I feel a little woozy. The glass walkway takes us to another building. This one also has a large number of rooms and different areas. But there's one difference I notice immediately: almost everyone we encounter here is middle-aged.

"This is basically the main base of the Tempes," Ty explains, and I look at him cluelessly. "We're the Tempes hunters," he says, but I still don't understand. Eventually the penny drops.

"You mean, the way the Noctu have a name, we're called the Tempes?"

He nods and doesn't seem to know where to even begin, considering the obvious gaps in my knowledge.

"It's lucky I'm here to explain a few things to you. If you didn't even know what we call ourselves..." He shakes his head. "What do they teach you in school? That would never have happened in my time," he grumbles, sounding like a crabby old man pining for the good old days. He makes me laugh for the first time, and I admit to myself that Ty also has a humorous side.

"I'll show you something you might find pretty useful."

We go down some stairs and pass several open doors. I can make out offices, a large conference room, and finally a library, where a few men and women are poring over books – apparently conducting research because they're taking a lot of notes.

"You'll find books here on pretty much any subject – history, math, literature, you name it. But also a lot of documentation on hunter deployments, Noctu attacks, information about our enemies, lists of our members, the history of the Tempes, and, of course, a lot of records relating to the school. So if you have any questions, you're sure to find the answers here."

"I never figured I'd have to comb through half a library to learn more about my new life."

"You can just ask me too. I'm happy to help if I can."

"Are students even allowed in here? This is the hunters' library, isn't it?"

He shrugs. "There's a school library too, but this one's way bigger and more comprehensive. Students hardly ever come here because they're generally shy about entering the hunters' wing. It's a kind of respect thing. But students are allowed to study in here. I mean, we need new blood, and it's better for us if the young talent is well educated and informed."

I let my gaze wander over the rows of shelves.

"Do you want to take a look around?"

I hesitate. "Can I find records of a particular person who used to work for the school?"

Ty raises his eyebrows in surprise.

"My great aunt. I inherited my key from her. But I never met her, and I'd love to find out more about her and get an idea of what she was like."

She's the only reason I have Yoru. This school, my new friends, this whole world would have remained hidden from me forever if it weren't for her.

Ty scratches his chin thoughtfully. "If she was a Tempes who worked for the school, then I'm pretty sure there should be some documents in which she's mentioned by name. But to locate them all..."

His eyes wander around the library, and I see what he means. It would take more than just a few hours. Suddenly his face brightens.

"But you said she worked for the school. Was

she a teacher?"

I shake my head as he goes to a shelf and pulls out a few books.

"No, she was a secretary."

"That might make it harder. But who knows, maybe you'll get lucky." He puts the stack on a table in front of me. "These are a few of the year-books."

I open the first one and flip through it. I don't hold out much hope of finding secretaries in it, but it's worth a try.

"What was her name?"

"Frida Harper."

To my astonishment, he sits down beside me and takes another book from the stack. So many strange faces peer out at me. Students, confidently looking to the future, who have plans and can't wait to graduate. I have no idea what became of them. Maybe some of them stayed on as hunters. Others may still live in the city, studying or doing internships. And although they must be out there somewhere in the larger world, they'll always remain a part of this one, and they'll return, if necessary, to fight.

I'm about to close the yearbook and reach for another one when the last page catches my eye. There's a picture of an older woman sitting behind a desk. On the wall is a painting, the style of which is very familiar. So is her face, with all its wrinkles, gray hair pulled back in a bun, and a kind smile on her lips. I only know Frida from one photo, and she was younger in that one. But I instantly know it's her. My eyes wander to the text below the photo:

Frida Harper obituary:

This year we suffered a great loss. Our loyal employee, treasured colleague, and the heart and soul of the administration, Frida Harper, passed away after a brief but serious illness.

We thank her for the unforgettable years we shared, the joy she always brought to her work, her diligence, and her tireless commitment.

Principal Samuel Collins and the faculty at Siena Hartford Academy

I swallow hard and my eyes wander back up to the picture. I hope with all my heart that she didn't suffer, and I'm glad to read that she was beloved by her colleagues. Seeing another photo of her means a lot to me because now her face has a few new facets.

"Found something?" Ty asks, leaning toward me. "I vaguely remember her. I didn't have much to do with the admin when I was in school." He shrugs. "So I can't tell you much."

"It's okay," I say, closing the book and standing up. "This helped a lot. Thank you."

Ty's lips curve into a pleasant smile, and his eyes radiate warmth. "You're very welcome."

Chapter 17

What should we do tonight? Any ideas?" Lucia asks as we clear away our trays and weave our way to the door of the cafeteria.

It's midday Friday, so it's understandable that the two of them want to make plans. But the last few days have been exhausting, and when I think about the fact that we have training next period, I doubt I'll be in the mood for much tonight.

"How about a movie?" Max suggests, but she sounds unconvinced.

A message comes in on my phone. I quickly take it out of my pocket and find, to my relief, that it's only Kate asking me how I am. I quickly type a reply and hear Max scoff loudly beside me.

"Earth to Teresa! Did you hear me? We could go for pizza and then see a movie."

"I don't know. It's been a long week, and we still have training…"

Max rolls her eyes. "Lately, you've been a total…" She breaks off mid-sentence and glances sideways to stare at someone approaching us.

"Ty," I say, surprised, and Lucia's and Max's eyes instantly swivel back to me.

"You know a hunter?" Lucia whispers incredulously.

There are a lot of new things in my life that I've started to get used to lately, but this reverence toward the hunters still leaves me baffled. Why does everyone stare at them like they're supernatural beings? I guess a lot of students probably idolize them, like movie stars or rock stars. This effect isn't fully developed in Ayden because he's still a student and seems more like a normal mortal.

"Good, I was hoping I'd find you here," says Ty, with that mischievous smile of his. I see Lucia's and Max's jaws drop.

"What's up?" I ask tersely.

I don't try to hide the fact that I'm unhappy about him showing up like this. Hunters and students clearly don't cross paths a lot at this school, and I see no reason why I should be the one to break this unspoken rule. Max flinches at my rude tone and looks appalled.

"I was wondering if you have any plans tonight?"

I raise my eyebrows and probably look just as astonished as my girlfriends.

"We have training next period. And later, I want to work on an assignment, an essay we're supposed to write for history. After that I plan to sleep. I'm already pretty drained."

"Don't listen to her," Max interjects, putting an arm around my shoulders. "Sometimes she just needs to have her arm twisted. So what are you thinking?" Max asks in a syrupy tone, smiling broadly.

"I'll tell you, but you can't spread it around. The Council doesn't like students knowing about hunter activities."

Max and Lucia quickly nod, and now they're hanging on his every word.

"As you may have heard," Ty says to me, "a couple of hunters and I recently defeated a few Noctu. We're celebrating with a couple of friends."

"A hunter party?" Lucia blurts, her voice almost

cracking.

Ty looks from Max to Lucia, then back at me.

"Your friends can come too. We're meeting at DNA around ten. They're all friends of mine. I'm sure they'll turn a blind eye if they know it was me who invited you."

"We'll be there," Max says quickly. She squeezes me even tighter, as if to say she'll strangle me if I express the slightest dissent.

"Great, see you later then." Ty raises a hand in farewell and leaves.

Lucia and Max wait until he disappears around a corner before exploding with excitement. They jump up and down and squeal, unable to contain their elation.

"I can't believe it! We're going to a hunter party!" Lucia exclaims.

"This is awesome! We get to spend a whole evening with them, get to know them, and listen to them talk about their missions and the fights they've been in. They might even have one or two tips on how to increase our chances of getting accepted into their ranks," Max enthuses.

I wave my hand to remind them I'm here. "Er… I'm not planning on going. I already told you, I'm tired, and I have loads of work."

Also, Ayden will probably be there, and we

agreed to try and stay out of each other's way.

"You can't refuse an invitation like this!" Lucia is incensed. "He came over here especially to ask you…"

"How do you even know him?" Max asks.

I wave my hand in a dismissive gesture. "We just met by chance."

She gives me a look that tells me she's anything but satisfied with this answer but that she'll leave it alone for now. Because there are more important things to discuss.

"YOU ARE COMING WITH US! Even if we have to physically drag you there!"

Lucia gives me an extremely stern look too. I sigh, realizing I have no chance of escaping this. "Fine, but I won't stay long."

Lucia hugs me and gives me a peck on the cheek. "We'll see about that."

It's late afternoon, and I'm tired as I sit down at my desk. Training was strenuous, as I knew it would be, and as usual, Amber did her best to shatter my peace of mind. But after arriving home, eating a sandwich, and making myself a coffee, I feel slightly better.

For the rest of the day, Max and Lucia were so overexcited and fired up about the party that my skepticism about the whole thing waned a little. We'll have fun, even if we're surrounded by hunters.

But first, I want to get a start on my history essay, so I take out my writing pad, pen, and laptop. I try to recall the name of the street and the few details I know about the murder. In 2011, Phil Kennwood was on his way home from work. He was supposedly ambushed near Albion Street and dragged into a small side street, where he was killed. They went through his possessions and stole some valuables.

So I start by searching for 'Phil Kennwood murder', but other than a few weird Facebook profiles and the customer support page of a large company, I don't find much associated with the name. And there's nothing about a murder investigation. I refine my search by including the year and the name of the street – still no luck.

I frown and lean back in my chair. It's kind of weird. Why can't I find anything on the case? Next, I try online news archives and scour a few articles. But there are no matches – for the name Phil Kennwood, or the date, or even the street.

"I just don't get it," I mutter aloud. Did Kate make a mistake? Is one of the details wrong? But I've also searched the databases for all murder cases and accident reports. There was nothing that matched. I pick up my phone and send Kate a message.

"I need some help with a big assignment. I was thinking of writing an essay on the Phil Kennwood thing, but I can't find any information about him. Can you tell me how you found out about it? Or where I could try searching?"

I put my phone down and close my laptop. It's probably just a mix-up in the name or the year. Hopefully Kate can shed some light.

It's getting late, so I decide to get ready for the party. I shower and change into black jeans and a sequined top – which I figure looks nice but not too over-the-top. Then, I put on a little makeup. I take one last look in the mirror before I head out, hoping that my friends and I will wind up having a fun night.

Chapter 18

The club is down a side street, but the area's not totally unfamiliar to me, because the hospital where Mom works is near here. I arranged to meet my friends at a bus stop nearby, and we walk the last stretch together.

Thanks to our fake IDs, we're let into the club without any major fuss. We're greeted by thumping bass, and the dance floor is already pretty full. Young people are moving energetically to the music, swinging their arms and swaying their bodies to the rhythm. Beside the dance floor are a number of tables, all occupied.

We soon notice a large, animated group. They've pushed three tables together and are whistling encouragement to the dancers and talking loudly among themselves. Max leads the way, pushing through the crowd.

Before we even reach them, Ty jumps up and waves us over enthusiastically.

"Teresa! Good to see you!"

My gaze only lingers on him for a moment before it's automatically drawn to Ayden, who's probably wondering what I'm doing here. I'm acutely aware of what I promised him, and now here I am. Vicky is sitting on his right, and she looks anything but happy to see us.

Ayden stands up and strides over to me. "Can you come with me for a moment?"

I reluctantly follow him to the other end of the club, to a corner where the music is not so loud.

"What are you doing here?" he asks. "First, you say you're going to stay away from us, and now you show up here?! Are you trying to suck up to the hunters, like your girlfriends, to increase your chances of getting selected in the future? Or were you just too weak to say no when they insisted on dragging you here?"

I can't believe what I'm hearing. Okay, he's right

about the first part – that I promised to keep my distance from him and the other hunters. But seriously! Does he actually think that's why I'm here?! I can feel his piercing gaze cut through every fiber of my being, as if it's burning into my bones.

"Don't try telling me that's not the reason Max and Lucia are here."

"Do you think I have any interest in becoming a hunter? You think I don't know how much of a wimp I am when it comes to fighting? When you all keep reminding me of it constantly?" I shake my head sadly. "Is that what you think of me? Or are you just trying to insult me?"

Ty joins us and puts his arm around Ayden's shoulders.

"I never figured you'd be so upset about this. I invited her."

He looks at me and jerks his head toward the tables. I quickly go back to Max and Lucia, who are sitting at the table, waving me over. Max points to an empty seat next to her, and I sit down. She immediately focuses her attention on the guy opposite of her. He has dark hair and designer stubble.

"So, you're all here to celebrate a victory over the Noctu. How was the fight? How many of you were there? Did you use a lot of odeon? Which hexes did you use?"

The young man laughs and nudges the guy next to him. "Reminds me of my school days. Remember training? Constantly analyzing everything." He shakes his head and says to Max with a smirk, "We're not supposed to discuss it with you, but since Ty invited you and we're all enjoying each other's company..." he winks suggestively. "We act more on instinct in a fight. It's something you hone over time and learn to rely on."

"I guess these three haven't honed theirs, or they wouldn't have come. What are a bunch of schoolgirls doing here with us?" Vicky wrinkles her nose as if there's some nasty smell coming off us.

"Don't you start now," Ty interjects. He's just returned with Ayden. "I invited them; they're my guests. Be nice." He sits down and sips his drink. As far as he's concerned, the issue is resolved.

But I just want to get up and leave. What are we doing here? We're obviously not wanted, and the guy Max is talking to only seems interested in having his ego stroked. But my friends show no sign of wanting to leave, so I try to keep myself in check for their sake.

Ayden sits down between Ty and Vicky. She gives him an enchanting smile and, to my surprise, scoots closer to him – a lot closer. I can't help raising my eyebrows doubtfully when I see this.

"This is the girl you tested and found wanting, right?" she asks Ayden, turning toward him and intimately resting her hand on his arm.

He nods. "Yeah, but to her credit, she's pretty hard-nosed. That makes up for some of her weaknesses."

"Thanks for the generous compliment," I grumble.

"Ooh, and she's feisty too," observes the guy with the designer stubble.

"As we all know, that only gets you in trouble," says Vicky. "You haven't been at the Siena Hartford for long, have you?"

"A few weeks," I reply, bracing myself for the next dig.

She nods, tilts her head, and looks at me with those icy blue eyes as she strokes Ayden's thigh possessively.

"And you figure it's better to spend your time partying instead of training and working on your weak points? I mean, it sounds like you're pretty far behind in school." She looks up at Ayden and says, "But I guess it's up to each individual how they choose to spend their own time."

She rests her head on his shoulder and wraps her hands around his arm. Her gestures look so natural and intimate. I swallow hard and stand up to go get a drink.

"Do you guys want anything?" I ask Max and Lucia, who both nod and ask for cokes.

I breathe a sigh of relief when I get away from the tables. But I feel this burning in my gut, a feeling of anger and disappointment so strong that it makes me want to scream. What the hell am I doing here? Why don't I just leave?! I know it's a mistake, but I can't help it: my stupid pride is what keeps me here. I won't let anyone treat me that way. I won't be intimidated. Not like that.

I manage to compose myself a little before returning to our table with the drinks. Vicky's still hanging off Ayden, holding him tight. But what really cuts me to the quick is the way he looks at her. There's so much warmth and intimacy in his eyes. I sense the mood changing when I return. There's so much tension in the air that it makes the hairs on my arms stand on end.

"So, once again, congratulations on the victory. That was a really successful deployment," says the guy with the stubble, raising his glass. The others raise theirs too in a toast to Ayden, Vicky, and Ty.

We all clink glasses.

"So it was you guys who defeated the Noctu?" Lucia asks Ty quietly.

He nods. "We released some odeon to lure them out. There were more than we expected, but in the end, it was over pretty fast, and we managed to neutralize them all."

"I guess you've seen a lot of fights in your time," says Max, full of admiration.

Ty nods. "Yeah, a few."

"Did you feel like school prepared you well for your role as a hunter? Are there any areas you'd recommend working on?"

Vicky chuckles, but it seems unrelated to what Max is saying. She's probably not even listening, because she's absorbed in a conversation with Ayden, who's talking to her with that seductive smile on his face. I look at his beautiful face, that amazing sparkle in his eyes, which seem totally focused Vicky right now. Are they together? Or is something developing between them? Just thinking about it makes me uncomfortable. But having to watch too… I immediately picture Ayden and the way he pretended to have feelings for me, how close we got. It hurts me to see that there are other people he genuinely has these feelings for. Why does it have to be Vicky? Okay, so she's beautiful and has an incredible body, she's a good fighter, and, according to Ty, she and Ayden have been friends for a long time. She's the perfect candidate. Sure, she's totally condescending to me, but what do I know about her? Maybe she's normally a really good person. I don't want to make the same mistake as her and judge her too quickly.

"Teresa?" The voice snaps me out of my reverie. I look at Ty, a little flustered. "All good?" he asks.

I nod and try to smile. "Yeah, I'm fine. I was just thinking about an assignment."

"How diligent," says Vicky. Apparently, she's half listening to our conversation after all.

"Turns out even I have a good side," I retort sarcastically.

"What amazing self-awareness."

"Leave her alone," says Ty. "Hey, I keep meaning to ask you where you're from and if you feel like you're settling in here in San Francisco?"

I frown, then I can't help smiling. It's sweet of Ty to try and redirect the conversation.

"I'm from Tucson. And yeah, I really like it here."

"Oh, Arizona. I lived in Phoenix for a while," says the guy with the stubble. He tells us that he spent time there with his parents growing up. "My mother was a key carrier. My father's from this world too, but the key didn't choose him. When my grandfather died, I got his key, and my parents wanted me to go to Siena Hartford to get the best education possible. So we moved to San Francisco. I was lucky – it was an easy transition for me, and I settled in quickly at school too. I mean, I'd already learned a lot from my parents."

And then a really interesting conversation develops in the group, about how each key carrier came by their key and their individual experiences of their time in school. At least the hunters seem a little more approachable and friendly now. I'm grateful to Ty for introducing the subject. Three of his friends are now sharing a story from their school days and laughing their asses off. Ty shoots me a conspiratorial look, and I nod gratefully.

Vicky refrains from making any more digs at my expense, but that's probably because she's so preoccupied with Ayden that she doesn't even register anything else.

I look at his profile again, his straight nose, his luscious lips curved into a smile, his symmetrical face, which is undeniably good-looking and alluring. Unfortunately, it still hasn't lost its effect on me. And then, his eyes wander in my direction. They pierce me like a bolt of lightning, and my stomach clenches. Why am I staring at him like this? I go to take a sip of my coke, but my glass is empty.

I need a break, so I decide to use the bathroom

and then get myself another drink. The bathroom is small, with only two stalls, but at least it's clean and tidy.

There's only one other woman there. When I go to wash my hands, she's just finishing up and leaves the room. Then the door opens again and someone else enters. Vicky. I stifle an irritated groan and try to ignore her, which isn't easy, because she's standing right beside me, staring at me.

"I admit, you're different from what I had imagined."

I turn off the faucet. "I'm surprised I take up so much of your headspace. I didn't even know you existed until a few days ago."

I try to walk past her, hoping that's the end of it. But I hear her icy voice say, "You realize you'll be forced to leave the school sooner or later, right?"

"I don't see why. I'm giving it my best, and nobody can expect more than that from me. I'm not a bad student; I'm doing well in most subjects. The fact that I'm a little behind in combat training is understandable, and I'm making progress there too."

"Oh, yeah, so much that they had to assign another student to help you."

"What do you care?" Is she for real? She's not a student anymore. Why is she so interested in how

I'm doing in school?

"Do you even realize how much of a burden you are for Ayden? First, he had to spend all that time with you, testing you, pretending to be interested and friendly." Her icy smile pierces my heart. "And it sounds like you fell for him pretty bad."

I can't breathe anymore; everything's spinning. I hear Ayden's wonderful laugh, his beautiful voice whispering my name; I feel his hands on my skin. And the whole time, there's this one phrase thundering through my head: Vicky knows. He told her everything!

"And then, you keep putting him in danger, and he has to save you from the Noctu. You can't even defend yourself, so you force other people to risk their lives for you."

"I didn't ask for his help. He didn't have to do that."

Vicky snorts contemptuously. "Right, and you figure he had a choice? That he could just leave you there to die? He has a strong sense of responsibility and would never stand by and let somebody get killed."

My hands are shaking; my whole body is trembling with rage. Every word this woman utters is like an arrowhead drilling into me. I can't take it anymore.

"Don't worry, I'll steer clear of him. That's what you want, right? I'll take care of myself. I never asked for his help."

I try to push past her.

"What I want is for you to leave the school because you obviously don't belong. Ayden saw that from the start. And everything that's happened since proves he was right. You'll always be a problem for us because you just don't respect boundaries."

"Great, so now I know. Can I go now?"

I look at her, and her cold eyes scare me for a moment.

She shakes her head sadly. "You don't understand anything. Ayden's worried that even if you handed in your key, the Noctu could still have you in their scopes. He'll always be there for you in an emergency, and you'll never be much help… There's no way I'm going to stand by and watch him risk his life for you. But that's exactly what's going to happen. We'll all suffer because of you. I don't believe for a second that you didn't rat us out to Noah."

So that's the bombshell. And I feel it blast my heart to pieces. Ayden even told her about that. He promised to keep it to himself! Vicky knows everything. She knows about Noah; she knows that he used me and how stupid I was.

"How can anyone fall for a Noctu? Especially one like Noah?! That just says it all."

Nothing can hold me back now. I dash past her, fling open the door, and shove my way through the crowd as fast as I can. I think I see a pair of green eyes flash at me, but I ignore them. He betrayed me. Again! And this time, it almost hurts more because as much as I hate to admit it, part of me thought maybe I could trust Ayden again, just a little, or at least learn to get along with him somehow. But now, that's all been blown sky high.

Tears stream down my face as I open the door and storm out onto the street. I can't forgive him for that. Not ever.

Chapter 19

What an idiot, I keep thinking, rebuking both him and myself. I'll never forget how he lied to me, but I was starting to believe we could somehow learn to get along. At times, I even had the feeling he wanted to help me and wasn't as much of an asshole as I thought. But now...

I have no idea where I'm going. I just continue straight ahead down some street. Past other pedestrians, street lamps, brightly lit houses. Right now, I just want to be alone so I can make sense of the emotional chaos in me. I cross at a zebra crossing, continue down the street, then turn right. There are still too many people around. It's so hard holding back the tears and this searing pain that's gnawing at my insides. Damn you, Vicky! Why does she get such a kick out of hurting me? And I didn't hide the fact that she'd hit the bullseye.

The next time I look up, I realize I've subconsciously taken the route to the hospital. I can already see it up ahead. I shake my head. Mom's working there now. Should I go to her? Cry on her shoulder? I keep walking. It would be nice not to be alone, to have her arms around me. I could tell her everything – what Ayden did to me… the thing with Vicky…

I stop abruptly and bite my lip. I can't be completely honest with her. I'd have to tell her a modified version of the story, spin a bunch of lies. There's already so much she doesn't know, and right now, my thoughts are a mess. What if I let something slip that she's not supposed to know? If she found out about Noah, how dangerous he is…

It's too much for me right now. Way too much. I turn around, and I'm about walk in the opposite direction when I hear a voice that chills me to my marrow.

"Teresa? Wow, I didn't expect to see you again

so soon. Did you come looking for me to ask for another training session?"

I slowly turn to face him, and for a moment, I just stare at him. It really is him! Right now, he's the last person I want to see – okay, with maybe with one exception.

He looks back at me, and the provocative grin abruptly disappears from his face. "Tess," he says, taking a step toward me and stretching out his hand.

"Leave me alone!" I shout and start running. I can't deal with his shit right now. I just can't! If he's going to provoke me into fighting him again, then not now, no way.

So I run as fast as I can down the street. I keep glancing over my shoulder and see that he's still hot on my heels. He calls my name a few times, but I don't slow down.

I dart around corners, hoping to shake him off somehow. I dash across the next zebra crossing and turn left into an alley that turns out to be a cul-de-sac.

"Teresa." Noah holds up his hands as if he's trying to approach a wounded animal and slowly walks toward me. "I just want to talk."

His eyes are warm, and they look at me without any guile or malice. I still remember seeing what I thought were assurance and safety in them. Like I did with another pair of eyes. And both times, I was wrong.

"Stop right there!" I say slowly. But Noah doesn't listen. I clench my fists. Unbridled rage bubbles up in me. Why does no one ever do as I ask? Why are my needs always ignored?!

"I said stop right there!" I scream, so forcefully I surprise myself. Yoru appears at my side and transforms. I just want some peace and quiet, for everyone to disappear, and Yoru seems to understand that. We're facing an enemy, and he knows to use the odeon I'm sending him. He hurls several fireballs at Noah, who leaps out of the way and winds up on the ground. But he immediately has to evade another attack from my key spirit.

"Teresa, what's up with you? I honestly just want to talk. What happened?"

I don't believe him, and I hope with all my heart that Yoru hits his mark soon and makes this guy stop trying to talk to me so I can finally be alone.

Yoru doesn't let up but neither does Noah – he keeps trying to reason with me. And then, I suddenly hear another sound. I turn around, as if in a trance, to see dark shapes emerging from the shadows. Noctu, I realize. But it's too late. A dark, wavering orb is racing toward me, and all I can do is gasp in surprise. It explodes right in front of me. The force knocks me off my feet, and I land on the cold pavement.

When I look up, I see Noah standing protectively in front of me. Rain is by his side. Was that him? Did he destroy the orb with a hex? No. Way.

"Clear off!" Noah snarls at the three Noctu, who are circling me like starving wolves. "This is your final warning: if you don't beat it right now, all bets are off!"

The Noctu hesitate. They seem as surprised as I am and willing to test his resolve. But Noah's not messing around. A burning orb appears in his hand wreathed in dark smoke.

One of the Noctu growls, tenses its muscles, then charges. Noah doesn't hesitate. In a flash, he rushes at the shadowy figure with Rain at his side, raises his fist, and throws the fireball at his opponent. The Noctu yelps in surprise, and as the flames hit him, his eyes roll back, cracks appear all over his body, and he collapses to the ground, where he slowly dissolves into a sticky dark mass.

Rain leaps over Noah and bites the second Noctu's arm. He tears the arm off without hesitation and attacks the creature again. Rain is smaller than the Noctu, but his strength apparently knows no limits. He shreds his adversary to pieces. Meanwhile, Noah summons one last fireball, which eerily illuminates his face. The third Noctu doesn't stand a chance, and within seconds, it too transforms into a sticky goop.

Silence descends on the alley. All I can hear is my own wheezing breath.

"Why... why did you do that?" I ask. "You killed your own people and... saved me."

He slowly turns to face me. I've never seen such a serious expression on his face.

"I couldn't let them hurt you. I've told you so many times – I don't want anything to happen to you." He says the words slowly, as if to make sure that they sink in through the veil of shock. "I may be a Noctu, but that doesn't mean I agree with everything they do. I have my own mind, my own plans, and I stick to them. I answer to no one."

He walks toward me very cautiously, and when he's standing in front of me, he reaches out and takes my hand. It's such a tentative and considerate action that I actually let it happen. The shock may also have something to do with it. I look at him, baffled, with no idea what's going on.

"I've been watching you for a while. Pretty much since you arrived in San Francisco. We keep tabs on potential key carriers too. I followed you and kept an eye on you."

I take a deep breath. I'm reminded of the open window in my room when I was sure I'd closed it. The uneasy feeling of being watched as I walked the streets. The ride on Ayden's motorcycle and the abrupt end to our date on the hill when we almost kissed. Did Noah follow me everywhere?

"You spied on me, and when that wasn't enough, you had to insert yourself in my life and pretend to be my friend." I shake my head. "What's wrong with you? And who told you to do that?"

"Teresa, it's not like that. I was trying to find out more about you, it's true. We Noctu are always looking out for new key carriers, and we keep track of them. All I did was inform the Assembly that you'd joined the Tempes, nothing more. Do you really think after everything that's happened that I want to hurt you or that I'm a danger to you? I just want to be your friend and help you."

Assembly, I think. So the Noctu also have a hierarchy and leaders who issue orders. I shake my head and back away from him.

"I don't know what to believe."

"I know it's hard, but you can trust me," he says. "I'm not like the other Noctu. I'm on your side."

"If you figure anyone in their right mind would believe your bullshit, then you're a total moron!"

At that moment, a hex speeds past me. It ruffles

my hair, and I feel a rush of heat pass by me. Noah glances at me one last time, and for a moment, I see melancholy and pain in his eyes. Or am I mistaken?

"See you around," he says. The key is already in his hand. "Later!" The door opens and Noah disappears before Ayden's attack reaches him.

"Damn it!" Ayden hisses.

Chapter 20

W hat are you doing here?" I stare at Ayden in disbelief.

"What am I doing here?" he parrots angrily. "I saw you storm off in a huff, and then when Snow sensed the odeon, we left immediately. I had a hunch it was something to do with you. But Noah showing up like that..." He shoots me a look that I can't read, but it makes me avoid his gaze for a moment. "How did he find you? Surely, you're not so clueless that you'd just release some odeon for no reason?"

I shake my head. "No, that's not what happened."

"You can tell me later. First, I'm taking you to the school where you'll be safe," he says. He takes my hand and pulls me away.

It takes a moment for his words to sink in. "Wait! Why do I need to go to school?"

Ayden turns and glares at me. "Do you really need to ask that? We need to figure out if Noah found you by chance or if he knows something. I mean, he did just threaten you, and say you'd see him again soon, and if I there's one thing I know about him, it's that he doesn't make empty threats."

"Is that all?" I scoff. "He's often in the hospital where my mom works. He's seen me there before."

Ayden stops abruptly and very slowly turns to face me. "Are you telling me it's not the first time you've run into him there? He knows your mother works at this hospital, right?"

I nod hesitantly. "It's okay. He's known for ages, and he's never done anything to me in all that time. Just now, he was the one saving me from the Noctu. He didn't want to hurt me. He... protected me."

Even I don't fully understand that.

Ayden looks at me as if I've lost my mind. "Believe me, he's just trying to lull you into a false sense of security. If he knows things about your life, then that's a huge risk to you. He'll use it against you."

"He knows everything about me, okay?!" I blurt. I've finally had enough. This conversation is really getting on my nerves. The whole night has been one big nightmare, and I want it to end. I just want to go home to bed and forget everything.

Ayden frowns and hesitates. "What's that supposed to mean?"

I snort and tell him, "Noah knows my mom. He's met her a bunch of times in the hospital. And he knows where I live. He walked me home one time."

"You can't be serious!"

"I didn't know at the time that he was a Noctu. How many times do I need to say that?! I thought he was a friend, so why shouldn't he know where I live?"

"Okay, that changes everything." Ayden continues walking. "We need to talk to my dad in the morning. You can spend the night in the residence. You'll be safe there."

"I'm sorry?! You realize he's never done anything to hurt me this whole time, right?"

"But that could change at any moment. He could share what he knows with other Noctu. It's just too dangerous."

"What about my mom? How am I supposed to explain to her that I'm not coming home? Is she even safe at home alone?"

"The Noctu are only interested in key carriers, not unsuspecting family members. Nothing will happen to her. But your situation is different. Just message her and tell her you're staying over at a girlfriend's."

He comes a step closer and puts a hand on my shoulder. The frostiness is gone from his expression. His eyes look warm and... soft.

"Come on, I'm serious. You can't go home. What if Noah's waiting for you there? Or other Noctu? They could get to you at any time."

I know it's true, but I just can't imagine it. And yet I know he won't just let me go. So I eventually nod and follow him. Part of me still wants to run away. I don't want to sleep at school. But I'm too tired, and I have no energy left to argue. I'll talk to the principal tomorrow, then I can go home again.

My eyes wander ahead to Ayden, who's walking in front of me, continually glancing back to make sure I'm still following him.

"You told Vicky," I say quietly, and I feel my emotions bubble up again.

He frowns. "What are you talking about?"

"Are you kidding me?! Or is it that you don't know what part I mean exactly because you told her absolutely everything about me? She knows about Amber helping me in training and that your assessment of me wasn't exactly positive. What do you think hurts the most? Maybe the fact that you lied to my face when you said you didn't tell anyone about what happened!"

"I said I didn't tell my father."

I'm stunned. "Oh, then in that case, please forgive me. It was just a misunderstanding. Everything's totally fine then, and I have no problem with you venting about me to Vicky. Do I drive you so crazy that you need to vent about me to anyone who'll listen?"

He shakes his head. "What I say to Vicky is none of your business. Keep her out of it."

I can't believe what I'm hearing. "*I* should keep *her* out of it?! She came to me and threw all this in my face. She was trying to humiliate me. And in case you didn't notice, she was trying to provoke me the whole evening. Then, she followed me to the bathroom and dealt the deathblow."

"Deathblow." He laughs derisively. "You've got her all wrong. She's not like that."

"How blind can you be?"

"Let's just drop it."

"Oh yeah, we can't talk about Saint Vicky. But of course it's totally fine for you two to discuss me behind my back."

"Believe me, we have better things to do than discuss you."

He says it in such a suggestive way that I instantly start picturing things that I really don't want in my head.

"Thanks for the information," I mutter, swallowing hard. Why can't we act normally with each other? Why do we always have to fight?

Ayden sighs and says, "She shouldn't have given you a hard time about that. It's not really your fault. Noah can be pretty devious. That's why we need to take precautions and get you to safety."

He seems to think that's the end of the matter. But I'm fuming. I just hope we're almost there, so I can lie down, sleep, and forget about the whole thing until morning. We walk the rest of the way in silence, which is totally fine by me. We definitely said everything that needed to be said.

It's pretty late by the time we arrive at the school. We approach from the back and go in through the entrance that leads to the residence. Our key spirits finally show themselves again. Snow trots beside Ayden, alert, and Yoru looks up at me questioningly. The corridors are quiet, deserted at this hour. There's not a sound to be heard apart from our footsteps.

Ayden stops in front of a door, takes a key out of his pocket, and unlocks it. He steps into the room, and I just stand in the corridor, confused.

"What are you waiting for? Come in!" Ayden says.

"Is this… your room?" I ask.

He raises an eyebrow and says, "Yes, and you can sleep here tonight." He throws his jacket over a chair and takes off his shoes.

My dismay helps me regain my powers of speech.

"I thought you were going to take me to one of the teachers. Or your father. Or a guest room."

"Guest room?" He takes a blanket out of a cupboard. "This isn't a hotel. There are just the students' rooms. My dad doesn't live here. He has an apartment nearby. So you need to wait until morning to talk to him."

He throws the blanket at me and points at a sofa. "You can sleep there."

Even as he's speaking, he pulls his sweater over his head, and as hard as I try, I can't look away. I'm sure it must be because of the shock and has nothing to do with the way his muscles ripple so impressively under his skin. When he unbuttons his jeans, then throws them in a corner and stands there in nothing but his boxer shorts, I'm about as stunned as I've ever been in my life. I don't know where to look. Without another word, he goes over to the big bed and lies down.

"If you're thinking about leaving, don't. Snow will wake up instantly. So just lie down and try get some sleep."

With that, he turns his naked back toward me, and it looks as if he actually intends to sleep.

I'm still standing here, blanket in hand, unsure what to do. Surely I can't stay here?! In Ayden's room!

My eyes wander around the room. The city lights shine through the window. I glance at Ayden's bed, which is really big for just one person. Did he choose it himself, or is that standard here? I doubt it, and I wonder how many girls he's already had in it. Not that I'd want to sleep in it. I'd rather lie naked on the bathroom tiles.

But it just shows, again, how ungracious he is. He'd rather sleep in the bed himself than offer it to me and take the sofa. Shit, what was I just thinking about? Oh, yeah, the nightstand by the bed, and the white rug in front of it. Snow has curled up on it.

His head is resting on the rug, but his eyes are

open, watching me. There's no doubt about it – he knows what his job is, and he won't let me leave.

Opposite the bed, behind me, are a large cupboard in one corner and a very comfortable looking sofa. In fact, the whole room has really pleasant vibe – bright and friendly – not like Ayden at all. I can't see any pictures. But there are a few sheets of paper with handwriting on them pinned above the desk, which stands against the wall to the right of the bed.

I take a deep breath and go to the sofa. Since I clearly have no choice with Snow's watchful eyes on me, I lie down and wrap the blanket around myself. Sleep is out of the question, and not just because Ayden's a few meters away from me. I keep thinking about everything that happened today. How am I supposed to face the principal tomorrow?

I pull the blanket up to my nose and breathe deeply. It's smells like Ayden. It smells so damn good. I quickly let go of the corner of the blanket and tell myself to get a grip.

Yoru comes and curls up beside me. I stroke his warm fur and some of my tension melts away. My eyes swivel in Ayden's direction again, and he seems to be sound asleep. He's turned to face me, and now I can see his face clearly. He looks so relaxed, so peaceful, and so... breathtakingly beautiful, like an illustration of some Greek hero. With that thought, I close my eyes and hold the image close to my heart.

Chapter 21

Rushing water. I'm floating on a wave. I'm enveloped by warmth and this perfect aroma. I feel so good, so safe and snug. I could stay here forever, enveloped in this wonderful feeling. Blue light shines through the waves at me, a deep and stormy hue, like the ocean. The deeper I sink, the darker it becomes, and the color changes to green. Green like an emerald.

The rushing sound of the water stops. My eyes fly open, and I jump, almost falling off the sofa. Where the hell…? Then I remember: I'm in Ayden's room. And he's coming out of the bathroom with a towel around his waist. Damn, does this guy have to constantly walk around half naked in front of me? His stomach is flawless, just like the rest of his body, which is now illuminated by the morning sun, as if he's standing under a spotlight, shooting some commercial.

"Sleep okay?"

I stand up and instantly feel an ache in all my limbs. As comfortable as the sofa looked, I guess lying on it for that long didn't do me any good.

"Yeah, okay I guess," I say, trying to tear my eyes away from his perfect six-pack.

"The bathroom's free if you want to take a shower. There's a fresh toothbrush by the wash-basin."

Well, if that's not a clue that he has a lot of visitors... I mean, who the hell has an unused toothbrush just lying around?! Hopefully, it was just meant to replace his own, but somehow, I doubt it.

I groan quietly. I don't want to stand under Ayden's shower, but spending the whole day unwashed is something I want even less. So I accept the offer. I lock the door behind me, although I doubt even he would burst in on me. I lean against the door for a moment and check out the room. He's laid out a towel – which was never a given. Shower gel, shampoo… Oh man, I'm going to smell like him all day.

I undress and get under the deliciously hot stream of water. The shower gel actually does smell like Ayden. What am I thinking? I should be preparing myself for my conversation with Mr. Collins. How am I going to explain to him that I ended up in another fight? And this time almost deliberately.

When I'm done, I go back into Ayden's room, where he's waiting for me. "Let's get some breakfast. Dad won't be here for at least an hour."

I'm hungry, and I'm keen to see what food they have here.

The cafeteria looks a lot like the school one. Only a little smaller and cozier. As soon as we enter, eyes swivel in our direction. We get suspicious looks, and I try not to imagine what's going through these students' heads right now.

I walk alongside Ayden, grab myself a bagel, jam, bacon, and a couple of pancakes. After that horrible night, I have a huge appetite. We sit down, and I wrap my hands around my large cup of coffee.

Snow sits watchfully beside Ayden, and Yoru ogles me expectantly. Or rather, he ogles the bacon on my plate. I give him a piece, and he devours it with relish.

Ayden sips his coffee and shakes his head, appalled.

"He's hungry too, and bacon's his favorite food," I explain, trying not to shrug off the fact that Yoru's a little different in that regard. Because I've now learned that key spirits don't normally eat anything.

"He's supposed to nourish himself from your odeon," Ayden points out. "I've never heard of a key spirit that eats human food."

"Well, maybe you should try it sometime. Snow might turn out to be a foodie too."

A hint of a smile crosses his lips. "I'll pass, thanks. One spoiled key spirit in this school is enough."

I ignore his dig and give Yoru another morsel, which he evidently enjoys. After we clear away our trays, Ayden escorts me to his father.

"Dad should be here by now," he says.

"For some reason I assumed you lived with him," I say with a sideways glance at him.

"No, I've had a room here for several years. My father was hardly ever home anyway – always in Council meetings or working late here at school. So I figured I may as well save myself the travel time, and I moved in here."

"And I guess as a hunter you're often away on assignments too," I say, thinking back to when we both attended the Urban School of San Francisco.

He nods. "The candidates often live outside of San Francisco, so we have to relocate to wherever they are during the testing phase. The Council has empty apartments scattered all over – not just here in San Francisco – and we use those. But sometimes it makes sense to move into one of the apartments in this city."

We arrive at his father's office and enter the reception area. The secretary isn't here yet, so we go straight to his door and knock.

"Come in."

Ayden turns the handle and enters the room.

Mr. Collins is holding a couple of files in his hands, which he's just pulled down from a shelf. His eyes narrow in surprise.

"Ayden and Teresa. You two showing up this early means something must have happened." He sits in the chair behind his desk and folds his hands. "What is it?"

"Teresa was attacked last night, by Noah," Ayden explains.

I open my mouth to contradict him. Because that's not true. But what does it matter? I don't even know why Noah helped me. How am I supposed to explain to Mr. Collins something I don't understand myself? No one would believe me. But I have to say something.

Mr. Collins scrutinizes me. "I see you didn't sustain any injuries. That's something at least."

I'm about to answer, but Ayden intervenes.

"Noah got away again, unfortunately. We think he knows a lot about Teresa's living environment."

The principal raises his eyebrows. "That's not good. What makes you think that?"

"He's been seen several times at the hospital where her mother works. In fact, they know each other, and Teresa saw him near her house once. She wasn't totally sure, so she didn't say anything at the time."

I blatant lie from Ayden. And I don't understand why he's trying to protect me. Or is he just trying to keep himself out of trouble? He's already lied to his father by withholding the fact that Noah and I exchanged messages and that I even went on a date with him.

Vicky pops into my head. He told her everything, kept nothing back. And that knowledge burrows into my flesh like a sharp thorn. He obviously trusts her a lot.

"That kind of information about a key carrier is immensely valuable to the Noctu and puts us all at great risk. We need to act immediately."

Mr. Collins takes a sheet of paper out of his desk and begins to write on it.

"We'll arrange a room for you here in the residence. I'll speak to your mother personally to convince her of your need to move."

I must have misheard him. I'm supposed to move? Move in here? He can't decide for me just like that. Not without at least asking me how I feel about it.

"Mr. Collins, I don't want to move. I really like my home, and I feel safe there. Noah's known all this for a long time, and he's never tried to do anything to harm me."

"Until last night when he attacked you. Not to mention your unfortunate encounter with him a couple of weeks back." He shakes his head. "No, I'm sorry. We have no idea when and where he'll attack next, but it will happen. We need to protect you. And I see no other way to do that."

I feel my cheeks getting hot. "And my opinion's irrelevant?"

He puts down his pen, folds his hands again, and looks me in the eye. His gaze is unyielding, hard, and he radiates such authority that, for the first time, I'm aware of the high position he must hold in the world of the Tempes.

"Honestly, no. You're too young and inexperienced to be able to judge this situation. You know too little about our way of life, the Noctu, and our struggle against them. I can only urge you to accept my decision. It's what's best for you."

I meet his penetrating stare, clench my fists, and can't refrain from asking, "What if I don't?"

Without any trace of emotion, he replies, "Then we'll take the next best course of action to protect you. We'll be forced to take away your key and return your fox to the Odyss. You'll leave the school and no longer be a part of our world." He pauses. My heart flutters, and all I can do is stare at him incredulously. "It's your decision."

I swallow hard, and a steel wire tightens around my heart. We both know that's not an option. My hands are tied – I'll never give up Yoru and turn my back on this world, as dangerous as it is.

"Then, I guess I have to accept it," I reply through gritted teeth.

"I'll arrange everything and speak to your mother. She'll understand. It's best if you move in today. Anything else would be too risky."

With that, he returns his attention to the sheet of paper, signaling to me that the conversation is over.

Ayden and I leave the room. I can't put into

words what's going through my head right and how it makes me feel. I feel totally sidelined, forced into something I don't want.

"It's the right decision, you'll see," says Ayden, which only adds fuel to the fire.

"Even if it is, don't you think it should be my decision?" A red-hot wave of intense anger surges inside me, ready to destroy everything. "If you kept your mouth shut, it wouldn't have come to this."

Ayden's lips narrow and he holds his breath for a moment, then he says, "I'm trying to save your life, which you keep gambling recklessly. You have no idea what you've gotten yourself into. And if you behaved a little less suicidally, then other people wouldn't have to keep risking their necks for you."

With that, he leaves me standing here. His words settle like burning acid in every part of my body. Is he right? Am I endangering people's lives? Ayden's already been forced to come to my aid several times. But I never asked him to. Would I be alive if it weren't for him? Shit. Damn it! What am I supposed to do? I take a deep, slow breath. I have no choice. The next step is already decided, and I'll make the best of it. I won't let it get me down.

The evening presents a difficult predicament. I've spent the whole day thinking about how to bring up the subject with my mother of me having to move.

Mr. Collins said he'd talk to her, but unfortunately, he kept me completely in the dark about exactly what he intended to say to her. So I have no idea what mood Mom will be in.

When I arrive home after a long day and open the door, I hear noises coming from the kitchen. I go through and see that Mom's cooked mac and cheese – a meal we usually have when she's pressed for time or too anxious to focus on a recipe.

"Hey, Mom," I say. She's just begun to set the table and pauses with a plate in her hand.

"Tess." She puts the plate down and hugs me. "You should have told me you were having problems in school," she says. "I know how hard all this must be for you."

"Mr. Collins talked to you?" I probe before going into any detail about the purported school problems.

"I knew you were a little behind in sports – you told me yourself – but I had no idea you were struggling with the workload in your other subjects."

Her voice is very soft. She must feel like she's

walking across a minefield and has to approach the subject gently so I don't explode.

"The principal called me at the hospital today. He said they want to offer you a few supplementary courses to deepen your understanding of the material. But that means you'll need to spend even more time at school." She takes a deep breath and comes to the point. "He wants to offer you a place in the boarding residence. As we can't cover the full cost ourselves, the school will pay most of it out of a fund set up for this kind of thing. A room just became available, and they're offering it to you. But we need to decide right away. Obviously, they have a bunch of applicants that want to attend the school. But as you're already a student there, they're giving you first option."

He really thought of everything. Mr. Collins has cast doubt on my academic performance. Without any concrete test results, which I obviously don't have yet, I can't exactly convince Mom otherwise. And why would I want to? I don't have a choice about moving into the residence. The situation feels like a nasty splinter under my skin. Does he have to make me out to be the ultimate loser? But this way, Mom has no wiggle room. She has to give me permission to move so that my grades improve and I can stay in the school.

"He already discussed it with you, he said."

It sounds like a question, and I nod slowly. "Yes, he did." The next words don't come easy, but they need to be said, as hard as it is for me to say them. "I'd prefer to stay here, but I really think it's best if I accept the offer."

Mom hugs me. I can see how much she's battling internally with this. She nods silently into my shoulder, wipes tears from the corners of her eyes, and smiles bravely.

"Well, you've been practically living alone all this time anyway. And I'll do everything I can to make sure we see each other regularly in future, I promise."

I know she's right, but that doesn't make it any easier. However, I also know that I need to do this.

Chapter 22

I put down the last box. It contains a few books, clothes, and a potted plant Mom gave me. "Something green to brighten your room." I actually moved a few days ago, but I kept a bunch of stuff at home because I still had to organize a few things, pack, and buy furniture. Now, I just have this last box to unpack, then I'll be done, and I can settle into my new home.

It feels strange because although I'm allowed to arrange the room however I like, everything still feels unfamiliar. The room is painted white and has two large windows. The bed was already here, and it's comfortable and totally adequate. The large, heavy wardrobe with a mirror, and the desk, also came with the room. All I had to get were the shelf in the corner, a table, and four chairs. I arranged the furniture the way I wanted it, hung a couple of Frida's pictures on the walls, made the bed, and did everything I could to make the place feel like home. But it's not easy, because I don't really want to be here.

My phone rings. It's Alex.

"How was the move? You done? Can we start your housewarming party already?"

Although I've been at the Siena Hartford Academy a while and even live here now, I haven't lost contact with Alex, Kate, and Chrissy, fortunately. I know it won't be easy to maintain these friendships because there are so many things in my life that I can't talk to them about. But I mean to stay in touch with them.

"Yeah, I'm done, you can come tonight," I reply.

I already asked Max and Lucia if outsiders are allowed inside the school or the residence.

"Only late afternoons at school, when classes are over, but that's just about not disturbing the school day," Lucia explains. "If you're worried about the key spirits, you know normal people can't see their true form. And the spirits are pretty savvy about staying out of sight when they need to. So, don't worry. If you want to bring someone here, obviously you're allowed. But I recommend after hours when most students are in their rooms and it's quieter."

"Actually, hardly anyone ever brings outsiders into the school or the residence," Max pipes up. "They're just such different worlds, and even if it's not officially against the rules, we try not to mix them."

Lucia elbows her lightly on the side and rolls her eyes. "That's just because most of us aren't friends with those people. But there's no reason you shouldn't be, and you're allowed to bring them here if you'd like."

"Just because something's officially allowed doesn't mean you have to do it."

Lucia sighs. "As you can tell, Max has a really strong view on this. But don't let her put you off."

I don't plan to. Still, I don't want to annoy anyone, so I'm keeping the party small. I've invited my friends but only those three.

"Great, around eight?" Alex suggests.

"Sure, works for me. Can you tell Chrissy?"

"Yup. I'm so excited. I can't believe you live alone now. The freedom! I hope you realize how lucky you are and make the most of it. I'd already be thinking of a thousand things I want to do. Need any inspiration?"

I laugh and say, "You can give me some tonight."

We say goodbye, and I message Kate, letting her know what time to come.

I put my phone away and go to unpack my last box. The sweaters look like they've been lying in a drawer for a while. I sniff them and sigh. I need to wash them before putting them away. I glance at the full laundry basket and decide to use this time to take care of that. I usually did my own laundry at home, so it's nothing new. But carrying it all the way through a huge building is.

After starting the washing machine, I return to my room. As I'm fishing my key out of my pocket, another door opens three doors down, and to my surprise, Ayden steps out. He closes the door behind him, then notices me and looks just as surprised as I am. So, it seems like he didn't know which room I was moving into. But I guess it could have occurred to me because I spent the night in his room only a few days ago. In my defense, the residence is huge, and all the corridors look the same, at least to me.

Ayden approaches me and doesn't look daggers at me, for a change. I guess this is my grace period because he must know it wasn't easy for me to make the move.

"So this is your room," he observes. "Have you had a chance to settle in?"

"Kind of," I reply. "It's not easy in a place where you don't even want to be."

"Try not to see it that way," says Ayden, and to my astonishment, there's no sharpness in his voice. "Focus on all the advantages you have now: no more long trips between home and school, which means more free time. And here, you're surrounded by people you don't need to fake it with; you can be yourself and so can your fox."

I glance at Yoru, who's sitting beside me and staring into the distance. He's probably spotted Snow. Ayden's key spirit doesn't reveal himself to me, but I'm sure he must be around here somewhere.

I frown and try to read Ayden's expression.

"Are you sick? Are you about to head out on a mission you may not return from alive, or why else are you suddenly being so friendly?"

"I only ever speak the truth, but people often don't want to hear it and think I'm being unfriendly."

There's that impish glint in his eye again that I know so well.

I think about what he just said and then reply,

"No, it's not what you say, it's how you say it, and I'm telling you, your tone is usually pretty harsh."

Ayden grins. "I'm not about to take lessons from you."

"Oh, don't worry, I wouldn't dream of it. If we practiced together, we'd probably be at each other's throats in a matter of minutes."

"A teacher who has no patience with her students..."

"A teacher who can't muster any patience with *one particular* student because he always winds her up too quickly."

"I wonder why."

"Probably because he's a master of his subject," I retort, looking straight at him.

His eyes immediately captivate me – on one hand, they're as dark as the densest forest, and at the same time, there's this light in them, like bright sunlight warming the world and melting any ice it comes in contact with. His incredible lips are drawn up into a smile.

I remember all too well how easily that smile can mesmerize me.

"And he's incredibly good at using other people for his own ends," I hear myself say, revealing what's deep in my heart. A wound that may never heal.

He's still looking at me, nodding slowly.

"I can understand if it seems that way to you, and maybe you're right." The green of his eyes appears to grow darker, and the radiance disappears from them. "I hope you'll give your new home a chance for your own sake. It's not so bad."

With that, he turns away, and I stare after him until he disappears down another corridor.

I will make this my home. What choice do I have?

Chapter 23

I survey my room. I haven't been here long, so I haven't had a chance to mess the place up. But I cleaned and tidied again anyway. It's only a single room, but from now on, I'll be living alone, and for the first time, I have a place of my own. I never expected it to happen so soon.

I glance at the table where I've set out a bowl of chips, some other snacks, and a few drinks. I put napkins on the table, then there's a knock at the door.

"Kate," I greet her cheerfully and give her a hug.

"I'm so glad you could make it."

She wasn't sure until the last minute if she could actually get away from her mother.

"Mom thinks I'm studying at the library. I told her I might be late. But I shouldn't push my luck."

I nod. "Just say when you need to go."

Kate walks into the room and looks around with a smile. "Looks great. You must love it here. I mean, the school looks really impressive even from the outside, but this... is really nice."

Not everyone would be so enthusiastic about my room, but Kate has a difficult time living with her mother. She has to discuss every aspect of her life with her and can't even decorate her own room the way she wants. She lives in a pink, little girl's dream, which for a seventeen-year-old is pure horror. For Kate, boarding at school would be totally liberating.

I offer her something to drink.

"Have you heard from Chrissy and Alex? I thought you were all coming together."

"Alex messaged to say she and Chrissy would be here later. She has something to take care of."

I raise my eyebrows, and a smile appears across Kate's lips.

"Well, if you ask me, I figure Alex is planning something, and Chrissy's trying to make sure it doesn't spiral completely out of control."

I laugh. "That sounds like Alex."

Kate doesn't reply because her phone has started vibrating. She takes it out of her pocket and reads a message, then quickly types a reply.

"Sorry, Mom wanted to know if I'd arrived safe."

I'm about to say a few sympathetic words when her phone starts ringing. She doesn't even need to check the display to know who's trying to reach her.

"Yes, Mom, I am. I just messaged you. Yes, it's important... I won't know until later, I already told you that. I'll try to hurry, but like I said, it's for an assignment, and it could take a while. No, of course not, don't worry... I will. See you later."

She ends the call. Her cheeks are slightly red, and I can't tell if it's anxiety or embarrassment.

"My mother. Reminding me not to stay out too late."

At least that's the official version. I suspect that for Kate's mom it's about controlling her.

"You really don't have it easy," I say, putting a soothing hand on her arm.

I can see that Kate's wrestling with herself. She bites her lip. "She doesn't mean to be like that. She just worries a lot."

"Worries that you'll get mixed up with the wrong people, i.e. me," I say, recalling the first time I met her mom. She made it pretty clear what she thought of me and my mother.

"It's not that. Or not just that." Kate sits on a chair and wrings her hands. "She's just afraid for me."

"Okay, but you're not a child anymore, and she can't protect you from the world. You've got to make your own way, and that means being free to make mistakes."

"I know, but she's just so clingy."

I raise my eyebrows. "Interesting way of putting it."

Kate's smile becomes melancholy as she says, "I guess it's not obvious at first glance, but she does it all for me. And she wasn't always like this."

"I'm not sure I understand," I say, taking a seat beside her.

Kate takes a deep breath and stares at the floor, as if she can see images of the distant past there.

"Mom never used to be this strict, and certainly not this controlling. But when I was five, I got sick. I had a serious lung infection and spent time in intensive care. Things looked really bad for me for a while, and the doctors were worried I wouldn't make it. The fear almost killed my mother. She stayed at my bedside day and night, held my hand, and prayed that I'd somehow survive. And then, the doctors actually did save my life, and I recovered. But that period really affected Mom. Since then, she's been super scared of losing me."

I stare at Kate incredulously, then give her a hug. "That must have been really hard for you too."

Kate laughs. "The parts I can remember weren't all that dramatic. I was in hospital for a long time, and I knew I was unwell, but I had fun, read lots of books, played with the nurses. I recall a lot of nice moments. I wasn't aware of how serious it was at the time."

"Unlike your mom."

I can totally understand her anxiety. It must have been terrible nearly losing her child and having to stand by helplessly and watch it happen. But although I understand her fear, the way she restricts Kate so much is unfathomable to me. Isn't it even more important, now that she's been given a second chance in life, to actually live that life? I guess her mom doesn't see it that way. She wants to keep her daughter's life on the straight and narrow, and she'll do whatever it takes to minimize the risk of anything happening to her again.

"So now you know the reason and why it's not always easy for me to stand up to my mom.

Because she's just doing it out of fear."

Just like you, I want to say, but I keep my comment to myself because I can sympathize with Kate's dilemma. She doesn't want to cause her mother any more suffering. And anyway, she's already taking steps to free herself from her mother's stifling control.

Kate stands up, helps herself to a cola, and takes a few sips.

"You've made this room really cozy," she mutters, as if trying to shake off the gloomy thoughts.

She goes over to my desk and looks at the school books and notes I've jotted down for my homework.

"Oh, we're doing this in math too. But I guess you guys will tackle it more extensively and have tougher assignments. The ones we have are enough for me."

It's hard for me to lie to my friend. But she can't know that this isn't really a school for gifted students and that our math class is no different from hers.

"What's this? Homework?" She points at the worksheet we were given in history. And then, it dawns on me that I was intending to talk to Kate about that anyway.

"Yeah, right. I messaged you about that recently.

We have to write an essay on the history of San Francisco. We can choose an unusual event as a topic. And I thought of the story you told me about that murder. You know the one I mean – Phil Kennwood, attacked and killed near Albion Street. I couldn't find any information on the case online. Do you remember how you found out about it?"

Kate frowns pensively. She avoids looking at me and glances evasively at the clock.

"Honestly, I can't remember. Maybe Dad told me about it. Or I might have mixed up the name or the date."

She smiles apologetically.

"Yeah, I thought of that. So I tried searching separately for the name, the street, and the year. But even then, I couldn't find anything."

"Well, sometimes these things aren't made public." She lowers her head and paces around the room. "San Francisco's a big city. I guess not every murder case is reported in the newspapers, especially not if some other issue was really big at the time. Then, something like that could get overlooked. But I can ask Dad if you'd like. Maybe he knows something about it."

I'm not sure why her father would know anything about the case. He's in IT.

"It's okay, I'll find another topic."

"Maybe I can help with that," she offers. "I mean, I know San Francisco pretty well, and I promise this time I'll only give you information I'm sure is one hundred percent correct."

"Thanks for offering. But I'm sure I'll come up with something."

"Okay. Let me know if you change your mind. Sounds like a really interesting assignment. I wish we did essays on stuff like that."

I'm about to say something when we hear a knock on the door.

Chapter 24

As soon as I open the door, Alex storms in. Chrissy follows her, looking red-faced and flustered. I guess it wasn't easy keeping our exuberant Alex in check. Alex strides to the table with the snacks and drinks and opens her backpack.

"I gotta say, you have really weird teachers here," she babbles. "First you think: great, he's young and even kind of hot. Something you only ever see in private schools – teachers as walking advertisements. I guess it makes the students more interested in going to class."

I stand by helplessly, unable to follow her train of thought.

"But then you realize you can never trust a good-looking façade." She puts a couple of beers on the table. "I was worried he was going to find these treasures in my backpack when he insisted on looking inside. Luckily, they were well hidden."

Okay, I'm starting to get the picture, and it's a little unsettling. "You met a teacher who wanted to look in your bag?"

Chrissy's been silent so far, and now she nods. "He even wanted to know our names, where we were from, and who we were visiting."

She still looks a little pale around the nose, which is understandable. If the teacher had found alcohol on them, it would have probably spelled trouble – we're underage after all.

"It felt like an interrogation," Alex says indignantly, grabbing a handful of chips and shoving them in her mouth.

"Lucky you weren't caught with those," Kate replies, glancing disapprovingly at the beers.

Alex waves dismissively. "I know what to do when I'm being searched."

"Is that something you should be bragging about?" Kate asks, but Alex has already moved on.

She's checking out my room.

"This is really nice, I like it." She sits backward on a chair. "I wish I could move out of home. It must be awesome being able to do whatever you want."

"Well, I'm in a school residence, and as you just found out, there is some supervision."

"It's pretty sad that they're so suspicious of everyone," she sighs. Then, she reaches into her bag and takes out a package with a lopsided bow, which she hands to me. "A small house warming gift from us." She winks at Chrissy, who rubs her neck and looks abashed.

"I didn't have much to do with it," she says. It can't be anything good, judging by her embarrassed expression.

I open the package and find a colorful collection of stuff inside. The most harmless thing is a block of chocolate.

"Brain food, which I'm sure you'll need," says Alex.

"Uh-huh. And what am I supposed to do with thumbtacks and liquor?"

"It's all stuff to help you survive your time at this school. Kate told us Ayden's here too, which doesn't exactly make things easier. So if he pisses you off, you can pay him back. A few thumbtacks on his chair or in his shoes. And the liquor's for emergencies in case nothing else works."

"So you're trying to turn her into an alcoholic," Kate says, rolling her eyes.

I peer into a small carton and can't help laughing. "Laxatives?! You're giving me laxatives? You're that suspicious of the cafeteria food?"

Alex shrugs. "I was thinking more for Ayden. He can't drive you nuts if he's stuck on the toilet all day."

I raise my eyebrows when I take out the last two items. A postcard and a pack of condoms. "Plenty of other fish in the sea," I read with a frown. "Very original."

"A little mantra to remind you that he's not the only guy in the world," explains Alex. "And the condoms are in case you catch one of those other fish," she adds with a wink.

I look at her in bewilderment and can't help laughing again. "You've really put a lot of thought into this."

"Count yourself lucky – there was a bunch of other stuff I managed to talk her out of," Chrissy comments.

"You guys have no imagination and too many moral hang-ups," Alex complains as she picks up one of the beers. "Anyway, now you're well-armed, and if you need any help," she rolls her eyes knowingly, "then I'm an endless source of knowledge."

"What more could I want?" I say, giving her a hug.

Suddenly, there's a knock on the door, and we all look at each other in surprise.

"Did you invite someone else?" asks Alex.

I shake my head and hope ardently that it's not the proverbial devil at the door.

I open it to find Ty standing there.

"What are you doing here?"

He raises his hand in greeting and cranes to peer past me into the room. "You're hosting a party?"

"Uh, yeah," I admit. "Is that a problem?"

He looks at me for a moment, then nods and says, "Definitely." He walks past me into the room. "Because you didn't invite me."

My friends are stunned and look at Ty as if the devil himself just walked into the room. They all try to position themselves so that the beer is hidden from him. Alex contorts herself so much that she only succeeds in drawing more attention to it.

"They do random room inspections?" Chrissy asks quietly.

"Hardcore," Alex mutters. "The teachers even show up in your room."

I look at Ty in surprise. His eyes widen with dismay.

"You thought I was a teacher?! How old do you think I am?" He runs his hand over the seven metal rings in his right ear. "Do your teachers look like this?"

Now it's my friends' turn to look confused.

"You're... not a teacher?" Chrissy asks.

"No, I'm Teresa's pal," he declares cheerfully, putting his arm around my shoulders and pulling me in close as if it's the most natural thing in the world.

"Oh, really?" I ask.

"Sure."

"Okay," Alex mutters, evidently confused. "And you're... uh... still a student here? I didn't think it was possible to repeat a year that many times, but I guess things are a little different at this school."

Ty's expression is priceless. A mixture of utter horror, disbelief, and pained bewilderment. "Again, how old do you think I am? I'm 22. I live in the next wing, and I visit Tess all the time."

"The next wing? What's that?" Alex asks.

Ty's mouth opens, then closes again. He's talked himself into a corner.

"Well," he scratches the back of his head sheepishly. "It's nothing exciting. I... I mean, obviously

I don't live there alone. There are a bunch of us, like, a group, and we, uh..."

"It's the college. Ty studies there," I say, coming to his aid.

"There's a college here too?!" asks Kate. "I had no idea."

I nod. "Yeah, it's only for students who graduated from this high school first. So you wouldn't find much info on it."

"It must have been a real honor for you to be accepted. And I guess it's an amazing place to study," she says to Ty.

"Uh, yeah, sure. Lots to do... learning and stuff.

I suppress a grin. Keeping secrets doesn't seem to be one of his strengths.

"Coming back to the teacher thing..." Alex interrupts. She clearly still has a bone to pick with him. "You should have told us you weren't a teacher. That was totally uncool. And then you searched through our stuff."

"You did what?" I ask. "Why did you do that?"

"I met them just now in the corridor, and I figured they were looking for something, so I asked them. They said they were on their way to see you."

"Yeah, and then he was really critical, like, 'So this is some kind of party?' And he had this weird grin like he'd had one too many tokes on a joint."

"It's amazing the stuff that goes through teenagers' heads these days," Ty mutters, sounding like an old man.

"So why did you search her bag?" I ask.

"It just came up in the conversation," he replies, scratching the back of his head. "I knew about your house warming. Just wanted to know if it was going to get interesting." There's that grin again.

Meanwhile, Alex has opened another beer, and she hands it to Ty. "You really scared the shit out of us."

"Sorry, I didn't mean to," he says, taking a gulp.

Chrissy helps herself to a drink too. Kate sticks to the chips. She keeps glancing at Ty and scrutinizing him mistrustfully. Or is it more a kind of admiration because he allegedly attends college here?

"Okay, tell me, how did you two meet? Obviously, you don't have any classes together." Alex has made herself comfortable cross-legged on my bed. Her expression makes me uneasy.

"We met through a mutual friend," says Ty, shooting me a grin, which is supposed to be teasing, but I doubt that's how my girlfriends interpret it.

"A mutual friend. So do you and Tess hang out

a lot?"

"Now and then. We recently went to a club together."

"Aha," says Alex. She looks back and forth between the two of us. "You guys don't need to be secretive on our account. I think it's cool if you're together. After all that stuff with Ayden, a new guy would do her good." She raises her beer in a toast. "You have my blessing."

Ty laughs. "Not the worst idea. Hey, what do you say?" he jokes, putting his arm around me. "I doubt everyone would be as understanding about it as your friend here."

I shake my head and shrug him off. "I have no idea what we are, but let's get one thing clear: we're not a couple. Ty's a friend of Ayden's, and we only met recently. Since then, I haven't been able to shake him off." I shoot him a mischievous smirk.

"Ouch," he retorts. "Don't listen to her. We're buddies."

"Buddies don't invite you to a club where no one wants you around. And they for sure don't let other people insult you once you're there," I declare.

His smile vanishes abruptly. It's replaced by an expression resembling guilt. "You guys were welcome there, trust me. You got along well with most of our crew."

I have no idea if Ty is really that blind or if he just refuses to believe that the other hunters were either making fun of us or basking in Max and Lucia's admiration.

"And if you're referring to the thing with Vicky, I have no idea what happened between you two. But I'm guessing it wasn't fun."

"You could say that," I retort, peripherally aware of my friends' puzzled looks. They're obviously listening intently to our prickly exchange.

"Vicky doesn't mean to be like that. When it comes to Ayden, she's just... I don't know, let's call it sensitive. She doesn't like her territory being invaded."

I raise my eyebrows. "That's a nice way of putting it. And while we're on that analogy, you can't tell her from me that she can have her whole forest and all the stags in it for herself. I'm not interested in them."

"She's just concerned. Don't hold it against her. You've seen how ambitious and driven she is. Vicky just isn't too understanding of anyone who's different from her."

"Oh-ho, now it's getting interesting," Alex pipes up, throwing a handful of chips in her mouth.

And she's right: I'm close to exploding.

"Are you trying to say I'm lazy and have no ambition? And that's why the conscientious Vicky can't stand me?!"

He holds up his hands defensively. "No, that's not what I'm saying. You two are just really different, and she doesn't know you at all. All she knows is what Ayden's told her, and he didn't want you to come here initially."

"Right. In their eyes I'm a..." I'm about to say 'danger,' but I remind myself that my friends are here and listening to everything we say. "They both think I don't deserve a place at this school and that everyone who tries to support me is wasting their time."

For a moment, Ty says nothing and just stares at me in bewilderment. Then, he shakes his head.

"No, it's not like that."

"Oh really?! Well, one thing's for sure: Ayden never wanted me here."

"Yeah, but he knows you're putting in a lot of effort and that you've made progress." He breaks off and sighs. "Ayden's not as bad as you think."

"He toyed with my emotions," I remind him.

"Yes, and you know his reasons."

"That doesn't make it any better," I point out.

"Sure. But Ayden has a job to do, and he takes it really seriously. He has to. I realize that doesn't change how it made you feel. But look at it from his point of view. It's impossible to go down that road without shutting people out, keeping people at arm's length. It's a difficult life, and things have never been easy for Ayden. He's had to live up to high expectations from a young age, had to work hard and never had any time for himself. Just try to put yourself in his position for a moment."

It's true – I know almost nothing about Ayden's life or his past. But that's not my fault. Back at our old school, I tried to get to know him better, but he wouldn't let me in – and never intended to. He could have told me the truth about some aspects of his life. But he just piled on the lies. No, there are only a few people, like Ty and Vicky, who are important to Ayden, and they're the only ones he lets in. Why should I even try to get through to him? The lines are already drawn, and I can't cross them.

"He's not the only one who's under a lot of pressure and high expectations," I remind Ty. "You have the same responsibilities. Do you take such a vicious approach? I find it hard to imagine."

Ty looks away guiltily. "I'm not Ayden. Everyone has to figure out their own way of dealing with things."

Those few words tell me all I need to know. I

just nod, and Ty stares at the beer in his hand. He takes a sip. He looks up as if he's just remembered we're not alone in the room.

"This school sounds really hardcore," Alex observes. "What kind of work are you talking about, where you have to be vicious?"

"Science competitions," I say. "It can get really heated."

Ty stands up. "I didn't mean to disrupt your party, and now I've killed the mood." He puts down his bottle. "Maybe it's better if I leave." He forces a smile and raises his hand in farewell. "I hope you guys have a nice evening anyway. It was nice to meet you all."

We all watch him leave the room.

"What was all that about?" asks Alex the moment the door clicks shut.

I shrug. "I don't know, that's just Ty. He's a little odd."

"And a friend of Ayden's," says Chrissy. "So what does he want with you?"

"You heard him," Alex interjects. "He's into her."

I roll my eyes and wonder which conversation she was just listening to. "No way."

"He's way older than Tess," Kate says disapprovingly.

"Pfff," says Alex, waving her hand as if to swat the words out of the air. "But hey, tell us, what were you guys talking about? What are these science competitions?"

"It's just an elective subject. You can compete with other schools. You get assignments and questions on scientific topics," I lie, helping myself to a beer. "Let's talk about something else. I'm tired of discussing school."

I can see that Alex still has a thousand questions. It takes a lot of effort, but she swallows them and claps her hands together.

"Okay, let's get this party started."

I can't help smiling as I watch her take out her phone to play music. For the rest of the evening, we don't talk about Ayden, his friends, or school. We just have fun laughing and enjoying each other's company.

"I thought he'd lost his mind. I mean, can you imagine?" Alex laughs as she regales us with anecdotes.

I'm about to say something when a phone rings. Kate instantly jumps up and frantically fishes it out of her pocket.

She answers after two rings.

"Hi Mom. Yeah, I'm still studying. Yeah, right. We may need to look up some more stuff. It's a big essay, so it requires a lot of research." Kate's pacing up and down the room like a caged animal. I can see how tense she is. "I won't stay much longer. There's at least one thing we still need to check... Yeah, I get that, but we wanted to at least make a decent start... Uh, yeah, okay. If you think so." Kate looks sad. "Yeah, I understand. I'll leave now."

She ends the call and stares down at the phone in her hand, then looks at us. She's wearing a forced smile, but embarrassment is written all over her face.

"Your mom?" asks Alex.

Kate nods. "I gotta go. She says it's late." Kate picks up her bag and adds apologetically, "I'm really sorry; I was hoping to stay a while longer."

We can all see and feel how uncomfortable the situation is for her. Alex puts a comforting arm around her shoulders.

"Don't worry about it. My mom always has these phases too, where she decides she needs to be stricter." She stands up and looks at the clock. "And it is pretty late. Maybe we should all think about going."

Chrissy nods, and I think it's incredibly cool the way they're supporting Kate. I hug them all and say, "It was great having you guys. Let's catch up again soon."

"Totally, and next time we'll party hard," Alex promises.

I escort them out of the residence and wave goodbye. It was a nice evening, even if parts of it didn't exactly go according to plan.

I linger outside a while and breathe in the cool air. There are no stars visible in the sky. The city lights are too bright. There are streetlamps everywhere. I can still see a few brightly lit windows here and there. I take a short walk and start to feel the tiredness creep through my body. With Yoru at my side, I go back into the building, which looks totally dead. There's not a soul around, not even a key spirit. It's as if Yoru and I are the only living beings that still exist here. A strange feeling. I'm about to unlock my door when I hear footsteps. Instantly alert, I glance sideways.

Ayden's shuffling along the corridor, his head down, looking totally beat. He heads toward his room, swaying slightly, and briefly leans against the wall. That's when he looks up and sees me. He straightens his posture, obviously trying to hide his ragged state. He fishes his key out of his pocket and inserts it in the lock.

"Hard night?" I ask.

His smile doesn't look genuine. "Kind of. But

that's just how it goes sometimes."

"The way you look, sometimes is probably often enough."

Ayden shakes his head wryly. "Do I look that bad?"

I scrutinize him. "Well, I wouldn't recommend running a marathon just now."

"I had no intention of doing that at this time of night." He gives me a wave, opens the door and says, "Sleep well," then he goes into his room.

I wonder where Ayden's just come from. Was he out partying? Did he meet up with friends? Or was he on one of his missions? Either way, he looks like he's had a long night. But it's not my problem, so I push the thought aside, lie down in my bed, and close my eyes.

Chapter 25

I admit I'm a little distracted, although I'm trying really hard to focus on the front of the class, where our teacher is rapidly writing up formulas for determining odeon concentration in key spirit hexes. But I keep pausing and glancing at Ayden, who appears to have fallen asleep at his desk. His head keeps sliding off his hand and then jerking up when he wakes with a start. I guess he had a really rough night. Looks like he was partying hard. He didn't sound drunk last night in the corridor, but we only exchanged a few words.

Lucia elbows me and nods at Ayden. "Someone went hard last night."

"Looks that way. Why does he even bother showing up to class in that state?"

She shrugs. "It's not that simple. You need a sick note from a doctor, and the doc would immediately know what was up."

She's probably right. I glance at Ayden again, who seems to have given up the charade entirely and is now resting his head on his arm. He's lucky the teacher is too busy writing and facing the front.

"I guess he'll never learn," says Lucia, returning her attention to the whiteboard.

"Does it happen a lot?"

"Seriously? You should know by now that Ayden's a fun-loving guy. He's always out partying, meeting girls, going home with them. He's smart enough not to bring them back here. He has his fun, and then he's done with them. He's not interested in anything long term."

Lucia says it so casually, as if that's totally normal.

"I thought he and Vicky had a thing."

Lucia shrugs. "Neither of them are relationship types. Friends with benefits, you could say."

Surprised, I raise my eyebrows and glance at him again. It's becoming increasingly clear to me that there was no truth to the persona he presented when we first met.

In history class, I actually manage to get Ayden out of my head because I have a much more pressing issue. I still haven't settled on an essay topic.

"You've all had time to think about your essays, and I hope by now you've chosen a topic. I'd like you to write them down for me, so I can offer advice if necessary. If any of you still don't know what you want to write about, please let me know," says Mr. Brian.

The others all get to work. Pens start scratching on paper all around me. I really should have given it more thought, but there was the hunter party and then the move. I probably shouldn't mention the former excuse to Mr. Brian.

Eventually, I get a couple of sentences down on paper around the topic of the Golden Gate Bridge, but I'm not really satisfied. I wanted to write about some darker aspect of the city, but that amounted to nothing.

We're supposed to spend the rest of the class working on our essays while Mr. Brian reads through the topics we've chosen. Everyone else seems to be getting into it, conducting online research on the school laptops and taking notes. I begin to realize how boring my topic is. The article I'm currently reading doesn't contain any especially fascinating facts. Eventually, I'm saved by the bell, and I pack my things away.

"Miss Franklin, can I speak to you for a moment?" asks Mr. Brian.

I go to him at his lectern. The teacher's holding the sheet of paper with my essay topic and looking at me doubtfully.

"The main points you've chosen to focus on are still a little vague. Can I help you in some way? I mean, there are various ways you could approach the subject of the Golden Gate Bridge. But it really depends on what interests you."

"Uh, honestly, I still need to think about that," I admit.

Mr. Brian's face darkens. He clearly suspects I haven't given it any thought, which isn't far from the truth.

"I haven't gotten that far yet," I continue. "I actually had another topic in mind, but in the end that didn't work out."

"Oh? Can I ask why not?"

"I couldn't find enough information."

"Maybe I can help you. I could recommend a few books and other resources. What was the topic?"

I doubt Mr. Brian can help me, but it's worth a try.

"I wanted to show the more sinister aspects of

a big city and how they're dealt with. How do they affect society? How are they tackled and what conclusions does politics draw from them? I wanted to discuss an example – a murder that happened in 2011. A guy called Phil Kennwood who was attacked and killed on his way home from work one evening. He didn't stand a chance. The killer was never caught. I wanted to write about that case."

"Phil Kennwood," Mr. Brian murmurs to himself, stroking his chin thoughtfully.

"Yeah, it's supposed to have happened near Albion Street. Someone ambushed him, went through his clothes, and stole his valuables."

Mr. Brian's head suddenly jerks up. "Phil Kennwood, Albion Street," he repeats.

I nod. "So, you read about it?"

He ignores my question and instead asks in a stern voice, "How did you hear about it?"

I've never seen Mr. Brian like this. His eyes are narrowed, as if he doesn't trust me.

"I... I'm not sure," I lie, unsure what to make of the situation.

"Surely you remember how you heard about the murder?!" He's trying to remain calm, but I can hear in his voice how important my answer is to him.

"I don't know, maybe I heard a couple of students talking about it. I don't really remember," I reply evasively. Some instinct tells me I should keep Kate out of this.

"A couple of students," he parrots. I'm not sure if he believes me, but he seems pretty suspicious. "I think it's best if you choose another topic. It shouldn't be hard to find another murder case. But an analysis of the darker side of the city and how it's dealt with politically would most likely lead to an ethical discussion, which doesn't really fit with what the essay is supposed to be about."

"Doesn't history keep showing us how important ethics and morality are? Isn't the past exactly where we should look to learn more about that and try to apply it to the future?"

Mr. Brian laughs and shakes his head. "Good argument. Maybe you should consider taking philosophy. I'm sure Ms. Thornten would enjoy your input."

I'm not sure how to interpret his comment, so I just nod.

"I'll note down a couple of books that deal with the history of the Golden Gate Bridge, and in particular what the bridge meant for the city's infrastructure. Take a look at the situation with the ferries and the law suit filed by the ferry operators. That could be an interesting angle." I nod, and Mr.

Brian adds," If you need any help, let me know."

"Thanks, I will," I reply. As I leave the class-room, I have the feeling a pair of eyes are following me.

Chapter 26

After lunch, I find a note in my locker asking me to report to the school secretary. There are a couple more documents related to the move that I need to fill out. I roll my eyes. Just what I need. I check the time. I won't make it there before afternoon training. I'll take care of it afterward.

I enter the gym with everyone else. The other students spread out and start their training exercises, and I go to Amber, who's already waiting for me.

"Ready?" she asks listlessly. Lancelot is back at her side and looks healthy again.

"Sure," I say, glancing at Yoru, who's sitting beside me.

"I was thinking maybe you could try some combat practice today."

I'm surprised she wants to try it again, but I guess Amber's not someone to give up easily. She assumes the position, sends odeon to her spirit, and he quickly transforms. He immediately launches his first attack.

I command Yoru to summon fire, and he succeeds in sending out such a powerful stream that it blasts away the wind. Another gust is hurled at us, and I have to run to dodge it. I do as Noah taught me and try to use all my senses. I detect a faint hissing sound to my right and resist the instinct to turn toward it, instead throwing myself to the left. Just in time because a powerful gust rushes past me. Amber's standing a short distance away from me with her arms folded. Her kestrel Lancelot dances in the air.

"You're not going to win this time," she declares with a cruel smile on her lips.

Great, I think. I don't have time to think about anything else because the two of them are already attacking me again. This time, I'm lashed by a storm that sweeps me off my feet and hurls me across the hall. I wind up lying dazed on the floor. I feel the air in front of me grow colder. I quickly call to Yoru, who sends out more fireballs and intercepts the gust of wind headed toward me. I get back on my feet and run at Amber, who looks surprised. Out of the corner of my eye I see Lancelot in a nose dive. I raise my fist to strike her because I don't see why it should just be my key spirit fighting. Her spirit instantly rushes to protect her. I grin, and my arm stops in mid-air. Meanwhile, Yoru attacks our opponents from behind, raining down fire on Amber. She barely has time to turn around. Just before the flames reach her, Yoru makes the fire disappear to avoid seriously injuring her. She just stands there looking mortified and breathing hard. A grin spreads across my lips – and then suddenly, it's wiped off my face. A violent fountain of water surrounds me, sweeps me off my feet, hurls me up in the air, and then drags me across the floor. I don't even know which way is up or down. The water swirls around me, and I can't breathe. I'm spun around again and flung against a wall, where I just lie for a while, sapped of energy.

"You never learn," Monica hisses in my ear. "You have one minor victory, and then you rest on your laurels. You didn't even consider that you might have more than one opponent. You should always think about that in a fight."

"True," I pant. I still don't know where my head is at. I feel dizzy.

"You still need lots of practice," says Amber.

"Thanks for the tip," I mutter, trying to stand on my shaky legs, which isn't entirely successful. I stagger. Then I realize the teachers are watching me.

"You demonstrated some good techniques," says Mr. Laydon as he and Ms. Rupert stride toward me.

"Yes, but also some critical mistakes," says the other teacher.

I nod wearily. All I want to do is go to the locker room, shower, and get changed. My whole body hurts.

"Take a short break," says Mr. Laydon. "Then, we'll analyze the fight with you."

He turns his back on me, and I slump back to the floor. I'm still gasping for breath.

Lucia hands me a water bottle, and I drink greedily from it.

"Amber orchestrated that well," I hear a voice say beside me. I turn to see Ayden standing a few steps away with another boy. Apparently, he has nothing better to do than analyze my fight – in a loud voice. "Teresa should have seen the attack coming. But her wall of fire was pretty impressive, wouldn't you say, Thomas?"

Thomas raises his eyebrows, looking slightly bewildered. Then he nods.

"Uh, yeah, sure. That was well done."

"And she noticed right away that there was another attack coming. The way she dodged it wasn't bad at all. I also get the feeling she's getting better at coordinating with her spirit."

"Good observation," Mr. Laydon agrees. "Her communication with her key spirit does show improvement."

"She demonstrated some really good reflexes," says Thomas, who seems to feel like he has to contribute something to the discussion.

"For sure. Especially when you think about how things were looking a couple of weeks ago," says Ayden, rolling his eyes. Okay, now he's overdoing it.

Ms. Rupert holds her finger to her chin in a thoughtful gesture. "I agree, she's getting faster. But still..."

"Obviously, she should have reacted to Monica's attack. Her fox could easily have protected her from the water," Ayden observes, and I shoot him a withering look.

What's going on here? Where's he going with this?

"But she did manage to intercept and vaporize a couple of attacks. That takes strength as I know from personal experience."

He glances at me and winks almost imperceptibly. Weirdly, this makes my heart leap. He's trying to help me?

"Yes, she seems to be consistently sending her fox more odeon now. Not bad," Mr. Laydon agrees. "But there's no denying she still has a lot of training ahead of her."

Ayden nods. "Sure. But still, it shows the extra coaching has helped."

I can't believe what I'm hearing. Is he now praising Amber's tyranny? If this is his idea of helping me, then he can forget it. What an asshole!

"Absolutely. Miss Mitchell's efforts seem to have paid off. You should be very grateful for her help," Ms. Rupert says to me.

"Words can't express how grateful I am," I grumble, wishing I could assassinate Ayden with a glance.

"Yeah, it's always a big help to be able to learn directly from another student. Thomas, you trained with Brick at some point, right?" Ayden asks his classmate.

Thomas nods again, still bewildered. "We trained together for a couple of weeks, and he helped me progress a bit."

"You learned pretty fast during that time," Mr. Laydon recalls.

"Brick was a huge help, Thomas. You took a lot away from that and then applied it in your own personal practice," Ms. Rupert remarks.

"Yeah, true," Ayden chimes in again, "at some point, you have enough new information. Then it's best to spend some time working alone to apply what you've learned."

"Exactly. Brick helped me a lot in terms of sending the right amount of odeon. Before that, I always used it all up at once. But after training with him, I got better at rationing it. Then it was up to me to practice on my own until it was second nature."

Thomas keeps looking to Ayden for his cues. He doesn't seem to understand exactly where this conversation is going. But I guess he's catching on.

"But it wasn't just Brick who helped you. Mr. Laydon and Ms. Rupert were always available to share their insight with you. That was a big help too, right?"

Thomas nods. "Uh, yeah, right. They were always coming to me and giving me tips." He glances over at the teachers and mumbles, "Thanks for that."

The two teachers smile with pleasure and Mr. Laydon runs his hand through his hair, looking slightly abashed. "That's what we're here for."

Ayden looks at me. "Anyway, you did well today. If Amber were your only opponent, you would have won."

The radiance in his eyes is indescribable. I find it just as disconcerting as his friendliness. Then he walks away and returns his attention to his own training.

"We should get together later and discuss it," Mr. Laydon says to Ms. Rupert. "Miss Franklin has certainly made some progress, and she managed to defend herself well today. Maybe she should focus on consolidating what she's learned for now and putting it into practice. We can take her under our wing again."

Ms. Rupert considers this and eventually nods.

"Good idea. That'd probably be the best course of action for her at this point."

I can't believe what I'm hearing. Is my coaching horror at an end?!

"Well, Miss Franklin, it looks like you're ready to start training alone again," says Mr. Laydon. "Do you feel okay with that?"

"I have your support, so what could go wrong?"

I hope that didn't sound as sarcastic as it felt. My heart leaps. I can scarcely believe it. I'm free! It's finally over. Amber gives me a curt nod. She's probably just as relieved to be rid of me.

"Alright, Ms. Rupert and I will talk it over, but I think we'll let you train on your own again for now and see how that goes."

I feel like jumping for joy. But I control myself and glance sideways at Ayden. He's smiling, warmly even, and right now, I'm happy to let him take the credit. Yeah, I even enjoy it. Ayden stuck up for me, and all I feel is gratitude.

I'm still in high spirits at the end of class. I'm so immensely happy to be done with Amber. On the way to the locker rooms I pass Ayden, who's apparently staying after hours to train longer.

"I just wanted to thank you," I say.

I look up at him, and his deep green eyes are simply breathtaking. So is his gorgeous face, and I can totally understand why he's so attractive to women.

"You deserve a break," he says with a smile. "You've certainly improved."

"In that case, I hope I haven't totally destroyed your worldview. I mean, you were convinced I'd never make it."

"True, I didn't think you'd come this far," he

admits, which kind of sounds like a concession. On the other hand, he's implying that he hasn't completely changed his mind. But right now, I don't care. He can think whatever he wants.

"Anyway, I'm so glad I don't have to work with Amber anymore," I continue.

He nods. "She didn't make it easy for you." There it is again, that piercing gaze, his eyes looking into me so deeply it feels as if they're exploring every corner of me. "I guess you had a breakthrough. You've improved a lot recently anyway. Some people might assume it's thanks to Amber's help."

I can't help thinking of Noah. He fought me once – or trained with me as he called it. And I must admit I learned a lot from that. I raise my eyebrows and shake my head.

"No, it wasn't Amber. Even though she really tried to make my life as difficult as possible. And then there was her weirdo friend Monica. Does she take steroids or some kind of magic potion I should know about? I mean, she fights like she's possessed."

"At least you could defeat Amber."

I'm not sure if that's appreciation in his voice or doubt.

"I guess I just worked hard and modeled myself on you. Training after school seems to help in the long term, but I guess you know that."

He nods slowly but doesn't look convinced.

"Are you about to throw yourself back into your training?"

I consider it for a moment, then shake my head.

"No, I figure I deserve a break."

I can't help thinking it could do him some good to rest after his boozy night, but that's none of my business. He nods. I raise my hand in farewell and head to the locker room.

My phone beeps, and I take it out.

"I've figured out that you don't live at home anymore. And when I couldn't find you, I realized where you must have fled to. I'm not entirely sure why, and I'd appreciate if you could explain it to me. I really hope it has nothing to do with me. I know where your old house is and that your mother still lives there, but I've never done anything to threaten her. We really need to talk. And if you want a sparring partner, I'm always available. I'll go to your mom's house tonight. As far as I know, she's working the nightshift. I'll be there at seven. Hope to see you there. Noah."

I can't believe it. The letters dance in front of my eyes, and I read through the message again, line by line. Its tone seems flippant, harmless even, but the malice in it is unmistakable: he still knows where my mother lives and works. Just because I've moved out of home doesn't mean I can dodge him forever. He can hurt my mom whenever he wants, and I guess that's what he's trying to prove by forcing me to go and meet him. He knows I'll show up. I have no choice. I'd never forgive myself if anything happened to my mother. So I'll go, but not to talk to him. He can have his fight, and this time I'll use everything at my disposal to make it clear that I want him gone from my life. I'm under no illusions that I can defeat him. But maybe I can injure him or find out something about him that will help me shake him off permanently. It's the only chance I have.

"Teresa?" I hear Ayden's voice say behind me.

I'm still standing in the gym a few steps away from the locker rooms, holding my phone in my hand.

"Bad news?"

The horror that Noah's message has triggered in me is probably written all over my face. I paste on a smile and reply, "All good. Just a friend from my old school in Tucson. She had a fight with her boyfriend and needs someone to talk to. I'll give her a call."

I try to smile again, and for a moment, I think Ayden's about to come closer. He looks concerned, but then he just nods, and I quickly disappear into the locker room.

Noah's message has really gotten under my skin, but there's no use running straight to my mother's house. It's way too early, and he won't be there yet. So I try to take the rest of the day one step at a time. First, I'll go to the secretary's office and take care of that paperwork.

The door's open, so I go in. But the secretary is nowhere in sight. I guess she's already left for the day. I sigh irritably and turn to go, but then I hear voices. They're coming from the principal's office, so I guess he's still here.

"I still don't understand how she found out about it. These incidents don't normally get leaked, especially not to the students."

I immediately recognize Mr. Brian's voice. My heart skips a couple of beats, and I stop in my tracks.

"She's full of surprises," Mr. Collins replies.

"How do you want to handle this? Do you think I should talk to her again and try to ascertain how she found out about it? I find it hard to believe she heard it from other students as she claims."

"We can't entirely rule it out," says the principal.

"But... I mean, how? How could this happen? And she suggested there were several students discussing it on school premises!" I can picture Mr. Brian shaking his head. "No, I really don't buy it. We place so much emphasis on discretion. And somehow a thing like this gets out?!"

"In any case, I don't see how we'll ever to get to the bottom of it. And I don't think it's worth the effort. You can't get something out of their heads once it's in there. Drawing attention to it will only make things worse," says Mr. Collins.

Mr. Brian doesn't seem to like this answer, judging by the long silence that follows.

"But thank you for bringing this straight to me," says Mr. Collins, making it clear that the conversation is over.

Before the door opens, I quickly slip out of the secretary's office and hurry down the corridor. What the hell was that? Why did Mr. Brian take it up with the principal? It was only a stupid essay topic. Or was their conversation about something else entirely? No, that would be too much of a coincidence. But what does Mr. Brian know about the murder? And why does he want to conceal the information from me?

I replay the conversation in my head. I have a sneaking suspicion, which frightens me. But it makes sense. I'm not sure how, but I need to find out more about it.

Chapter 27

I keep checking the time. Still fifteen minutes. I'm way too early, but I just couldn't bear to sit around in my room any longer. Mom's at work, so in theory I could wait in the house for Noah. But the idea of him walking up to my door and ringing the bell... No way, he's not some normal guy coming to pay us a visit. He's an enemy who tried to kill me. But did he really? He's actually saved my life more than once and killed his own kind. Doesn't that say it all?! Who kills their own people? I just can't figure him out, and that's what bothers me more than anything.

I sigh again and keep walking. I continue past my house, then cross the street and choose a strategic spot under a tree. From here, I hope to see Noah coming so I have time to react. I doubt he'd attack me out in the open, but he did mention sparring with me. What does he want from me? What am I letting myself in for? I guess I'll find out soon enough.

I cross the street again and walk back to our house. I can't stand all this waiting. Where is he anyway? I check the time again. Five more minutes. Why does the time have to pass so slowly?

Something falls out of a tree and hits my head. Probably a twig, I think, reaching up to pull it out of my hair.

"Peanut shells?" Confused, I raise my head and glance around. Another one hits me. I quickly turn to my right, the direction it came from, but see nothing.

"It's really entertaining watching you," I hear a voice say. I crane my neck and finally see him. He's sitting on a roof, as if it's the most normal thing in the world. He's picking at something in his hands. Peanuts. I'm stumped. What is with this guy?!

"What are you doing? And how did you even get up there?"

"Do you really need to ask that?" he says, taking something out of his pocket. It flashes in the sunlight; his hand makes a rapid movement, and a door opens, through which he disappears.

Right, the key. He can go anywhere with that. I look around for him. I'm sure he's about to reappear somewhere. He'll materialize next to me and...

I scream as he grabs me and pulls me backward. I've never experienced anything so terrifying. First, I fall for what feels like an eternity – although it's probably only a fraction of a second. Then, I recognize the Odyss. Darkness filled with countless doors. Noah still has his arms around me. He reaches out with his left hand, and one of the doors glides toward us as if by magic. He unlocks it and pulls me through it. I struggle to breathe. Colors, another fall, then cold wind lashing at my face, and I'm staring down into an all-consuming abyss.

I scream in panic and do the very thing I never wanted to do again: I cling to Noah like I'm possessed. I even try to climb up him, just to get a little farther away from the devastating drop below me.

"Oh my god oh my god," I shriek.

Noah laughs in my ear as the wind whistles by, and I feel another gust buffet us as if it's trying to throw us off this steel girder.

Below me, I can make out tiny cars moving along the streets, the occupants of which have no idea what's going on right above them.

"This can't be happening," I say, unable to tear my eyes away from the scene below me. "This is a nightmare, a horrible, terrifying nightmare."

"It's not that bad," he whispers into my ear, still holding me tight. "You'll get used to the height in a few minutes. Just enjoy the view. This is a special place – San Francisco's most famous landmark, and you get to experience it right up close."

My panic turns into disbelief and finally rage.

"You're crazy! First you abduct me and drag me through the Odyss, only to maroon me in the middle of one of the highest girders on the Golden Gate Bridge. I mean, are you totally nuts?! If you're trying to kill me, just do it – you don't need scare the shit out of me first."

"I just wanted to talk to you undisturbed," he replies.

"Okay, you've definitely lost your mind."

"It's nice up here. We have a great view of the Bay and the city, away from the hustle and bustle, where we can be all alone."

"Yeah, because I can't get away. That's what this is about, right?"

Noah tilts his head and grins. "Partly." I can't stand that smile, and I feel like punching him.

"Get me down from here now!"

He snorts indignantly. "Since you ask so nicely."

He grips me around the waist with one hand and takes out his key with the other, and before I know what's happening, I'm falling back into the Odyss. Another door magically appears directly in front of us. It opens, and I feel like I'm being squeezed through a keyhole. I fall and fall and fall, and I brace myself for the impact even though I should know better by now.

Firm ground beneath my feet. I stagger back a few steps and gasp for air. A harsh wind buffets me – sea air, and I hear the sound of waves crashing, breaking against a rugged cliff. I turn to look at Noah and see Alcatraz behind him.

I fold my arms in front of my chest and glare furiously at him. "Great spot you've picked out. Are you hinting at something?"

Noah quickly holds up his hands defensively. "Just a little sightseeing – my own special tour. I thought you'd like it."

"I've already been here with a friend, so no need."

My eyes dart around, looking for an escape route, but of course, there's no escape from Alcatraz. I guess Noah thought of that when he chose the locations. I still don't understand what's going on. What the hell does he want from me?

Obviously, I have no choice but to stick around and find out.

"Can you please quit your little games? I only came to meet you because you threatened my mother. So just spit it out. What do you want from me?"

My voice is caught by the wind and blown away, but Noah understood me clearly.

His mouth opens slightly, and he looks at me with dismay. "You think I was threatening your mother?" He sighs and runs a hand through his hair. "You still don't get it. I've helped you again and again, protected you from my own people, and even helped you hone your fighting technique. But you refuse to see all that; you just cling stubbornly to your rigid opinion of me. What a shame."

Is he serious?!

"Are you trying to convince me we're on the same side?! You fight against the Tempes, and I'm one of them. You try to kill them. You wanted to kill Ayden. And you're seriously trying to tell me you weren't threatening my mother in your last message?"

A smirk appears on his lips. "You can read whatever you want into that. But I didn't say anything about threatening your mother."

Actually, he's right.

"But you knew that's how I'd interpret it and that I'd come."

"Hey, a guy has to recognize and exploit his advantages."

"Which brings us back to my question: why did we meet and what do you want from me? You worm your way into my life and pretend to be my friend to spy on me. And you tell me you'd never hurt me. Why? Why do I matter to you? And what happened to your plans for me?"

He avoids my gaze, obviously struggling internally with something. I can see his mind working and that he's suddenly unsure of himself. He doesn't know how to answer that. Or is he wondering how much he can risk revealing to me?

"I know it's hard to understand," he replies without a trace of mischief in his expression. "But you can believe me when I say that my plans are irrelevant now. I realize I'm putting you in a difficult situation when I refuse to give you the straight answer you want. But I hope my behavior makes it clear to you how I feel about you. You can trust me."

The sound of the crashing waves mingling with

Noah's words makes them sound more dramatic.

"What?!"

"I'm your friend – maybe the only person who understands your new life and is on your side."

"I have enough friends at my new school," I correct him. "I don't need a friend who works for the enemy." I tilt my head and consider pushing him off the cliff, but thanks to his key, that would be pointless. "When we met you pretended to be someone you're not, just to squeeze me for information about the Tempes."

Noah waves his hand impatiently. "And yet I stuck up for you, helped you, and even killed some of the fallen to protect you."

"What does that say about you? That you're someone with no scruples who's willing to kill his friends."

"They weren't my friends. You should know: just because I'm a Noctu doesn't mean I agree with all of the Assembly's decisions or that I follow their rules. I have a mind of my own, and I make my own decisions."

"And nobody has a problem with you massacring a few Noctu?"

"Sure, but the truth is malleable."

"See? That's where we disagree. I don't see it that way at all. There's only ever one truth."

"Do you always have to be so black and white about everything?" Noah mutters. "Teresa..." He comes a few steps closer. "You're an incredibly interesting and special person. At first, I just wanted to learn more about you and find out if you were a key carrier. The longer I observed you, the clearer it became that there was a lot more to you and that you were someone I wanted to be there for. You're not as out of touch as the other Tempes. You weren't indoctrinated from a young age to believe we're the enemy. There's still a chance with you that we could come together."

I raise my eyebrows. Did I just hear that right? "If you're angling for a Romeo and Juliet story, you can forget it. I prefer modern literature."

He rolls his eyes. "That's not what I meant; I was just..."

He takes another couple of steps toward me, but I'm thinking about what he just said: *the longer I observed you...* I know he was stalking me and keeping tabs on me. I'm aware of that. But hearing him say it to me straight doesn't exactly help. I'm reminded of my open window, the hasty getaway on Ayden's motorbike when we were being pursued, the interrupted kiss.

I can't stand thinking about it. I can't stand Noah!

"You're nothing but a danger to me," I whisper, outraged, and take a few steps back. I can't believe how stupid I was.

"Teresa, you're not listening to me. I just wanted to... Stop! Teresa, stay where you are!"

But I can't. I take another step back, which is a grave mistake. I totally forgot where I'm standing. I feel my foot step into nothingness, flail my arms, struggle to regain my balance – in vain. I scream and feel the wind all around me, hear the roaring sea behind me, and then I fall. There's no escaping it now. I experience something strange at that moment – I'm barely aware of my body. No thoughts, no memories flashing through my mind like a movie. Just pure horror and fear.

Suddenly I'm grabbed; I feel that horrible pull again. I'm falling, then I land on soft grass.

At first, I just lie still, feel the ground beneath me, breathe – and I can hardly believe it when my lungs fill with air. It's quiet – all can hear is the chirping of crickets, and it's the most wonderful sound I've ever heard.

I slowly turn my head and see the city lights in the distance. This place feels somehow familiar.

"You okay?" Noah's kneeling nearby. He keeps his distance and looks at me with warmth in his eyes.

I nod slowly and look around me again.

"It really was you," I say.

If I ever had any doubt, it's now completely dispelled. Noah followed me to the place where Ayden took me on our date. Where he would have kissed me if we weren't being watched.

"I already suspected, but to have it confirmed like this..." I take in my surroundings, and the memories flood back. "You followed us here," I murmur in disgust.

"Not both of you. Just you. Like I said, I wanted to find out more about you."

"And our conversations weren't enough for you?"

"You know I was just trying to form an impression of you and your abilities. But in the process, I got to know you as a person too. I understand if you don't have a high opinion of me right now. But I don't want any secrets between us."

"Why?" I ask again.

"In the world of the Noctu, I do my own thing. Just like you do with the Tempes. I've never met anyone who's so similar to me in that regard."

Is he really just looking for an ally? More importantly, should I pretend to buy it? It could be a way to find out more about him and whether he has ulterior motives. Clearly, I can't easily shake him off. So what's the point in trying to run away? Wouldn't it be better to let him get a little closer so I can keep tabs on him? It's a dangerous game I'm getting myself into. I'm fully aware of that. But what other options do I have?

Ayden. I could tell him everything... And he'd head straight out with his friends, spoiling for a fight. No, I need to go it alone. I need to find out how much of what Noah's telling me is true.

"You're relentless," I reply, shaking my head.

"I've been called worse," he says, sitting down beside me. A warm smile spreads across his lips. I struggle to overcome my unease at his closeness.

"How do you do it?" I ask after a period of silence.

"What do you mean?"

"The thing with the key and the doors. You can move around so fast with them."

He gestures dismissively. "You could do it too. It's not some special ability, if that's what you're thinking."

I raise my eyebrows. "We Tempes can use our keys in the same way?"

"Well, you need to really know your way around the Odyss. In particular, you need to be familiar with the doors. Each one leads to a different location. Once you know which door will take you to your destination, it's not difficult to summon the door you need."

"First, you use your key to open the door to the Odyss," I say.

He nods. "Once I'm there, I think of the door I want and kind of reach for it with my odeon. It's as if they're all attached to rubber bands. I pull the door toward me, open it, go through it, and then it snaps back to its usual place."

I shake my head. "I'm not really the rubber band type. I prefer bag clips."

Noah laughs and shakes his head. "Anyway, it's not difficult. As long as you know your way around. But the Odyss is the domain of the Noctu, so it's really dangerous for Tempes to be there."

"And that's why an experienced Tempes always accompanies a new key carrier to find their spirit there."

"Right." That mischievous smile reappears on his lips. "But they don't have a Noctu with them, especially not one who knows the Odyss like the back of his hand and knows a few corners where you're not likely to be found." He winks at me. "I could show you."

I hold up my hands in a gesture of refusal. "Not right now, thanks. This is a lot to take in, and I'm not even sure it's a good idea to be talking to you here. An excursion into the Odyss would be too much of a good thing."

"I get it. Just let me know if you change your mind."

He'll be waiting a long time for that. It would mean putting myself totally at his mercy, which will never happen. I've already had enough of being dragged through all those doors. There's no way I'm taking another trip with him.

Silence prevails again for a while, which is surprisingly not uncomfortable at all. I gaze out over the city lights glittering so beautifully, and I'm reminded again of the last time I was here. Not a nice memory.

"If you want me to trust you, then tell me a bit about yourself," I say, hoping that if I can get him talking, he'll give something away. "Where do you live? In the Odyss? Do you have parents?"

To my astonishment, Noah replies without hesitation. "My parents are both Noctu and members of the Assembly. It's similar to the Tempes' Council. Assembly members are responsible for making all the most important decisions. My key was passed down to me by my grandfather when I was five. My parents used to spend a lot of time in the Odyss back then, and they still do. That's how I know it so well. But I've always felt more at home in the human world, which is why I live here. The apartment officially belongs to my parents, but I hardly ever see them, so it's pretty much mine. A lot of Noctu don't actually live in the Odyss. That makes it easier to conduct our work. Just like you, we track down key carriers, and we also capture the breath of dying people."

"And wage some kind of war against the Tempes on the side," I add.

Noah laughs and shakes his head. "I guess you could look at it that way. But I go to a totally normal public school – I wasn't lying about that – and it's also true that I want to study medicine although my parents have other plans for me."

"Something to do with the Assembly?" I probe.

"Their main concern right now is that I respect the Assembly's decisions and stop being so headstrong. But they're glad I became a scout – which is basically equivalent to your hunters – and that I try to fulfill my obligations as best I can if not quite in the way they envisioned."

He looks at me with his pale, candid eyes, and I wonder how much I can trust him. I don't think he's lying to me right now. And given what I already know about him, I believe him when he says he doesn't like to be stereotyped.

Out of the corner of my eye, I see Yoru moving

behind a bush, watching me. It's good to know he's still with me after all those jumps. I can't see Rain anywhere, but I'm sure he must be nearby too.

"I couldn't imagine living in the Odyss. It's so dark there, so gloomy and depressing, not to mention all the fallen."

He shrugs. "They were once just like us. But they accidentally merged with their spirits – or some of them did it deliberately. They're harmless to us. And the Odyss isn't as gloomy as you may think. But you need to see that for yourself," he says with a smile. "Since we're talking about our lives, how are things going for you? How's school? We haven't had much contact lately, so I don't what your life looks like these days."

I hesitate but see no reason not to talk to him about it. As long as I don't say anything about training or the Tempes, it shouldn't be a problem. But I try to choose my words carefully.

"I'm still enjoying school, although it's not always easy. You know that I moved."

"That means at least one of the Tempes knows that we're in contact," he surmises.

I'm not about to give him any more details about that, so I just nod, but he's seems satisfied with that.

"And do you feel at home there?"

I nod. "I guess so."

"You don't sound convinced."

"It's a big change. But I'll get used to it," I reply. "Anyway, I'm not alone. I have good friends, and I appreciate being at that school."

"I'm happy for you," says Noah. He sounds surprisingly genuine.

"What about you? What's it like going to a normal school as a Noctu?"

He shrugs. "A lot of Noctu lead totally normal lives."

I can't imagine it being easy to conceal your true nature from everyone, but he seems to manage somehow.

"I guess our school is no different from a normal high school, apart from the key spirits and the combat training. We have annoying teachers, dry subjects, exams, homework." That reminds me of the essay, and I pull a face. "I don't suppose you can tell me anything about the origins of the Golden Gate Bridge? It could save me a lot of work."

He shakes his head wryly. "Can't help you there, sorry. Bridge engineering isn't my strong suit."

"Nor mine."

"Essay topic?"

I nod and marvel at the fact that we're sitting

here together talking about stuff like this. He's supposed to be my enemy, and yet for the first time in ages I feel like I can relax and talk openly with someone.

"Sounds pretty dry."

"Yeah, I wanted to write about something else, but..." I shake my head and recall the weird conversation between Mr. Brian and the principal.

"But?" Noah probes.

I pause and wonder what parts of it are safe to mention to him. I begin cautiously.

"Well, I actually wanted to explore the darker side of San Francisco, looking at an unsolved murder as an example – a guy called Phil Kennwood who was killed in 2011. It happened near Albion Street. The killer was never caught. I searched online but couldn't find anything on the case. No mention in the media, absolutely nothing. And when I mentioned it to my teacher, he was kind of..." I break off, trying to find the right word.

"Agitated?" asks Noah.

I look at him in surprise and nod. "Exactly. Do you know something about it?"

Noah doesn't hesitate. "Phil Kennwood was a Noctu. The Tempes ambushed him and killed him. Apparently, he had no chance of defending himself. One of their key spirits must have tracked him down, and they exploited the opportunity."

I look away and gaze over the city. I had a hunch ever since overhearing the conversation between Mr. Brian and Mr. Collins. Now that I know for sure... I'm almost disappointed. But that instantly brings up another, much more burning and important question: how did Kate know about it?

"The Tempes don't like students getting involved in the fight against the Noctu. And part of that is making sure they don't hear anything about the deployments. They figure students are too young to understand everything and that they might go around looking for fights to prove themselves or out of some misguided sense of duty."

The incident with Max – when she provoked a fight a few weeks back and then left me in the lurch – proves that they're not totally wrong about that.

"Everything okay?" he asks.

I'm wrenched out of my reverie, which revolves around Kate. I urgently need to talk to her. In fact, I should message her tonight and say that we need to catch up as soon as possible.

"I'm just tired. It's been a long day," I say, forcing a weak smile.

"Sure, it's getting late. I should take you home."

"Thanks, but there's no need. I'm still not totally

comfortable with this key travel thing. I think I'd rather take public transport."

We're a long way from the city center, and it'll take me a while to walk to a bus stop, but I need that time to organize my thoughts.

Noah seems to understand.

"Okay."

He stands up and holds out his hand. It feels firm and warm. There's an intimacy in his grip that I really don't want to feel.

Chapter 28

I lie awake half the night, and it's not just thoughts of Noah wrecking my head. I can't stop thinking about what he told me about Phil Kennwood. Especially because I have no explanation for how Kate knows about it. The Tempes apparently do everything in their power to keep their fights with the Noctu under wraps. It's morning now, and I reply to Kate's message. She's promised to pay me a visit after school today. I have a thousand burning questions, and a small part of me is afraid of the answers.

I get up, shower, and get ready for school. Before classes start, I want to take care of the bureaucratic formalities.

I knock on the door to the secretary's office and hope I'll have more luck this time. I want to sort out all the paperwork from my move. To my relief, the school secretary is sitting at her desk, and she looks up as I enter.

"What can I do for you?"

"My name's Teresa Franklin. I moved into the residence recently, and I got a message that I need to sign some more forms."

"Oh, yes, of course," says the woman. She looks like she's in her early forties. She begins searching distractedly through a stack of paperwork, and her delicate fingers flip hastily through the folders.

"Where are they?" she murmurs. "I had them out especially. Franklin, right?"

I nod, and she eventually finds the documents. Her red lipstick curves into a smile.

"Here you go. I marked the places you need to sign."

I skim-read the text and apply my signature to the marked lines.

"Thank you so much," says the secretary, taking the documents from me. "I'll just have the principal sign them, and then I'll bring you back your copies."

She stands up, knocks on the principal's door, and enters. I wait, still wrestling with the questions that kept me awake half the night. Will Kate actually give me any answers tonight? Will she be honest and tell me the truth? And my thoughts keep going back to my meeting with Noah yesterday. Was it a mistake to go meet him? He didn't do anything to threaten me. In fact, the opposite – he was the first person in a long time to give me answers, and he shed light on what happened to Phil Kennwood.

I sigh and glance around, and my eye is drawn to the wall behind the secretary's desk. A picture hangs there, the style of which is very familiar to me. Houses that look like they could be from Western Addition, a night sky filled with dark clouds. Everything is bathed in the light of the streetlamps, and there are lights in some of the windows. And when you know what to look for, you can also make out all those glowing eyes hiding behind trees and shrubs. I recognize the picture immediately: I saw it in the photo that accompanied Frida's obituary in the yearbook.

The secretary returns and gives me an apologetic smile.

"Sorry, that took a while."

She seems to notice my eyes are focused elsewhere.

"Oh, yes, the picture. It's beautiful, isn't it? My predecessor painted it. Unfortunately, she fell ill and died in the space of a few months. She hung it there, and I left it on the wall to honor her memory."

I respect her for not simply removing every trace of her predecessor.

"Yes, it's lovely," I agree. "I've hung some of her paintings at home. Frida was my great aunt."

"Oh." The secretary looks disconcerted. "I didn't know. I hope you don't think it's inappropriate." The situation clearly makes her uncomfortable. "If you want to take the picture..." Her eyes dart between me and the wall.

"No, it's alright. I think it's great that one of Frida's paintings has a place here."

"That reminds me, there's something else of hers."

She goes to a noticeboard with a few postcards pinned to it. At the top right-hand corner is an envelope. She brings it down and shows it to me.

"This is a get-well card that was sent to your great aunt, but it seems she never received it. I found it on the mail pile when I started here. It's signed by all her colleagues. And, well, I couldn't bring myself to throw it away."

Her nervousness increases with every word, and she draws back the card in her hand.

"I don't know. Maybe it's not such a good idea. I mean, I don't want to bring up painful memories for you. But I thought, since you're family... you should know that Frida was well loved by everyone and, uh, they wished her all the best. But unfortunately... uh, in the end I suppose it didn't help, and she never saw the card."

I smile and hold out my hand for the envelope.

"That's really nice of you, and I'd be happy to take the card on Frida's behalf. I'm sure she would have appreciated it."

The secretary hands me the envelope with a smile.

"Again, my condolences."

She also hands me my copies of the documents signed by the director. I leave the office and slide the card out of its envelope. Sure enough, it looks as if all the teachers have signed it and written get-well wishes. A smile spreads across my lips because the words are incredibly heart-felt. I'm sure Frida would have enjoyed reading it. My mother and I know so little about Frida's life and her death. All we know is that she had cancer, but we never found out what kind or how long she lived after her diagnosis.

I put the card back in the envelope and pause for a moment. I reread the address on it and can't believe my eyes. Frida was in San Francisco General Hospital, where my mother works. I'm sure that's news to my mom. Maybe it'll help us find out more about Frida and how she died. My mother could ask her colleagues. Some of them might even remember Frida, or Mom could look through the files. My heart pounds excitedly. I know that's a lot of ifs and maybes, but it's a start. Frida left her key to me, worked at this school, was a key carrier, and had a spirit at her side. I know so little about her, so I'm grateful for even the smallest pieces of information.

I agreed to meet Kate at my mom's house, as she doesn't have much time and it's not as far for her to go there.

When I arrive at the house after school, I cook myself some instant noodles. But I don't eat much. I'm too tense, and I keep glancing at the clock. The time seems to pass incredibly slowly. I try everything I can think of to distract myself. I hand wash the dishes and vacuum downstairs. Eventually, I hear the key in the door. It's Mom.

"Teresa, how lovely," she says, giving me a hug.

"Is your friend here yet?"

I shake my head. "But she should be here at any moment."

We go into the kitchen, where she pours herself a glass of water and sits at the table.

"I just made myself noodles."

Mom waves her hand. "I ate in the canteen."

She smiles and looks me up and down as if she hasn't seen me in years and wants to see if I've changed in that time.

"Do you still like boarding school? You know if you don't like it there..."

I interrupt her. "No, it's good. I miss you a lot, but living at school has some advantages, and it's starting to feel like home."

She nods, and I can see her wrestling with herself. On one hand, she's relieved that everything's okay, but she also misses me.

"I had to go to the secretary's office today to sign a few forms."

I've been burning to tell her about it. I take out the card and hand it to her.

"The teaching staff at my school sent this to Frida. But it never arrived in time. In any case, Frida didn't receive it, and the new secretary kept it for us."

Mom takes the envelope, reads the address,

and raises her eyebrows. "I didn't know she was a patient at San Francisco General." She glances at me. "And you're hoping we can find out a bit more about her?"

I nod. "Maybe. I mean, we know almost nothing about her. And she did so much for us. I'd really like to get a better sense of who she was."

Mom reads the address again. "I could ask Chloe. She said she worked in oncology for a while. Maybe she was there at the same time or knows a colleague who can help. She's working the nightshift tonight, so I won't see her until the day after tomorrow."

"Thanks, that would be great," I say, giving her a quick hug. I'm about to say something else, but the doorbell rings.

"I'll go lie down for a while. It's been a tiring day. Have fun, you two," Mom says. Then she heads upstairs.

I run to the door, almost slip on the floor, and fling it open. I'm not sure if Kate's stunned expression is due to my dramatic appearance or because she can guess what I want to discuss with her.

"You okay?" she asks.

I nod and step aside to let her in.

"I don't have much time," she reminds me again.

"I know. It won't take long. Should we go up to

my room? We can talk freely there."

She nods and follows me hesitantly. I can see that she feels uncomfortable. She hesitates before sitting on the soft carpet, avoiding my eyes. Yoru goes to her and puts his head on her lap. She slowly begins to stroke his fur.

"So, what's up? Your message made it sound really urgent."

I sit in front of her and try to catch her eye, but she continues to evade me.

"I think you know what I want to talk to you about."

"Is it about that essay? You want me to help you find a new topic?"

There's a hint of hopefulness in her voice.

"No, but you're not far off. I wanted to talk to you about the murder of that guy Phil Kennwood. How did you know about it? Where did you hear his name? I did some more digging and, uh, a teacher at my school who used to be in politics knew about the murder. He confirmed that the case was real, but it was swept under the rug because Kennwood was... let's just say he didn't exactly have a clean sheet, and they didn't want to stir up any dust."

I prepared this lie to force Kate into a corner. Because if I show her that I know at least part of the truth, she can't keep making excuses.

"I... I just can't believe it," she mutters. "That man... actually lived, and the murder really happened." She went even paler.

Her words leave me none the wiser, but I'm glad she's opening up and not denying everything.

"What do you mean?"

Kate seems to be wrestling internally with herself. Her fingers keep running through Yoru's fur, as if she hopes to find solace there or the strength to say what she has to say. She takes a few deep breaths, and I can tell she's wondering if she has a choice. Then, she finally comes out with it.

"I told you about how I spent a lot of time in hospital as a kid. That was back in Washington, where we lived before Dad was transferred to San Francisco. Anyway, I recovered from my lung infection, but there were all these complications and setbacks, so I still had to spend a lot of time in hospital. I didn't really have any friends. So I was really grateful for the nurses who took care of me and played with me. Some of them came up with fun ideas and tried to make my time there as pleasant as possible. I got along especially well with this one nurse. I often sat at my window and looked outside. I used to watch the people out there, the cars, the trees, the hospital grounds. My favorite nurse came up with an idea for a game. I was supposed to watch people really closely and imagine what their stories might be. We did that for hours and came up with loads of funny stuff. Over time, it got more and more detailed. I said names that came into my head, and obviously the reasons these people were there. I got pretty good at it. I realized just how good I was when I saw Caroline Smith. She was an old woman of 78 visiting her husband after he suffered a heart attack while pruning the roses in his garden. He loved his roses; he was so proud of them. And he was kneeling in front of a rose bush, about to cut one for Caroline, when he clutched his chest and tried to stand up but couldn't. He collapsed. Luckily, Caroline found him, and he was brought to the hospital, where she visited him every day. I met her during one of my rounds in the hospital corridors, which I wasn't really supposed to do, but they couldn't control me. I met her when she was searching for a vase for her husband's room. It turned out that her name was Carol Smithson, and she was 75. And her husband actually did have a heart attack while working in the garden and had to have several bypasses. He was feeling better by then and was about to be discharged. She was so nice to me, and I felt like we'd known each other for ages, which was true in a way because I'd spent so much time inventing her story. Since then, I've hit the mark several times. Sometimes, when I try to think about the lives of individual people, images and names pop into my head, and I imagine events they could have experienced. I always thought it was just coincidence that I get it right now and then. I mean, I still do it. It's like a bad habit. I get lost in thought, and then these names come to me, these stories. But not all of them are true."

She finally looks up at me.

"I know it sounds crazy, and I shouldn't have made it sound like it actually happened back there in that street. But it just came over me all of a sudden, this stupid whimsical notion. So I wasn't surprised when you told me you couldn't find any information on the case. But this changes everything."

I can hardly believe what I'm hearing. What does this mean? Could it all just be coincidence? But the name, the year... To me it sounds more like Kate can actually see things that happened at some point in the past – or at least fragments of them. As if she has... "Clairvoyant powers," I mutter to myself.

Kate's jaw literally drops when she hears those

words.

"You're kidding me, right? It's just a stupid game. Now and then, I hit the bullseye. But that's just statistical probability, right?"

I can see the fear in her eyes. She's imploring me to agree with her.

I bite my lip, and my mind races. What can I say? Is it possible that she has some kind of gift? Not long ago, I would have laughed at the idea, but now I know about the key spirits and I'm a key carrier myself. There's obviously more between heaven and earth than first meets the eye. So why shouldn't clairvoyance be possible?

I still don't know what to say or think. Can I talk to someone about it? Should I tell the principal? One of my teachers? Ayden? But that could get Kate mixed up in something she wants no part of. She obviously doesn't know what to make of this ability; she thinks it's a game, and wants to keep seeing it that way. Kate has enough problems in her life – does she really need to be burdened by something like this? No way. And anyway, what do I know? What can I tell her with any certainty?

I touch her hand and say, "It's just coincidence. You make up some story, and parts of it match reality. You seem to have really good powers of observation. Maybe that'll come in handy someday.

You could be a movie director or something." I give her an encouraging wink.

Kate exhales with relief and smiles bashfully. "Yeah, Mom would love that."

We giggle, and we both know that we'll never mention this again. It's like an unspoken agreement between us to protect our friendship, but above all, to protect Kate. From a truth she doesn't want to see or accept. And who am I to force her?

Chapter 29

I can't stop thinking about my conversation with Kate. Did I do the right thing pretending I thought it was all just coincidence? But what's the use of voicing my suspicion to her? I have no proof to back it up.

I pad across my room again, and Yoru lifts his sleepy head. Even my normally laid-back fox seems to be unsettled by me.

I need to get out of here. I need to stop thinking about it somehow. The envelope containing Frida's card catches my eye. Mom said she'd take care of it, but the hospital isn't far, and I could use the distraction. Chloe's supposed to be working tonight.

I quickly creep along the hallway and peer into Mom's room. She's sleeping, so I leave a note for her on the kitchen table. Then, I grab my jacket and leave. Yoru follows me at a distance, as usual, and hides whenever we pass someone. I'm constantly astonished at how skillfully he conceals himself.

I find an empty seat on the bus. My thoughts start racing again, and I'm glad to get out when I reach my stop.

It's only a few minutes' walk to the hospital. I focus on the questions I want answered.

Mom's still on the maternity award, and I assume Chloe is too, so I take the elevator to that floor. I follow the corridor until I come to a junction. The surgical ward is to the right and the maternity ward is on my left. I'm about to turn left when I see something out of the corner of my eye. A door opens and a figure darts out. He's holding a book in his right hand, and his left hand hastily pockets something. I realize it's Noah a moment before an alarm goes off. A shrill noise rings out, and a nurse hurries past me. She flings open the door to the room Noah just came out of, dashes inside, and calls out to her colleagues rushing to help, "Cardiac arrest."

No one pays any attention to me or Noah. A defibrillator is brought in, and a doctor rushes into the room.

I'm still standing rooted to the spot. Noah looks up and sees me. His face freezes, and I see a look of sheer horror in it, and something else: shame. That's what makes me realize he's done something terrible.

"You," I say, outraged. "What have you done?"

"Teresa, it's not what you think," he says quietly, walking toward me and extending his hand. "I'll explain it all to you. But not here. Let's go somewhere else."

He put his hand on my back and pushes me toward the stairwell. As soon as the door closes behind us, I shake him off.

"Tell me the truth, right now! Did you... do something to the person in that room?"

I'm scared stiff, and my pulse is thudding in my ears. I'm afraid of the answer, but I suspect I already know it.

"It's complicated," he says, reaching out to me, but I recoil in horror.

"Tell me!" I demand.

He scrutinizes me, his eyes narrow slightly, his body tenses, and I can see him suddenly close himself off to me.

He nods slowly. "You're aware that we Noctu capture people's dying breath. We need the final dose of energy that humans can give us to keep our world and the fallen Noctu alive. Without that, everything would collapse. You can't possibly understand the scope of it. You have no idea how important it is for us. We have to do it, for ourselves and our world."

I just shake my head. No excuses, no more talk. I don't want to hear any more.

"You killed a person to take their last breath. And I'm guessing it wasn't your first victim. How could do a thing like that? And I was stupid enough to actually consider trusting you again. You're a murderer who doesn't care about anything but annihilating the Tempes and sending sick, defenseless people to their deaths. All for the sake of self-preservation."

"It's easy for you to say," he says, looking straight at me.

His eyes are dark and threatening. Like black clouds scudding across a bright blue sky, heralding a storm on its way to destroy everything.

"For you, it's simple because your existence isn't at stake. But what would you do if your world, your family and friends were threatened with annihilation? Self-preservation is the oldest and most natural human instinct – and maybe the strongest."

"I don't care what excuses you come up with; it doesn't change the facts." I step back, reach for the door handle behind me, pull it open, and yell, "You're a murderer!" With that I storm out.

I hear Noah calling after me, "Teresa, you don't understand."

But I don't want to hear any more, and I just run. My heart's pounding as I sprint down to the next landing and rush out of the hospital and onto the street. I feel sick, and everything's spinning. I can't believe what just happened. Obviously, I knew in the back of my mind that Noah killed people – Tempes and ordinary people for their dying breath. But I ignored it. I wanted to ignore it. I was so stupid, so naïve.

I'm exhausted, and my knees are trembling as I take a seat in the bus and bury my hands in the pockets of my jacket. I fight back the tears and keep picturing Noah's face. How could he do something so horrible? The doctors will try to save the person, but they don't stand a chance. Because Noah took something from them that they need in order to live – I'm certain of that. How long has he been doing this? How many people has he killed? I finally realize how insidious his methods are. The 'Read and Dream' program opens all doors to him and gives him access to the seriously ill patients. It's so perfect, so scheming and so deeply abhorrent. He sits there at their bedsides and actually reads to some of them, then at some point he kills the person to capture the energy of their dying breath.

I bite my lip until I taste blood and fight back tears. Noah's probably not the only Noctu hanging around the hospital. How many more are there? How many people's lives are taken by Noctu every day?

I climb out of the bus in a daze and head back to the residence. There's nobody in the corridors, which is fine by me because I'm so overwrought. I need to calm my mind and figure out who to talk to about this. Because I can't remain silent, that much is clear.

I run down the corridor to my room and fumble for my key with trembling fingers, drop it, then try to insert it into the lock – unsuccessfully.

Suddenly there's a hand on my shoulder. I drop my key again and yell out in fright.

"Teresa? What's wrong?" Ayden turns me around and looks into my face, which must look stricken because his expression immediately softens. "What happened? Were you attacked?"

I shake my head and bite my lip again, unsure

what to tell him. Can I tell him about Noah? Something holds me back, something I can't put into words. Maybe it's just that I don't want to provoke more conflict between them.

"I was just in the hospital. Someone died, and I'm sure a Noctu was involved."

Ayden's eyebrows shoot up. "What makes you say that?"

"There... there was this guy. He came out of a patient's room. He pocketed something, and an alarm went off straight away. Nurses came running, and doctors..." I shake my head. "It was horrible."

Ayden puts his arm around me and pulls me against his warm, firm body. I inhale his smell, and he just holds me. It's so unbelievably comforting. Right now, I'm grateful for his soothing presence. His fingers stroke my back, and I let the tears flow.

"The Noctu have various ways of getting their hands on a person's dying breath," he explains quietly. "We try to intervene, to stop them. But they show up in so many different places and have so many ways of accessing their targets. It's impossible for us to prevent every case. We need to stop the Noctu altogether if we want them to finally leave people alone."

I know he's right. Because there are so many

places the Noctu could attack: hospitals, retirement homes, hospices, health clinics, rehab centers. And who knows where else they've gained access to.

"I'm sorry you had to see that," he says in a quiet, soothing voice.

His breath tickles my ear. He gently caresses me; his fingers wandering through my hair. I feel most of the tension melt away. I grow calmer, more relaxed, and simply enjoy the feeling of being held by another person.

His fingertips are cool and soft as they touch my cheek and wander over my hot skin.

"I wish I could tell you we'll find the guy and stop him." He pauses. "But it's not that easy."

I nod, knowing all too well what he means. But I'm grateful that he doesn't lie to me and give me false promises in an attempt to placate me. Honesty – that's all I want from him, and it's all I need right now. I nestle up to him. It feels so good just to smell him. When I move my hands, I feel the muscles of his torso, his warmth. For a moment, I allow myself to imagine that everything's different between us, that all these terrible things never happened.

He rests his cheek on my hair, and his breath rustles it and leaves me tingling. We're in a tight embrace, and I feel my heart begin to patter restlessly. I slowly run my fingers over his chest. I feel him flinch slightly when I first touch him, and he starts breathing faster.

"I know how hard this must be for you," he continues, and I'm not sure what he's referring to. "I know we haven't always seen eye to eye, but I'm here for you."

I swallow hard. Memories resurface. I see his face in front of me, hear the words he spoke to me when we were first getting to know one another. Picture us nearly kissing. I look up at him. He's stunning. Breathtakingly beautiful, almost perfect. But sadly, only on the outside because he's only human. With flaws and shortcomings. He's just as capable as anyone else of hurting people. And he hurt me more than anyone else ever has.

Tears well up in my eyes. I nod and say, "Thanks," in a husky voice. I reluctantly pull out of the embrace and turn back to my door. "I guess I'll try get some sleep."

He just nods and doesn't look disappointed or offended. He wanted to be here for me at a difficult time. No more, no less.

"I know it's hard, but try not to think about it. You have tomorrow to wreck your head over this, and you will. So give yourself a break."

There's that breathtaking smile again, which cuts

deep into my heart.

I nod, open the door, and quickly close it behind me. Then, I slump to the floor and feel the tears stream down my face.

Chapter 30

I delete Noah's message without reading it. It's not the first one he's sent. Since the incident in the hospital, he keeps messaging me, asking for a chance to explain himself. But how can I grant him that? It's as if my eyes have finally been opened. Even though I knew Noah was a Noctu, I refused to admit what that really meant. Now I know. I have no desire for his company, and I refuse to listen to any more of his lies. So I ignore his messages. I realize that's not without its risks, because he could bring my mother into it again, threaten her. But it seems important to him – for whatever reason – to save face with me and foster a certain impression. And he can only do that if he feigns innocence and doesn't do anything nasty. And that's what I'm counting on. He won't hurt my mother, I'm sure of that despite everything.

"Tess, what's up?" Lucia asks, putting a comforting arm around my shoulders. "You've been miserable for days. What happened? Guy problems?"

"No, nothing like that," I reply and continue poking around in my salad.

"Are you sure?" Max asks, studying my face closely. "Is it something to do with Ayden? You know you can talk to us."

My eyes automatically wander to him. He's sitting a few tables away from us, talking to friends and drinking cola.

We haven't spoken to each other since our encounter in the corridor, and I'm glad. We were far too intimate then. I don't want a repeat of that, even if I don't actually regret what happened. I needed someone, and Ayden was there for me. I'm grateful for that, end of story.

Max follows my gaze, and she frowns suspiciously. "Are you sure everything's okay?"

I nod and manage a smile.

"Say what you like. You've been in a bad mood lately. And we urgently need to do something about it. Let's go see a movie after school. Could be fun," Lucia suggests.

"I was kind of looking forward to a quiet night," I say.

"I won't take no for an answer. You need to get out and get your mind off things. It'll be great, I promise."

That evening, we make our way to the movies together. It was hard to agree on a film. Max wanted to see a schmaltzy romance, to which Lucia responded with a warning glance at me. They obviously both think I'm lovesick. Lucia had her way in the end, and we opted for a comedy. I mechanically stuff popcorn in my mouth, slurp my coke, and barely follow the movie at all. But I make an effort to laugh in the right places, so they'll leave me alone. And it works. Lucia looks at me contentedly after the movie. She puts an arm around me and says, "See? That did you good."

I nod. "Thanks for a nice evening."

We order burgers and eat them on the way home. They both live with their parents and not at the residence, so we part ways at my bus stop. I say goodbye and get on the bus. I wave again from the window. I'm so tired and drained. Things have been pretty exhausting lately. I just want to go to bed, and I hope to finally get some sleep tonight. I get out at my stop and only walk a few steps before I'm suddenly grabbed and feel myself falling. That long, terrifying fall that I'm all too familiar with. I can't believe it. I don't even have time to scream before I land roughly on hard, stony ground. I gasp for breath and turn around as my whole body tenses up.

"Noah!"

He's standing in front of me with his arms folded, glaring coldly at me. "I hope we can finally talk now."

My blood runs cold, and I glance around to see where he's brought me. To the Odyss. To the Noctu, to his world, from which I can't escape because to do that I need to take my key out, and I'm sure he'll take it from me before I have a chance to find a door.

"Get me out of here now!"

I don't want to stay a second longer in this creepy place, especially not with him.

"Sorry, I know you feel a little manhandled, but it was the only way. I just want you to listen to what I have to say."

"We have nothing to say to each other," I growl.

"So leave me alone."

I feel like turning and running – just to get away from him. But that would be suicide. There's a reason he brought me to the Odyss.

"None of this," he spreads his arms out, "could exist without the energy of people's dying breaths. We'd lose this special place, where so many key spirits live. And don't forget the Tempes get their spirits from here too."

I fold my arms and glare furiously at him.

"I realize you Noctu have your reasons. But killing people, singling out the vulnerable and exploiting their weakened state..." I shake my head. "There's no excuse for that."

"Everyone has to die sometime," Noah points out. "What you're forgetting is that it's not death that's painful. It's life. Sometimes the end brings relief and frees people from endless suffering."

I snort contemptuously. Is he really trying to justify his actions with that old chestnut?!

"And you're trying to tell me..." I begin in a scornful tone. But suddenly Noah's right beside me and pulls me in so close that I'm forced to look straight into his eyes. They're as clear as a fine day, and at the same time, they burn like a forest fire threatening to destroy everything in its path.

"I'm trying to tell you the truth. It's a fact that

many people yearn for it all to end. People who are in pain and no longer want to fight. Why shouldn't I help them? I see so many patients every day, and I don't take the decision lightly. I observe them over a long period, talk to them about their illness, their wishes. And what can I say? You'd be surprised how many of them have a grateful smile on their lips when I set them free."

For a moment, we just stare at each other. I'm speechless. I don't know what to think. I realize there are people in that situation. And I wouldn't want to suffer pain day in and day out if I knew I was going to die. The idea of that is horrible, and I don't even want to think about what my end will look like. I just hope it's a long way off.

"How... how do you do it?" I ask.

Noah's still staring at me, holding me captive with a look so penetrating, so intense, that it sends a cold shudder up my spine.

"We use a poison. A few drops orally is all it takes. The substance is absorbed by the mucous membranes and causes instant cardiac arrest. It's a very gentle death, without suffering, I promise. When they breathe their final breath, I'm there to capture it."

I swallow hard. What am I supposed to think? The worst thing is, I can kind of understand. A tiny part of me couldn't stand to watch that suffering either. But would I be able to kill another person, even if it was what they wanted? I doubt it, and I don't want to be in a position to make that decision.

"You have to believe me when I say that I only give this poison to people who I'm sure can't be cured and who want to die. I'd never kill someone who had a chance of recovering."

His eyes are bright and open. His words are sincere and seem to come from the bottom of his heart. But can I believe him? And more importantly...

"Maybe *you* only kill those who welcome death as a release. But what about the other Noctu? Do they have the same code?"

I watch his face closely, study every little movement, and I soon have my answer.

"They don't all share your principles. Am I right?"

"We all have principles, but it's up to the individual to determine what those are for themselves."

There's my answer. I turn around and demand: "Take me back. Or is there something else you want to tell me?"

I hear Noah sigh deeply. He puts a hand on my shoulder and summons one of the doors. It zooms toward us out of nowhere and opens when Noah inserts his key. We step through, fall, and then we're standing in the middle of the city. But in a small side street where no one can see us.

I immediately start walking. I just want to get to a busier street among other people.

"You can hold my own actions against me, but making me responsible for what others might do? I don't think that's fair. I mean, you'd expect the same from me, right?"

I pause. I'm only a few steps away from a sidewalk bustling with activity.

"What in this world is fair?" I retort, and I know my words will hurt him. But I can't help it. Why does he have to keep plunging me into such emotional turmoil? Why do I have to keep asking myself who's my friend and who's my enemy? Why does he always make it so hard for me?

I head for the busy sidewalk with a quick backward glance. Noah's still standing in the same spot, and it looks as if he doesn't intend to follow me. The city lights flash all around me; cars drive past; noises, voices – everything combines into a deafening cacophony. I rub my eyes and take a deep breath, and when I look up, I realize it's happening again: golden lights dance through the air. They wriggle through the night like filigree snakes. I feel dizzy. It's all too much – the chaotic lights, the unsettling noises.

"Tess, what's wrong?" I hear Noah say. He's suddenly beside me, holding me up. As much as I dislike it, I have no choice but to press my head against his chest to protect my eyes and ears.

"I'm seeing these lights everywhere," I pant. "Golden flashes swirling through the air. It's all too much."

He puts a soothing hand on my back.

"Come on, let's get you out of here."

He leads me back into the alley, takes off his jacket, and spreads it out on the ground for me to sit on. He sits beside me, keeping a protective arm around me. I need to feel that I'm not alone, and even if he's the last person I want to be around right now, I'm relieved not to feel so lost. The feeling that someone's there for me lessens my fear and helps me gradually calm down.

"Feeling better?"

I nod slowly.

"Can I ask what happened?"

"Vitreous opacity," I explain. "I see these bright lights everywhere, dancing through the air like pieces of string. And the noise – everything was suddenly so loud." I shake my head. "I guess I just haven't been coping well lately."

Noah studies my face. He's clearly not convinced I'm okay. His eyes bore into me, as if they're trying to look deep into my soul. But there's something else in them that I can't put finger on.

For a moment, I think it's something sinister, probing, but then I realize it's something else: anxiety maybe.

We sit for a while in silence. Noah's still holding me in his arms, and I let him because I don't have the strength to fight anymore. I just want to go home.

"Ready to go?"

I nod and stand up.

"I'm guessing you don't want me to escort you home?"

This question and his cheeky grin actually extract a smile from me.

I shake my head. "No way. Nice try though." I raise my arm in farewell and say, "See you soon." Because I'm clear about one thing: I won't get rid of Noah that easily.

Chapter 31

I no longer dread afternoon training. I'm reminded every time how liberating it is to not rely on others for help, to be independent, and most importantly, to be able to train the way I see fit.

Today, I try to work out the relationship between the amount odeon I send Yoru and the intensity of his attacks. If I send him a lot all at once, are his attacks more powerful? Or is it better to feed the odeon to him gradually. I notice that I feel way more sapped of strength if I send him one big burst of energy – and that makes Yoru's attacks less precise too.

I've learned a few things since I started at this school. But I doubt I'll ever be an exceptional fighter. And that's not my goal. I just want to be able to defend myself in emergencies. And there it is again – the thought that's been constantly on my mind for the last few days: Noah. I keep thinking back to our last encounter. I haven't seen or heard from him since. And I was so sure he'd show up again soon. Maybe that's his tactic: to keep his distance, thereby ensuring he takes up even more of my headspace.

"We all have principles, but it's up to the individual to determine what those are for themselves."

Who is he to make decisions about life and death, even if he is fulfilling the wishes of a patient? Again, I imagine a terminally ill patient watching death's fingers snatch at them. They lie there, suffering, longing for an end to their torment. Then the door opens, and Noah comes in.

"Watch out!" someone shouts.

But it's too late. A hex is speeding toward me. Yoru intercepts it, but he can't completely neutralize it. The gust of wind is so powerful and so unexpected that it sweeps me off my feet. I somersault through the air and can't tell which way is up and which way is down. My arms and legs are thrown around, and I can do nothing to stop it. I'm hurled through the air like a ragdoll. Finally, I smash into a wall. The air is knocked out of my lungs; I feel dizzy; I feel as if I've just been driven over by a truck. I gasp for air and try to orient myself. Mr. Laydon and Ms. Rupert are instantly at my side.

"Are you alright?" asks Mr. Laydon.

I'm not sure, but I nod. I touch my head and quickly discover a big lump. But no blood, to my relief. My arms seem okay too. But there's a shooting pain in my right foot.

"Let me see," says Ms. Rupert, examining my arms, ribs, and legs. When she comes to my foot, I draw a hissing breath. She carefully removes my shoe and sock. My ankle is a little swollen, but that's all. She moves it back and forth. I groan in pain again. She tests it again, then nods. It doesn't surprise me that these two have medical training.

"Can someone bring me a first-aid kit?" she asks. Lucia runs off and returns with one. Ms. Rupert smears a cooling gel on my ankle and applies a bandage.

"Just a slight sprain. You need to rest it," she says. "No more training for you today."

She stands up and scans the room. "Can

someone take Miss Franklin to her room and support her weight a little? She needs to avoid straining her ankle. Mr. Collins, would you mind?"

He nods and comes over. Why does it have to be Ayden? Probably because he's a hunter and doesn't really need these training sessions. And he lives in the residence. But I think I'd prefer if she chose someone else.

Ayden puts his arm around my waist. His touch is firm, warm, and strangely familiar. Lucia looks at me with a big grin, whereas Max looks like she wants to rip Ayden's head off. She knows we don't get along too well. Everyone stares at us as I limp out of the gym, supported by Ayden.

As soon as the door closes behind us, I shrug him off and say, "Thanks, but you don't need to come with me. I'll manage."

He rolls his eyes irritably. "Somehow, I knew even something as banal as this would lead to endless discussions."

"It's not that bad," I retort.

"Whatever," he says, putting his arm around me again and practically carrying me.

"Hey," I complain.

"If you want this to be over quickly, then let me help you. The more you scold, the longer it'll take."

I know he's right, but I can't leave it alone.

"Scold! You sound like you're taking your role as a knight in shining armor too seriously, using old-fashioned words like that!"

"If it makes you cooperate, then why not? So, M'lady, if it pleases you, I'd very much like to escort you to your chambers. After that, I'll fetch your lady's maid, so she can soothe your foot with a little cold water."

I can't help laughing. I shake my head in exasperation. "Idiot!"

"Charming as always," he replies.

We reach our corridor in the residence, and I feel the mood change a little. I've been enveloped in Ayden's scent the whole time, and now I become aware of where my hands are on him. My left is around his waist. I can feel his firm skin under it, his warmth. My right hand is on his arm, which is wrapped around my waist, and my fingers are touching his. Why do such small points of contact drive me so wild? It's as if little electric shocks are shooting across them. I keep my eyes in front and try to focus on the door to my room.

"How are you doing, by the way?" Ayden asks. The teasing tone is gone from his voice.

I look up at him and smirk. "I'd be doing better if I didn't just sprain my ankle."

He shakes his head. "You know what I mean."

Yes, I do. Apparently, he actually wants an answer and won't let me gloss over it with sarcasm. I shrug.

"I can't stop thinking about it. It's not easy, and sometimes..." I'm not sure if I should say it. But his gaze is warm, attentive, and open. He wants to know, and he wants to understand. "I can't help wondering whether death can be a release for some people. There are so many terminally ill patients in the hospital who can't be helped."

We stop in front of my door. Ayden's smoldering eyes are still fixed on mine.

"I get what you're saying," he says surprisingly calmly. "But the Noctu aren't like that. Obviously, it's possible in some cases that they're putting an end to their victim's suffering. But even if that's true, it's not their place to decide. No one has the right to take another person's life. And they're not killing them to end their suffering. They need their dying breath. That's all it's about for them, no more and no less. And they need loads of it. More than they can get from terminally ill patients in a hospital, trust me."

He's still staring at me. The truth blazes in his eyes. He's totally convinced, and he's probably right. If only it weren't for Noah. Why can't I figure the guy out?

"Teresa?" His voice makes my skin prickle. "Where were you just now? I've noticed it several times in the last few days – something's bothering you."

I swallow hard. Am I that transparent? I guess I am to Ayden – or that's what he figures. He told his father as much when he delivered his report on me.

He puts a hand on my cheek. His green eyes are so close, sparkling like gems, and they're no longer cold and aloof.

"I just have a lot on my mind right now," I reply evasively. I can't tell Ayden about Noah. I just can't – not anymore. He'll never understand why I kept it a secret from him all this time that I'm still in contact with Noah and that we've even met up.

"What happened in the hospital exactly? Did you recognize the Noctu?"

His gaze becomes more intense. It bores into me, imploring me not to close myself off to him. He's so close that our bodies are almost touching. The heat radiates from him, and his intoxicating proximity calls to me. Everything in me longs to press myself against him and put my hands on his body. My breathing is ragged, and my heart's in my mouth.

"Teresa." His breath brushes tantalizingly across my skin and his fingers wander over my lips. "I know it's not easy, but the information may be useful. It may even help us to identify them. Then, you'd be safe."

He leans even closer, his hand still gently tracing my lips, opening them slightly so that my panting breath can escape. Ayden rests his left hand on the wall behind me and moves his face close to mine.

"Teresa." His voice is persuasive, the feeling of his fingers on me sweeter than anything in the world. Those wonderful eyes. That delicious mouth forming the words of a kind of siren song.

But I'm not falling for that again. I remember that look and his touch all too well, and the main thing I hear is what he wants: he wants information. He packages his request nicely, in caresses and tender words, but all he wants from me is information. That's all it's ever been about for him.

"I get it," I say in a steady voice. "You're just trying to squeeze information out of me. Did your father send you, or are you just being an opportunist?"

Ayden studies my face, a smile appears on his lips, then he shakes his head.

"It's sad that you think that. But I guess your reaction's understandable after everything that's happened."

He withdraws his hand and only moves back a few inches, but it feels to me like there's now an unbridgeable chasm between us.

"No, I wasn't planning to tell my father anything. And he didn't send me. Maybe you haven't noticed, but he doesn't order me around, and I'm not his minion. I have certain duties as a hunter. But how I choose to carry them out is up to me."

I swallow hard and recall Noah's words. "Everyone has principles." I don't want to think about him! Not right now!

"I don't care how much freedom he gives you or whether you have a close relationship. In the end, you work for him and for the Tempes. Everything you do revolves around one thing. You try to glimpse behind people's facades, delve into their innermost thoughts and feelings, and draw your own conclusions. And now you think I have some secret, and that's why you're here."

He shakes his head. "So you think I'm spying on you for my father," he says, leaning toward me again.

I shrug. "What do I know? I don't even know you. So I have no idea how close you are to your father or how loyal you are to him. But for most people, family comes first."

My words are like sword thrusts. I know that. But I want him to leave me alone and stop confusing me, and above all, I want him to stop stirring up feelings that I'm trying to put behind me.

"You're right. But we all have things we keep private, and that's the way it should be. I'm not trying to extract your deepest, darkest secrets. But since that's obviously what you believe, let me tell you something about myself that you probably don't know. Something nobody at this school knows." He moves even closer, fixing me with this captivating gaze that I can't tear myself away from. Very slowly, his sweet breath whispers to me, "He's not my biological father. He adopted me as a baby."

I wasn't expecting that.

"I'm not trying to get anything out of you. I just figured it might help you to talk about whatever's bothering you. But it's okay if you don't want my help."

He finally steps back.

"Elevate your ankle and put an icepack on it. It should start to feel better soon."

He waves and disappears down the corridor.

Was I mistaken about him? Was Ayden really just trying to be there for me? As some kind of friend? My guilty conscience nags at me. Maybe I shouldn't have pushed him away like that.

Chapter 32

The rest of the afternoon seems to drag on interminably as I lie on my bed and cool my ankle, my thoughts going around in circles. I'm angry with myself and keep wondering if I should have behaved differently toward Ayden. Was I too hard on him? Maybe, but what do I even want from him? I can't deny that he still has an effect on me. But can I afford to give in to it? After everything that's happened? Anyway, I don't really believe Ayden takes me seriously. He has Vicky, and somehow, it's different with her. When they're together... You can just see that they have this connection, and he treats her totally differently from how he treats other girls, myself included.

So what do I want?! I hurl myself into my pillows, trying to halt this train of thought. I need to get out of here. I cautiously stand up. My ankle still hurts, but it'll be okay. There's no way I can sit around in my room like a prisoner and do nothing.

I'll visit Mom. It's not far from here, and I can take the bus most of the way. Maybe she's had a chance to talk to Chloe. Either way, visiting her will be a welcome distraction.

I grab my jacket and leave. I don't have to wait long for the bus, and I soon spot the hospital in the distance.

Once inside, I have to slow myself down because walking has put more strain on my sore ankle than I realized. I take the elevator up to the ward where my mom is working.

I glance up and down the corridor and see no one except for a new mother carrying her baby in her arms. So I go to the nurses' station, where two women are sitting. Chloe looks up at once, and a friendly smile appears on her face.

"Teresa, so nice to see you. Your mom's in an examination, but you can wait here if you'd like."

"Thanks," I say.

"Do you want something to drink?"

I shake my head, then I hear a baby cry. Probably the one belonging to the woman I saw in the corridor. Sure enough, she appears at the nurses' station.

"Do you mind helping me for a moment?"

"Sure," says Chloe's colleague. She follows the woman to her room.

"How are you?" Chloe asks me.

I nod. "Not bad. You?"

"Busy, as usual. Your mom and I have been meaning to meet up for ages, but with the current workload..." She shrugs. "A chat over coffee would be really nice. But either we have different shifts or we're so busy that we barely have time to exchange more than a few words."

"Oh, then I guess she hasn't had a chance to ask you about Frida?"

"Frida?" Chloe appears to have no idea who I'm talking about.

"Frida Mitchell," I reply. "I found out that she was here in the oncology ward and probably died here. Mom said you used to work there now and then and that maybe you knew her. Do you remember her?"

"Frida," Chloe whispers, dumbfounded. "Frida

was in this hospital?!"

Now I'm confused. "You knew her? And she wasn't in this hospital? That would explain why she never got the card."

Chloe's eyes narrow and she regards me suspiciously. She stands up and puts her hands on her hips.

"Why are you asking about her? Did you know Frida?"

"She... she was my great aunt," I reply, taken aback.

The color instantly drains out of Chloe's face. Pale as a corpse, she murmurs, "I can't believe it. You're... you're related to her." She stares at me as if she's searching for some clue in my face, then she suddenly stammers, "I... I'm really busy, I've got to go."

She's obviously trying to resist the temptation to run, but she hurries away from the nurses' station as fast as she can.

"Chloe, wait!"

I run after her. But Chloe's damn quick, and she disappears into the stairwell. With my sprained ankle, I have no chance of keeping up with her, so I stop at the door. I try to order my thoughts. What was that about? I don't get it. But one thing is clear: Chloe knew Frida. And the fact that she was related to me seemed to really unsettle Chloe.

"Teresa?" I hear a surprised voice say behind me. "What are you doing here?"

I turn around to see Mom coming out of a room, smiling cheerfully at me.

"I stopped by to visit you," I reply, glancing again at the door Chloe disappeared through.

"It's good to see you." She takes me in her arms. "Everything okay?"

"I... I just had a strange conversation with Chloe. I asked her about Frida."

"Right, I still haven't gotten around to that. And? What did she say? Was she on the ward at that time?"

"She seemed to know Frida. But I'm not sure how. Chloe said Frida was never at this hospital."

My mother frowns. "Are you sure"

I shrug. "Well, that's not exactly what she said, but that was my understanding."

"Maybe you were both talking at cross purposes," Mom says. "You should ask her again, or I can." She pauses and takes a deep breath. "It's possible they met somewhere else. An unusual coincidence but not out of the question."

"Then why did Chloe claim Frida was never in this hospital?"

Now it's Mom's turn to shrug cluelessly. "Maybe

she was here briefly, and Chloe didn't know about it. Just talk to her again. Where is she, anyway?"

That makes total sense, and I know it's the most likely explanation. But Chloe's reaction bothered me a lot more than what she actually said.

"I don't know where she went."

My thoughts race, and I keep going over the conversation in my head, but nothing adds up. I'm sure Chloe won't want to discuss the subject with me again. And if she does, I should at least know what I want to say to her and ask the right questions.

"Is Chloe working tomorrow?"

She nods. "Early shift. She has the following day off, and then she's back on the night shift. We were just comparing our schedules again because we want to catch up outside of work."

I bite my lip and think about it for a moment. I need to speak to her again as soon as possible. I guess my only option is to skip school tomorrow morning. I smile at Mom and nod.

"Then I'll try again sometime in the next few days."

I hug her and try not to let her see my limp as I make my way out. What a weird day, I keep thinking.

The feeling of unease and the knot in my stomach won't go away, and all I can think is: something's not right.

I barely sleep all night. I keep seeing Chloe's horrified face. When I wake the next morning, I still remember the last fragments of a confused dream, and Chloe's deranged laughter chasing me through it.

It's five thirty – a time when I would normally roll over and go back to sleep. But today, I feel awake and full of adrenaline. I'm not sure if Chloe will talk to me again. But I'm going to try.

Silence prevails in the corridors of the residence. The rooms are well insulated, and there's no one in sight. So, I head to the entrance without being seen and make my way to the bus stop. The whole time, I can't stop thinking about Chloe, and I can feel my heart pounding in my chest as I arrive at the hospital. At this hour, Chloe will have just started her shift – if she even showed up today, I can't help thinking. But would she really skip work just because I tried to talk to her about something uncomfortable? That seems far-fetched. I can't find her in the ward, and there's no sign of her at the nurses' station, so I ask a colleague.

"I'm looking for Chloe. Is she here?"

"She's with a patient just now. But I'm sure she'll be back soon."

I nod and say, "Okay, thanks."

Then, I leave the nurses' station and wander up and down the corridors for a while, in the hope of running into her. And sure enough, a door opens, and she comes out with a baby in a buggy. She turns right without seeing me and goes into another room. I quickly follow her. I reach for the door handle and, on impulse, open the door very cautiously and quietly.

Chloe has taken the baby out of the buggy and laid it on a changing table. She prods it with her finger and then begins to take off its clothes.

"Okay, we're just going to weigh you because we need to stick to the routine, although that won't help you now." She undresses the baby. "At first, I considered not coming in at all. Maggie's daughter really rattled me. But if there's one thing I've learned, it's the importance of keeping a cool head. She doesn't know anything and, as a student, I'm sure she's out of the loop. So there's no need to worry, and I can focus my attention on you." She looks at the little one and sighs. "It won't be long now."

I don't know what she's talking about, but my heart beats loudly as I watch her weigh the baby, dress it again, and lay it back in the buggy. I step back from the door before Chloe notices my presence and hurry back down the corridor. When I turn back, I see her take the baby back into its room, presumably to its mother.

I bolt into the stairwell, steady myself on the handrail, and take a few deep breaths. What does it all mean? I sit down on the steps and try to get my thoughts in order. I just heard Chloe say she's not afraid of me because I'm out of the loop. Is the school hiding something from me? And if so, what? I raise my head and glance at the door leading into the ward.

Is it possible? Could Chloe be a Noctu? I jump up, fling open the door, and in that moment, I hear a heart-rending scream, as if someone's insides are being crushed.

I freeze. I can't move. I see a woman lurch out of the room that Chloe just took the baby into. She has a little bundle in her arms. At first glance, it looks like a doll. So tiny, pale... and lifeless.

Tears well up in my eyes when I hear the mother's despair. She sinks to the floor. Nurses rush to help her and take the newborn from her arms. They try to resuscitate it. A doctor arrives on the scene and takes over the chest compressions. Doors open, and other new mothers peer out, but they go straight back into their rooms on the instructions of the nurses. The mother sits on the ground beside her baby, watching the doctor, who finally gives up.

"I'm sorry," he says. It seems to take the young woman a while to comprehend. Then, she picks up the tiny body, holds the baby close, and weeps. It breaks my heart. She screams in anguish, rocks back and forth with the child in her arms, gasps for air like a drowning person, and finally faints and collapses. The doctor quickly attends to her, taking the dead child and handing it to Chloe, who places it in the buggy.

She says coolly, "I'll take the little one next door until Ms. Irving wakes up."

The doctor nods. The young mother is lifted and carried to her room. An eerie stillness descends over the ward. The hairs on the back of my neck stand on end. My senses are numbed, and I can't think. The horror I've just witnessed is too terrible.

As if in a trance, I follow Chloe, and although my instincts warn me not to, I quietly open the door. Chloe stands over the buggy and does something I'll probably never forget.

She strokes the dead baby's pale face and says, "There was no other way. As sad as it is, some lives must be cut short."

She places her hand deliberately on the little

one's head and suddenly a golden light radiates through the child's skin. Chloe pulls back her hand a little, and the light follows it – a fine, glistening thread, very short. She pulls this thread of light all the way out of the little body, and the glow that was so intense, warm, and golden only a moment ago begins to darken and fade. Chloe winds the strange gray strand of light around her wrist, and it sinks into her skin and disappears.

"Rest in peace," she says, glancing again at the dead child.

I feel sick. I quietly close the door behind me. My legs feel weak, and I sway, feeling as if I'm about to throw up. I need to get out of here. As fast as possible. If Chloe finds me here... I stagger along the wall, supporting myself on it, and pray that Chloe doesn't suddenly appear.

Finally, I reach the stairwell, wrench open the door, and stagger through it. Then, I slump and weep silent tears. Could I have saved that baby? I shouldn't have left it in Chloe's hands. Those are the thoughts that keep running through my mind, and I keep hearing the mother's screams, which will probably haunt me forever.

Chapter 33

I have no recollection of returning to school. My feet must have automatically taken the familiar route. They knew my mind needed a break and that I needed to get somewhere safe where I could let the tears flow.

I traipse down the corridor as if in a trance, not even aware of where I am. I hear sounds all around me and register the vague outlines of people. Am I at school? What does it matter, anyway?

Something touches my shoulder, but I keep walking. I feel a hand on me again, but I shake it off.

Now there are two hands on my arms holding me still. I slowly lift my head and look into a familiar face.

"Teresa? What the hell is up with you?"

I stare into that face, the striking features, the green eyes smoldering and shooting sparks. Yes, I know those eyes, and the storm raging in them is familiar too.

"Ayden," I observe, and my voice sounds distant and strange.

He nods. "Come on, let's get you out of here."

He takes my hand, puts his other arm around my waist, and leads me away. I don't know how long we walk. A few minutes? Hours?

He opens a door and closes it again behind me, then he steers me toward a soft bed, and I let myself sink down on it. Ayden kneels in front of me, holds my hands, and looks up at me. He gently tucks a strand of hair behind my ear. My skin begins to tingle, and I feel the warmth returning to my body.

"Where were you? What happened? You look terrible if you don't mind me saying."

His hands grasp both of mine again and squeeze them, imparting strength and warmth.

My lips won't move at first, but then I hear myself say, "The hospital."

He nods slowly and doesn't take his eyes off me. "And something happened there?"

I nod.

"Was it a Noctu?"

"I... I think so," I murmur. "She... she killed a baby."

The tears begin to flow again. They pour out of me as if a dam has burst. Sobbing, I lean forward, and Ayden catches me. He puts his arms around me, holds me tight, and rubs my back. He doesn't say a word; he's just there, holding me – the anchor that keeps me from being swallowed up by this madness.

I tell him everything. At first, the words come out haltingly, then my speech accelerates, and the sentences come thick and fast as I describe the way Chloe took the golden light from that little person – the thread that I assume was its dying breath.

Ayden lets go of my hands. The tension in him is palpable.

"What..." I don't finish my sentence. He looks at me so piercingly that I quickly fall silent.

"This Chloe..." he says. "You're absolutely sure she put her hand on the child's head and then you saw the light?"

I nod, and Ayden leaps to his feet.

"I need to go to my father," he mutters.

I don't know what's going on, but I stand up and follow him.

"What are you talking about? Are you planning to go there with the other hunters because she's a Noctu? You can't attack her in a hospital."

"If my suspicions are correct," he says, "then she's no Noctu."

With that, he flings open the door and charges down the corridor.

I follow him without hesitation. We both head to the principal's office. Ayden's so fast that I can hardly keep up on my injured ankle. My mind is in turmoil. I don't know what's going on. But I have a definite sense that something pivotal has just happened.

Ayden runs past the secretary without saying a word, throws open the door to his father's office, and goes inside. Mr. Collins looks up from his desk in surprise.

"Ayden? What is it?"

"Teresa was just in San Francisco General Hospital. One of the nurses, by the name of Chloe, just took a thread of destiny from a dead infant in the maternity ward." He looks at me, and there's something in his eyes that I can't describe. "Teresa appears to have the ancient gift. She can see the threads and was able to identify a goddess of destiny."

I gasp and stare at him. "Goddess of destiny?"

His father jumps up. "There's no time to lose. Did the goddess – this Chloe person – see you? Does she know she was being watched?"

I shake my head and still have no idea what's going on.

"Then our chances aren't bad. I hope the Noctu aren't tracking her too." Mr. Collins thumps the desk with his fist and smiles. "We've finally got one in our sight, after all this time." He picks up the phone and says to Ayden, "I'll send out several hunters. You should be ready too. She won't get away from us – we'll make sure of it. Good work!"

I don't know if his praise includes me. Ayden and I leave the office. I'm more confused than ever.

"What the hell is a goddess of destiny?"

Ayden looks at me for a moment.

"They're not human – if they were, they'd have a heart and wouldn't cause us so much suffering. They're worse than any Noctu, and they have very special powers. It's our job to stop them. When we find one, we have to apprehend and destroy them. And that's exactly what we're about to do." His eyes are cold and dark. He looks so unapproachable, so distant that it almost frightens me. "And you'll stay here!" he adds, then turns and hurries away.

I'm left standing in the corridor with a pounding heart. There's one thing I'm sure of: whatever it is I'm caught up in is about to change my life forever.

Chapter 34

I couldn't, of course. How could I? I guess I should have listened to Ayden and stayed behind. But I want to understand what all this is about.

A goddess of destiny. I still have no idea what that is, but I'm going to find out. That's why I'm here. And Chloe's a friend of my mother's. What if she's done something to her?

After the conversation with Ayden, I went to my room and tried to put it out of my mind. But it was impossible. I can't stand being kept in the dark.

I hurry toward the hospital, which is already visible in the distance. Where are the hunters right now? How do they hope to apprehend Chloe without creating a scene? I have no idea, but I'll soon see.

I keep walking purposefully, hoping I'm not too late. But I left quickly, and the hunters will have needed time to prepare themselves.

I'm aware of Yoru following me and hiding behind shrubs, cars, and houses. Now and again, I see a bright streak as he runs to the next hiding place.

As I turn my attention back to the street, an arm wraps around my waist. I cry out in fright, but I'm quickly dragged behind the wall of a house.

"Damn it!" I yell.

The arm lets go of me. Noah takes a step back, holding up his hands apologetically.

"I didn't mean to scare you. But the street up ahead and the hospital are teeming with hunters. And believe me, you don't want to show your face there right now."

"Oh yeah? And why not?" I snap.

"Because a whole battalion of them has just stormed the place. I assume that's also why you're here. But trust me, if you interfere with their operation, whatever it is, then..." He shakes his head.

"You won't be attending that school much longer."

I take a deep breath and glance at the hospital. Noah could be right. I'm probably not welcome there right now. But can I let that stop me?

"You want to tell me why all those hunters are here? A big operation like this in plain view is pretty unusual for them. They're taking a big risk. I assume you know what it's about. Am I right?"

I feel his eyes on me, piercing, calculating, penetrating.

"And you think I won't be expelled for telling you?"

"If they knew you were still in contact with me, that alone would be grounds for expulsion. But they don't need to know that. But if you march straight into the hospital, they'll notice for sure."

I know he's right. Is there really no other way? I bite my lip and shake my head in resignation.

"You're probably right."

"Damn straight. So, what's going on? Are you going to tell me?" He moves a step closer, reaches out his hand and strokes my cheek. "You don't look so good. What happened?"

I swallow hard as the images flash through my mind. The events of the last few hours are so serious, so abysmal, that I'm struggling to believe them. I slowly shake my head.

Noah looks at me sadly and nods. "You still don't trust me."

I quickly look up and the expression on his face pierces my heart.

"It's... it's not that," I hear myself say, though I don't know why. Is that true? Do I trust Noah? He's supposed to be my enemy. But I have to admit that, in a way, I do. He was there for me and helped me on several occasions. And there are times when he seems totally genuine. But I'm still wary of him.

"It's okay," he says with a smile that's supposed to comfort me. "I just hope you can trust me one day."

He reaches out and tenderly strokes my hair and my cheek.

"I... I... I'm sorry," I stammer.

"Don't be. Your secrets are safe with me."

I laugh and shake my head. "What secrets?"

"For example, your special ability," he says.

I stare at him in shock.

"I always felt you were exceptional. But I never would have guessed you possessed one of the ancient gifts. They're very rare."

"What are you talking about?"

First Ayden and now Noah. Everyone seems to know more about my abilities than I do.

"You don't need to hide it anymore. I know."

He cocks his head and studies my face. "Or are you saying you actually have no idea what's up with you?"

"Spit it out," I demand.

He shakes his head in disbelief. "You can see destiny threads. Every person has one of these threads from birth. The threads vary in length depending on their life expectancy. Those lights you keep seeing..."

"... aren't vitreous opacity. They're destiny threads," I finish.

Noah nods.

I've had this ability since I was a child, but then it gradually disappeared. As if it became dormant in order to grow into the fully-fledged ability it was always meant to be.

"There used to be a lot of Tempes and Noctu with special abilities. Some were able to sense magic, which was useful in figuring out where and when a fight would take place. Others didn't need to rely on the power of their key spirits because they had magical powers themselves. They could move objects with their minds or even transport themselves from one place to another. And then, there were those with clairvoyant powers. And of course, the ones who could see the threads. That ability was important, but not always easy to live with."

"I can see how long the thread is," I summarize, "and know whether someone has a long or a short life ahead of them."

Noah nods again. "You didn't know any of this?"

I shake my head slowly. "Thank you for telling me."

Noah studies my face, as if he's not sure he's done the right thing. His words echo in my head. I think of all the special gifts he mentioned. One in particular grabs my attention.

"Are there also non-key carriers who have those abilities? For example, clairvoyance?"

Noah nods. "The Noctu and the Tempes are basically no different from other people. Except that they have odeon, which is a prerequisite for becoming a key carrier. But odeon's not a prerequisite for those gifts, so non-key carriers can also have them. But they're rare these days, in us and in ordinary humans."

I take a moment to digest this. "Are people with odeon always discovered by the Tempes or the Noctu?"

"I'd say so. Both sides put a lot of effort into that, keeping close tabs on the relatives of key carriers so they can show up at just the right time."

So Kate most likely has clairvoyant powers. And if there were key carriers in her family, then she and her parents would be on the radar. In which case, her special gift may also have come to light. But so far, it doesn't seem as if anyone's keeping tabs on her. So I can probably assume she's not a potential key carrier. Still, I need to keep an eye on her.

That's basically good news, right? It means she can get on with her life as usual. She never needs to know about our world. At least, that's what I hope. And I'll do everything in my power to ensure she gets to lead a normal life.

"Can you... tell me anything about the goddesses of destiny?"

He stares at me, and I see the hesitation in his eyes. Noah knows things about them, I can tell. But he shakes his head.

"Not now," he says. He looks up, and in that moment, I notice a number of people coming out of the hospital. But I'm too far away to see if they have someone in their custody.

"I gotta go." Noah takes out his key and opens a door in the air. "Take care, Teresa," he says in a husky voice. He looks at me with concern, then disappears.

Chapter 35

I rub my tired eyes and try to concentrate on Mr. Klein's class. A pretty arduous task because I was awake half the night. I spent most of yesterday trying to find information on the goddesses of destiny. By the time I got back, I'd missed all my morning classes and training had already started, so I couldn't show up there – not even to talk to my friends. Instead, I went online and then to the hunters' library. Considering students have access to that, it was hardly surprising that I couldn't find anything there either. In the end, I pinned my hopes on seeing Ayden and asking him how the operation went. In vain – he didn't return.

"What's up with you today?" Lucia asks, gently nudging me with her elbow. "Sleepless night?"

I just nod and rest my head on my arms again. That's how tired I am.

At lunch, I keep a lookout for Ayden, which my friends don't fail to notice.

"Looking for someone?" Max asks.

"I need to talk to Ayden," I say, and Max raises her eyebrows.

"What about? Have you guys had another tiff?"

"No, it's about a school thing," I reply evasively, but I can hear how unconvincing it sounds.

They both exchange a doubtful glance.

"Maybe we can help," suggests Max.

I don't know what to say.

"Have you read much about mythology?" I ask, thinking back to my online research.

"Er... no. Why would we?" asks Lucia.

"Uh, I'm thinking about writing a history essay about immigrants. Obviously, religion and old belief systems are a part of that. It turns out mythologies from different countries have a lot of similarities. For example, did you know there are so-called goddesses of destiny in Greek, Roman, Germanic, Slavic, and Etruscan mythology?"

"Okay," says Lucia after some hesitation. She looks baffled and seems to be waiting for me to say more. When I don't, she asks, "But surely you're not going to write an essay about mythology now?" She exchanges another confused glance with Max. "That's pretty far removed from the topic of San Francisco. Don't you think?"

"I guess you're right. I just thought it was interesting, and I was wondering if you knew anything about that aspect of mythology. Stuff like gods, immortality, goddesses of destiny, supernatural abilities..."

Max leans back in her seat and smiles. "Oh right, now I get it. Because some of the stuff in our world is supernatural. You're wondering if that's where they originated and whether some of the myths could be true."

I nod, and Lucia puts a comforting arm around my shoulders.

"I can tell you one thing for sure. Our life, our world, has nothing to do with old myths and definitely didn't originate there."

Her expression is full of pity, and I can't stand it. But at least now I know: neither of them has ever heard of the goddesses of destiny. Their existence is evidently kept secret from the students, just like the hunters' missions.

"What exactly were you going to ask Ayden?" Max probes. "I doubt he's an expert on the subject."

At that moment, I see him enter the cafeteria, and I instantly jump up. Without another word, I rush over to Ayden. Before he's even joined the line to be served, I grab his arm and drag him out of the cafeteria with me. I steer him into another corridor and glance around cautiously, but we're alone.

"Where were you yesterday? I waited up half the night for you."

Ayden raises an eyebrow. "Okay."

I roll my eyes. "Just tell me – what happened yesterday? Did you find Chloe?"

He folds his arms in front of his chest and regards me with that aloof expression that I can't stand.

"You don't need to worry about her."

I'm stumped. "What's that supposed to mean? Can't you speak plainly for once?"

"Putting it plainly: it's none of your business. You should never have been dragged into that. Students aren't supposed to know about those creatures. And it's not your job to deal with them. We know what needs to be done and how to handle them. The last thing we need is outsiders getting involved."

My jaw drops. What the hell? Why is he trying to shut me out?

"I'm the one who found Chloe. Without me, you wouldn't even know about her. I deserve to know what happened and what you're planning to do with her."

Ayden's eyes bore into mine. They look cold and distant. Finally, he gives a loud sigh.

"We have her. That's all you need to know."

Then he turns and walks off.

I stay rooted to the spot. They have Chloe. What does that mean? And what are they going to do with her? I feel a band of fear tighten around my ribcage, making it hard to breathe. What are they planning to do?

For the rest of the afternoon, I'm totally distracted, wondering what I should do. At training, I can't focus and struggle to even send my odeon to Yoru, so I use the time to run and train on the fitness equipment. I'm so relieved when the class finally ends and I can shower and go back to my room.

But now, I'm clear about one thing: I have to do something. I can't live with the uncertainty. I need someone to talk to me, to tell me the truth. And

I need to see Chloe. I can't expect any help from Ayden. But I think of someone else I could turn to.

I hurry to the hunters' wing and look for Ty. He's sitting with a few friends in one of the common rooms and looks puzzled when I storm in. But then, a smile spreads across his face.

"Teresa, what are you doing here?"

"I need to talk to you. Preferably right now. It's important."

"Oh, okay."

He casts a bewildered look at the others, then stands up and follows me out into the corridor. We walk a short way.

"What's it about? Did Ayden do something stupid?"

I'm not sure if I should be worried that everyone assumes all my problems lead back to Ayden.

"No," I say. "It's about the goddess of destiny."

Ty stops in his tracks, and his expression is suddenly serious. The lightheartedness disappears from his face and is replaced by something hard and unyielding.

"Teresa, I'm not allowed to talk to you about her."

"Why not? She was my mother's colleague – her friend even. I need to know more about her and figure out if she did anything to my mom, or if she was planning to. And I also want to know how she knew my great aunt. Please tell me what the deal is with the goddesses of destiny."

I look at him beseechingly, but Ty shakes his head.

"I can't, Teresa. Really. But I'm sure your mother's fine."

"Why? What makes you so sure? Ty, I'm not giving up. Either you help me, or I'll search for her myself. I'm pretty sure she's still here. I mean, the hunters live at this school, so there's probably no place that's more secure. It would make sense to bring her straight here."

"You want to go looking for her?" The horror is written all over his face.

"No one can stop me. I'll find her eventually."

Ty shakes his head. "No, you won't. If you try, you'll just turn a lot of people against you and get yourself expelled. Teresa, I'm begging you, don't do this."

"You don't understand. I have to see her. I need to talk to her so I can understand all this. She was in my house. She befriended my mother. I can't just let it go. I need closure."

Ty runs his hands over his face, takes a deep breath, and turns away from me for a moment.

"Teresa, do you have to drag me into this shit?"

"I'm asking for your help, but no one's forcing you. I'll find a way with or without you."

"No, I'm sorry, but you won't. You have absolutely no idea." He sighs again, pauses, and runs his hand furiously through his hair. Finally, he says, "You do exactly what I tell you. Do you understand? I'll take you to see her. You'll have two minutes to get your answers, but that's all."

I nod. "Thank you, Ty."

He shakes his head. "I must be insane, seriously. I must have completely lost my mind to get mixed up in this shit." He groans quietly and then says, "I'll come get you tonight. Be ready."

I nod and watch him stride back down the corridor. Tonight. I'm going to see Chloe again. I'll get to ask my questions.

Chapter 36

I've been pacing up and down my room for hours. It's one in the morning, and Ty still hasn't shown up. Will he still come? Or did he get cold feet? Whatever he's decided, I'm clear about one thing: I'm going in search of Chloe tonight. I need to find out more about her, and for that, I need to see her. I'm responsible for the fact that they found her. I can't help wondering how she's doing. What have they done with her? I just can't get these questions out of my head.

The knock on my door is so quiet that at first,

I wonder if I just imagined it. But I hurry to the door, fling it open, and find myself looking into Ty's face. He's not smiling; there's no mischief in his eyes – just this serious, tense expression. It's his way of making it clear to me how dangerous this situation is that I'm about to throw myself into.

"Come on, hurry up!"

No questions about whether I'm sure and no unnecessary warnings. We've already said everything there is to say.

The hallways and corridors are already familiar to me, but right now, they feel pretty spooky. It must be my nerves because I've come this way before at night without feeling a cold prickle like an icy hand on the back of my neck.

We walk silently along the corridors and reach the hunters' wing. We head for a stairwell, and, to my surprise, we don't head downstairs. Instead we go up one level. Ty's watching me out of the corner of his eye and must have noticed my doubtful expression.

"What? You figured we have her locked up in some dungeon in the catacombs under the school?"

He's pretty much hit the nail on the head. I shrug. "I don't have a lot of experience with the incarceration of supernatural beings. So I'm sorry if my expectations rely too heavily on what I've seen in movies."

He grins impishly, which does me a world of good and softens the tension a little.

We don't go all the way up but turn instead into a corridor with several doors leading off it. Ty stops in front of one of them, and I glance around in astonishment.

"Here?"

It looks so normal – similar to the wing I live in. Ty nods.

"There are no guards or anything?"

"I took care of that," he says cryptically, taking a key out of his pocket.

"Where did you get that? I assume not every hunter has access to this room."

"I'm not just any hunter. But you're right. Not everyone has a key. I had to stick my neck out pretty far to get it." He shrugs and inserts it in the lock. "You remember what we agreed?"

I nod and swallow hard. He gives me a penetrating stare, and I feel cold sweat break out on my back. What awaits me behind this door? I'm about to find out because Ty's turning the key and pushing the door open. I slowly enter with Ty close behind me.

Nothing I see matches the image I had in my

head. Everything looks... normal, but only at first glance. A small plain room, curtains over the windows, a lamp on a nightstand beside a bed with a dark colored bedspread, a wooden cupboard with rosette handles, shelves on the wall containing a few books. And in the middle of the room is a person sitting on a wooden chair. Her skin looks pallid in the diffuse lamplight. Her face is directed at the floor, and her dark hair hangs down over it. Her posture is upright and somehow unnatural. I do a double take and see that her hands and legs are tied to the chair. The ropes that bind her look strange. Am I imagining it, or are they emitting a silvery glow?

Ty has closed the door and is now standing against the wall.

"You have two minutes," he reminds me.

This snaps me out of my trance. My mouth is extremely dry, and I've forgotten what I wanted to say.

"I should have taken your presence more seriously," I hear Chloe say in a voice that sounds totally unfamiliar. She turns her head very slowly toward me, and I look into her eyes, which are now so dark it's as if they want to devour me. "It was a mistake to underestimate you."

I swallow hard. "Have you done something to

my mother? Why did you befriend her?"

Chloe tilts her head back, looks at the ceiling, and takes a deep breath.

"Creatures like me aren't supposed to have friendships or relationships of any kind. But Maggie just wouldn't let up. So, in the end, I gave in. It was only supposed to be a little diversion. But that turned out to be a serious mistake."

I can't believe what I'm hearing. She was only faking it with my mom. None of it meant anything to her. I inhale deeply and ask my next question.

"You... knew my great aunt, right? Tell me how you knew her."

She sighs deeply again before replying.

"I should have trusted my instincts and disappeared. But I guess I'd become careless after all those years." Another sigh. "There's no use beating myself up over it now. It is what it is, and I have to accept my mistake."

"Answer me, please," I demand.

She turns her face toward me again. Her expression is so creepy that I instinctively take a step back.

"Yes, you should be afraid," she murmurs. "You've gotten yourself mixed up in something you'll wish you stayed out of. But it's too late now. Frida paid a high price for her curiosity. Will it be the same for you?" She twists her neck and grins menacingly at me. "Your fate was sealed long ago. Just like mine."

"What... what's that supposed to mean?" I ask. "Did you do something to Frida? Was she not even sick? Or did you manipulate her destiny? Can you do that?"

I think about the information I found online. A goddess of destiny can determine the course of a life. Was she involved in determining mine?

She shakes her head wryly. "If that were the case, I wouldn't have made such a stupid mistake."

What's she talking about? I don't know what she means. I cautiously step closer and say, "Answer me properly! What have you done?" I need an explanation, so I move a little closer, kneel down in front of her, and look straight into her cold eyes. "What did you do to that baby? Why are you even here?"

Chloe snorts derisively. Her expression changes, darkens, becomes so cold and menacing that it takes my breath away. She looks past me at the door, and a grin spreads across her lips. Ty turns and glances at the door, but I'm only vaguely aware of him. All my senses are focused on Chloe. Suddenly, all the ropes around her body snap. Her skin turns deathly pale, as if the act of freeing herself has cost her all her strength. Moving as fast as lightning, she grabs my wrist and squeezes. I scream in fright, try to leap back, but Chloe's holding me tight. Her chilly breath brushes my face as she says, "Watch. Watch very closely!" Then, she suddenly lets go of me. A golden beam of light appears in her hand. It hisses through the air like a flashing blade, so fast that I don't even have time to fall backward. The blade hits its mark, and suddenly everything is bathed in red.

I just stare at Chloe and watch as she commanded me to. I have no choice. It's as if I'm paralyzed; dumbstruck by the horror in front of me. The blood is still spurting from her thin snow-white neck.

The door opens, and people stream in. I hear voices. Someone pulls me to my feet. But I keep staring at Chloe, who's bleeding out before my very eyes, a hideous smile on her lips.

"Watch. Watch very closely," her words echo in my head.

There's nothing worst she could have done to me. Does she hold me responsible for her capture and therefore her death? Is that what she's trying to tell me? This is the only way she could escape her tormentors.

Chapter 37

I'm standing in the principal's office. I feel sick, and I keep watching Chloe die over and over in my head. My heart's racing, and all I want to do is crawl into a corner and surrender to my emotions and the horror of it all. But I'm here. Mr. Collins sits behind his desk, his hands clasped together, looking at me sternly. Beside me, Ty looks as wretched as me, bracing himself for what's to come.

There are two men present whom I don't know. And Ayden. He's leaning against the wall, arms folded across his chest, looking angrier than I've ever seen him. And it's no wonder! Tracking down a goddess of destiny is far from easy, and then she takes her own life – right in front of me.

"I'm sure I don't need to tell you what a grave mistake you've both made," Mr. Collins begins. He looks back and forth between me and Ty.

"It wasn't Teresa's fault," Ty says quickly. "It was my idea. It wouldn't have occurred to her if it weren't for me, and she had no way of getting to the..."

Mr. Collins holds up a hand. "Save your breath. I know Miss Franklin well enough to guess what her role was in all of this. But I'm surprised you allowed yourself to be swayed by her – a highly trained hunter like you." He shakes his head in disappointment. "We'll discuss the consequences later."

Now he addresses me. "The death of the goddess is a great loss to us all. As I'm sure you're now aware, one of the Tempes' tasks is to find them before the Noctu do and apprehend them so they no longer pose a danger to humans. If too many people find out about this – including the students – not only would it make our work considerably more difficult, it would also incite fear and possibly result in panicked behavior, which won't serve anyone."

"You mean, because the goddesses determine our lives?"

I have no idea whether the old myths are true, but surely they can't be too far off the mark.

Mr. Collins scrutinizes me for a while. Eventually, he nods, which makes the two men beside him flinch visibly.

"That's correct in a sense, or rather, it may have been true in the past." He looks at me, seems to reflect on something for a moment, then leans forward and continues, "There were once three goddesses. Clotho spun the threads of life and wove destiny into them. She determined the course of a life and imbued it with happiness and suffering. The second, Lachesis, determined the length. The third was called Atropos. She cut the threads and thereby determined the manner of death. The home of the goddesses used to be in a temple in the Odyss. It was their world, the place they resided. Humans revered them, prayed to them, and feared them. But at some point, humans turned away from them, wanting to determine their own destinies and choose their own gods to believe in. Humans hunted the goddesses of destiny and tried to kill them. Sometimes, they succeeded. But the goddesses are part of life and can't be exterminated.

They're continuously reborn. Humans quickly realized this. But they also discovered that, if a goddess died an unnatural death, it took longer for her to be reborn. And she lost some of her power. If a goddess died a natural death, she passed on her power and knowledge to the next generation.

"The goddesses had to find a way to protect themselves. So they used some of their power to create the key spirits. They also imbued the keys with some of their magic and distributed them among the few humans who were still faithful to them. These became key carriers, protectors of the goddesses of destiny. These people came to their aid and prevented other humans from attacking them. But over time, things changed. Humans completely forgot the goddesses, dismissing them as a myth and rebelling against their prewritten destinies. The disposition of the goddesses that held sway at this time became increasingly sinister. Possibly because the murder of their predecessors had diminished their powers and contaminated the purity of their spirits. In any case, these goddesses were not the same as their predecessors. They had only one aim: seeking revenge on humanity for rejecting them and striving for self-determination. The goddesses wanted to inflict suffering. They actually took pleasure in watching their victims suffer. So, they wove great knowledge into some threads, setting humanity on a path of progress. The world became more complex, and life became harder. Disease, war, megalomania – this was all brought about by the destiny threads. Humanity was infected, filled with doubt and fear. They began to destroy themselves and their world.

"It soon became clear that the goddesses had to be stopped. And the key carriers recognized this. But there was one thing they couldn't agree on: one faction wanted to apprehend and kill the goddesses so their successors would become weaker and weaker. The others wanted to take their power for themselves – to capture the goddesses and use their magic for their own ends. That's how the two camps formed: the Tempes, who wanted to destroy the goddesses, and the Noctu, who didn't want their power to go to waste." Mr. Collins swallows hard. "This conflict was a terrible mistake. A kind of war broke out between the two camps. This alerted the goddesses to the danger they were in, and they seized the opportunity to flee. The Tempes and the Noctu now compete in their search for the descendants of the goddesses of destiny."

I can't believe what I'm hearing. I glance around at all the faces in the room. Ayden's arms are still folded and his eyes speak volumes – he didn't want me to know all this.

"And how do you find the goddesses?" I ask.

Mr. Collins clears his throat. "Over time, we've managed to identify certain clues, signs that make it easier for us to track them down. For one thing, they have a tendency toward magic and are often born into families with a history of special abilities. However, we've observed that, as soon as the godly powers become apparent, there's often a change in their personality. But that's another story. In any case, we keep a close eye on certain families. Our intention is to intervene in a timely manner to prevent the personality change, in the hope of working together with the goddess so that we don't need to resort to killing her."

I swallow. His words echo in my head. It all sounds so surreal.

"Why are you telling me all this?"

Mr. Collins looks at me with his piercing blue eyes. "It's become clear that you know far too little about our world, which potentially puts you in great danger. I've shared information with you that's normally withheld from our students. I expect you to keep this confidential, and I also hope you'll stay out of these matters in future. Leave the goddesses of destiny to those who are trained to deal with them."

"What... what about Chloe? Which goddess was she, and what did she do to that baby?"

Mr. Collins clears his throat and searches for the right words. "She was a Lachesis. She determined the length of the threads. That's what she was doing in the hospital. She gave some of the newborns their threads. She doesn't need to be there in person to do that, but as I said, they're weaker than they used to be. The closer they are to the person whose destiny they want to influence, the easier it is for them. During those periods when a goddess' powers haven't fully reawakened to the point where she can carry out her task, it's left up to nature to spin the threads." Mr. Collins takes a deep breath and swallows. The next part is hard for him to say. "And the baby you saw... Lachesis had already given the infant a very short thread – causing a great deal of suffering. When the newborn reached the end of its thread, she took it back."

I try to process all this, but it's impossible. Goddesses who influence people's lives? Who take pleasure in causing grief and torment?

"Thank you for telling me all this," I say. My eyes wander to Ayden, whose whole body appears to be electrically charged. He still hasn't said a word.

"We should start discussing the consequences,"

chimes in one of the men who have stood by in silence up to this point. His aversion to me is obvious from the expression on his face. "She persuaded a hunter to take part in a serious crime."

"She didn't persuade me," Ty insists, his face still very pale. "I organized it all without her knowledge and then took her there."

"You're saying this was all your idea and that you were just trying to impress the young lady?"

Ty nods without hesitation.

I can't believe he's trying to take all the blame.

"It wasn't..."

I break off mid-sentence when I see Ayden's eyes flash at me. He shakes his head very slowly, and I shut my mouth.

"May I introduce these two gentlemen?" asks Mr. Collins. "This here..." he indicates the man on his right, who's tall and has a full beard and cold blue eyes. "...is Mr. Fabrici. He's a member of the Council as is Mr. Cunningham." He nods toward the much shorter man, who's a little younger, with curly red hair. He too looks at me with obvious distaste.

"However it may have happened, there's no denying that the young lady got involved in something she should have never witnessed. Regardless of how she pulled it off, she appears to have a significant influence over Mr. Waydon. I hate to think what she may have promised in return."

I wince. What's the guy implying?! "What do you take me...?"

Ayden interrupts me. "Mr. Waydon and Miss Franklin are just friends, I assure you. This was all the result of curiosity," he explains in an astonishingly calm tone. "And it was Miss Franklin who drew our attention to the goddess of destiny. So it's only natural that she'd want to know how our operation went. I realize she should have stayed out of it and there have to be repercussions, but they should be appropriate. We should keep in mind the good work Mr. Waydon has done in his numerous deployments in the past. He's an incredible asset to the hunters. And Miss Franklin..." That piercing stare again. My pulse races, and I swallow. "Let's just say there's more to her than meets the eye."

"Ayden's right," agrees Mr. Collins. "Miss Franklin possesses one of the ancient gifts. She can see the destiny threads. The blood of our forefathers runs in her veins, which must not be underestimated. Her ability could be of great benefit to us."

The two Council members exchange a brief glance.

"We'll consult with Mr. Collins now."

We're dismissed. Ty, Ayden, and I leave the room and quickly distance ourselves from the office.

"Phew, that was a close call," says Ty, running his hand through his hair.

"Close call? They'll impose a curfew for sure, and you can count yourself lucky if that's all you get," says Ayden. "How could you be so stupid?!"

"If we students weren't kept in the dark about everything, it wouldn't have come to this. But all the secrets..."

Ayden interrupts me. "My father just explained to you why that's necessary. I don't get why you can't just leave things alone. You're always sticking your nose where it's not wanted and putting yourself in danger."

"Oh, yeah? You're forgetting that without me you'd have never found Chloe."

"And you're forgetting that you didn't even know who or what she was."

"Okay, okay, guys," Ty intervenes, holding up his hands. "I guess I'll leave you two alone. You seem to have a few things to get off your chest."

"I wish I could be as laid back as you," Ayden grumbles. "Do you realize how close you came to being stripped of your rank?"

Ty puts a comradely arm around Ayden's shoulders. "Oh, as long as I have advocates like you, what can go wrong?"

He gives Ayden a friendly punch and walks away. Ayden and I head back to the residential wing. Silence prevails, but you could cut the tension in the air with a knife.

"What'll happen to Chloe now?" I ask boldly.

Ayden raises his eyebrows. "Really? More questions? I thought we just established that your curiosity could get you killed?" He pauses. "She'll be reborn in another body. As another person, obviously, but with the same abilities. There'll soon be a young Lachesis."

I swallow hard and picture Chloe again, tied to the chair. Her words echo in my ears and I close my eyes briefly to push away the image. So much makes sense now. Including her intense reaction when I asked her about Frida and told her we were related. She must have known Frida was a Tempes and feared that I might be too. I recall the golden light, the blade that grew out of her hand, and the way she ran it across her throat. The blood, so much blood...

"I'll never get the images out of my head," I mutter, glancing at Ayden.

He sighs and says, "She would have been killed sooner or later. We need to weaken their descendants so they can't harm humans. It's the only way, and it's our duty. Her death will prevent a lot of suffering even though she'll be reborn eventually. But we'll search for her successor too, and we'll find her." He looks at me again. "That's not your responsibility, so don't worry about it. What happened was right, and her death is the only logical outcome."

We reach Ayden's room, and he opens the door. I don't understand how he can be so callous about all this.

"I can't just put it all behind me."

There's no warmth in his expression, no compassion. He just stands there, cold and distant.

"You have to if you want to stay here with us."

I know he's right, but it's so hard to swallow. How can I? Someone just died because of me. "Watch. Watch very closely" Chloe said to me. She knew I'd be haunted by her image forever. That was her punishment because I'm responsible for her death.

Chapter 38

E mpty hospital corridors stretch out in front of me. The overhead lighting casts a milky, ghostly light. The only sound is the echo of my solitary footsteps. I keep turning and randomly opening doors, my heart pounding. Where is everyone? And where's my mother? I came to visit her, but now I realize something's really wrong here.

Suddenly, I hear a noise – a quiet sing-song whisper that floods through my body and makes my blood run cold. I'm approaching the source. A door is ajar. I slowly push it open to see someone sitting on a chair in the center of the room. She has her back to me, but I recognize her figure, her hair, her eerie voice. My instincts tell me to run away as fast as I can. I don't want to see that face, don't want to hear the voice that's burning into my brain. But my feet have developed a life of their own and keep bringing me closer to the woman.

I'm breathing hard, as if I've just been sprinting. My heart's pounding in my chest, and my eyes are wide open, as if trying to capture every detail of Chloe's hideous expression. Her legs are tied to the chair, but her arms are free and they're holding a small baby. She rocks the tiny creature back and forth, singing a lullaby in a voice so chilling it makes my skin crawl. Suddenly, Chloe stops rocking the baby; its clear blue eyes fly open, and it whimpers.

"They'll figure it out, little one. Believe me. You can't keep up the charade and hide behind a lie forever," she purrs, stroking the baby's downy little head. "You'll die in the end, like all the rest. But until then, I won't let you forget what you've done to me."

She flings back her head, and her eyes bulge in their sockets as she wraps her hands around the tiny body and squeezes it. The baby screams in pain, but Chloe doesn't stop. She yells at me, "Watch! Watch very closely!"

I cry out and jump. Something nudges me and then nestles up to me, trying to soothe me. It's Yoru, I realize. I finally become aware of my surroundings. I'm in my room, safe. Nothing happened. It was just that dream again.

More than two weeks have passed since Chloe died, and I've been plagued by this dream ever since. It's as if she's haunting me – which didn't seem entirely absurd to me at first. But Ty assured me that, while goddesses of destiny are powerful, they definitely don't haunt people as ghosts. Unfortunately, that didn't stop the harrowing dreams. It's probably my guilty conscience plaguing me. I'm partly responsible for the death of a person – if you can call her that. I saw it with my own eyes – a woman tied to a chair, who saw no other way out of her predicament than to kill herself.

Did I do the wrong thing? Was it a mistake to tell Ayden about Chloe? But I didn't know what she was at the time. And she wasn't innocent. I think of the baby again. No, Chloe definitely wasn't harmless. She was the cause of so much suffering. Is there no other way to deal with the goddesses?

The last two weeks have been hard because I wasn't allowed to leave the school premises. That was my punishment for venturing into an unauthorized area. A light punishment, I know – and I probably have Mr. Collins to thank for putting in a good word in for me. Ty's house arrest and extra training sessions were lenient too.

It's five thirty. Until recently, I wouldn't normally be awake at this time. But the nights are terrifying.

I get up, shower, and get dressed. Then, I sit on the bed with Yoru and try to focus on a book, with minimal success. I'm relieved once school starts and I'm sitting in class. At least it's a distraction. But my thoughts begin to wander again in biology as Ms. Warren is explaining an exercise on genetics. I keep seeing things in my mind's eye that I wish I could forget.

"Miss Franklin?" The voice snaps me back to reality. I look up, as if waking from a dream. Every face is turned to toward me. The teacher frowns.

"Nice to have you back with us. I was just asking which of the characteristics in question two are hereditary and why?"

I haven't even opened my book. I try to find the right page. Ms. Warren shakes her head with a pinched expression.

"If this continues, your future at this school is doubtful."

She turns away and resumes her explanation. I

bite my lip, read the textbook, and try to concentrate. But I'm soon picturing Chloe's face again.

As I'm packing up my things at the end of class, I keep glancing at Ayden. He's chatting with a couple of friends. I need to talk to him. He's the only student who knows about the goddesses of destiny. Maybe I can confide in him about what's troubling me. Maybe he's struggled with the same doubts in the past and can tell me how he copes with it all. I need to pour my heart out to someone. I can't keep battling this out on my own.

I leave the classroom with the other students. Ayden's up ahead of me, still talking to his friends and looking totally unconcerned. How can he be so relaxed after everything we've experienced? I guess he's been through this kind of thing more than once, so it's probably desensitized him. Or is he just a good actor? More likely the latter – I know from personal experience what he's capable of.

"Ayden," I call out, trying to catch up to him. "Ayden, I need to talk to you."

He continues down the corridor with his friends. It's crowded, and I can't get to him. I call out his name again, but he doesn't hear me, and finally I stop. There's no time for a conversation like this in the short gap between periods. So I give up and go to my next class, hoping I'll somehow get through the day.

At the end of afternoon training, Ayden doesn't stay back after class like he usually does. Another missed opportunity to get him alone. I wait in my room the entire afternoon and evening, repeatedly knocking on his door. I must look pretty stunned when his door finally opens and I see him standing in front of me with his arms folded.

"Teresa, what are you doing here?"

I wasn't expecting him to be here, so I don't know what to say at first. I clear my throat and stammer, "I... I wanted to talk to you."

"Yeah, I figured. I mean, you're standing at my door."

I roll my eyes. I could really do without the dumb comments right now.

"It's about Chloe," I say, trying to choose my words carefully. "I keep picturing her. I can't get her out of my head. I feel like I'm going crazy, you know? I don't know what to do. I mean, I'm partly responsible for her death and..."

"Teresa," Ayden sighs irritably. "I get that it's not easy for you. Someone died right in front of you. But you shouldn't feel guilty. She killed herself; you didn't do anything. Don't even think of them as people. She was a goddess of destiny.

She caused so much misery in the world. She took pleasure in making people suffer – every single day. It's our job to stop these creatures and protect people from them. I know it's not easy, but that's why we're here. It's what we train for." He studies my face. "And that's exactly why only the hunters and the Council are supposed to know about this stuff."

I swallow hard. "You're saying I'm an outsider who's too feeble to understand it?"

"I'm saying you have no idea how much pain they dish out and that there's nothing human about them. It's the only path open to us, but nobody's forcing you to walk it. And you need to stop worrying about it. Try to get on with your life as normal. Leave the rest up to us."

My heart tightens. Why did I even come to him? What did I expect? That he'd take me in his arms? Hold me close, stroke my hair, and tell me everything would be alright? No, I guess not. But I hoped he'd show some understanding and listen to me. Instead, he just tries to play it all down.

"I have these nightmares," I say quietly, looking up at him. One last try, which I pin all my hopes on. I need him to understand that I'm not coping. "I keep seeing Chloe. She's holding the baby in her arms, then she kills it and speaks to me. She always says the same thing. She tells me to watch her die. She hopes I'll never get the image out of my head. And that's exactly what's happening."

Ayden's quiet for a moment, then he sighs and says, "You can't let it get to you. Just remind yourself you did the right thing and that her death is a relief to all of us. It'll take some time before her successor's ready to take her place. And until then, there's basically one less goddess plaguing humanity. Her death was good and right. Just keep telling yourself that."

He just doesn't understand. I look into his green eyes, so deep and fathomless, but I find no hint of empathy in them. They're as cold and distant as polished gems. I force a smile, and he doesn't even notice how fake it is.

"Thanks, I will," I say.

I turn on my heels and go back to my room. As soon as I'm inside, I throw myself on my bed and feel the tears well up in my eyes. Ayden has lived here for so many years; he's grown up with this fight. He'll never understand my situation. But the fact that he doesn't even try...

I reach absent-mindedly for my phone, look at the darkened display, then swipe my finger across it. I check my messages, hesitate for a moment, then type, "Hey, Noah. How are you?"

The emptiest phrases I've ever written. But he replies immediately.

"You okay?"

A tear runs down my cheek, and I quickly wipe it away and reply.

"What makes you think I wouldn't be?"

"Well, for one thing, you're messaging me. You haven't done that in a long time. And you're asking how I am. You're not normally one for small talk."

I chuckle and type, "Not great. Honestly, not good at all."

"Want to talk?"

I stare at the words and weigh them up. My fingers hover above the letters. Then, they finally begin to move.

"Yes."

And it's the truth. I want to talk to him. Noah knows this world, and he's the only other person I can confide in. But I know I need to be careful. No one can find out about this.

"Should we meet outside the hospital? At 9?"

I check the time and reply, "Thanks. See you soon."

I stand up and get changed. I glance at Yoru, whose eyes look almost reproachful. Or am I imagining it? Is it just my guilty conscience? Because part of me knows that I'm about to do something that should never happen.

Chapter 39

I hang around the hospital entrance and check the time again. Just before nine. I still don't see Noah, so I pace back and forth. The cool air does me good, and I use the time to clear my head. I still have a knot in my stomach when I think about what I'm about to do. I'm acutely aware that this is something the Tempes can never find out about. This really isn't a good idea. But here I am.

Nine o'clock. I look up and see someone walking toward me. This time he resists the temptation to materialize out of nowhere and walks toward me like an everyday person. There's a faint smile on his lips. As he comes closer, I also see the look in his eyes. They're full of concern, maybe even a trace of uncertainty.

"I wasn't sure you'd actually be here."

I shrug. "Honestly, neither was I."

My words prompt a tender smile.

"I'm glad you decided to come." He glances around. "Want to take a walk?"

"Are you afraid I've lured you into a trap? Watch out, the hunters are about to jump out from behind those cars."

Noah's expression darkens, but his eyes are radiant – as honest and open as a starry sky.

"I know you well enough to know you'd never do that. I trust you."

I quickly lower my eyes and take a deep breath. How can he say that? What does he really know about me? Why does he figure he knows me so well? How much did he learn from spying on me? That's what goes through my head, but in my heart, I feel something else entirely: warmth and connection.

"Let's take a walk," he repeats.

I nod, and we move off down the road. We walk side by side for a while with no particular destination, staring at the pavement, oblivious to our surroundings.

"Yoru's gotten much better at concealing himself," Noah observes. "It took me ages to spot him."

I glance around but can't see him anywhere, which is nothing new. I'm obviously not very good at locating key spirits.

"I wouldn't know," I say. "I rarely see him when he's following me. But I've developed a kind of sense. I can feel him near me."

Noah nods as if he knows exactly what I'm talking about. "That's good. You've made a lot of progress."

"Partly thanks to you," I admit.

He waves away the compliment. "I'm happy to help. Actually, I'd rather talk than spar. But if you ever want to train, I'm up for that too."

"No thanks," I reply. "Where's Rain?"

Noah nods toward a side street on his right where several cars are parked. "He's hiding in the shadow of that wall over there."

I still can't see him. "A master of disguise," I say with a smile.

"Years of practice," says Noah, smiling warmly at me.

"Thanks for coming," I reply, swallowing back the lump in my throat.

"You may not believe it, but I'm your friend. I'm here for you if you need me. And it's okay if you don't want to talk about what's on your mind. I can understand if you still don't trust me after everything that's happened. But I'm glad you reached out to me and that we're here. Maybe it'll help take your mind off things."

I look up at him in astonishment. He's right, I realize. I can't tell him about Chloe or what happened. If I did, I could be passing on information he's not supposed to know. He's a Noctu.

"Teresa," he says quietly.

He stands still. Apparently, I'm not in command of my feet, because they take their cue from him and halt instantly.

"You don't have to confide in me if you don't want to. But I hope you feel you can open up to me because I can see you're having a hard time, and I want to be here for you."

He slowly strokes my cheek. His fingers feel warm and soft against my skin. He wipes away a tear, and I look up in surprise, unaware I was even crying. I cautiously look into his face, which is so open, kind, and warm. Right now, I see just see Noah the person, not a Noctu, not a key carrier, and definitely not an enemy. He's a friend who wants to support me, and the only person who's told me everything and has no secrets lately.

He cups my face in his hands. They feel protective, offering warmth and security. I get goosebumps. The feeling is so sweet, such a relief, so liberating. I feel more tears running down my cheeks and hear myself sobbing quietly. Noah pulls me close, wraps his arms around me, and I finally feel I'm not alone.

"Chloe's dead," I say.

Noah nods slowly. "I figured as much."

I look up in astonishment. "What? How?"

A smile flickers across his lips. "You're forgetting that I spend a lot of time in the hospital. I know more than you might think. Chloe quit with no notice. Her resignation letter said something about a new job and having to relocate quickly. Pretty implausible if you ask me, but I guess the administration took it at face value."

"But..."

He shakes his head, and his breath caresses my skin. "We had a vague suspicion about Chloe. But in the end, the Tempes got to her first."

"The Noctu search for the goddesses too," I say, recalling what Mr. Collins told me.

Noah nods. "Yes, we do."

I'm glad he doesn't try to explain anything. He just remains open.

"The Tempes found out about Chloe through me. It was my fault that she... She killed herself right in front of me, and I can't get the image out of my head. I have nightmares every night, and I keep hearing her words."

Noah tightens his embrace, and I rest my face against his shirt. I breathe in his scent. I wish we could stay like this forever. No more barriers between us, no more animosity.

"You can't blame yourself. Chloe knew what she was doing."

I know Noah's right, but I also know that Chloe saw it differently. *Watch. Watch very closely.* She was making sure I'd never forget the part I played.

"I figured you'd find out about the goddesses sooner or later. I mean, you can see the destiny threads, so it was only a matter of time before you discovered one of them."

Something comes back to me. I quickly look up, recalling something he once said to me. That time Noah attacked me and Ayden, he said, "Do you really want to continue down this path? You have no idea what that means. Just wait until you're face to face with a goddess. Maybe then you'll finally recognize the truth. I just hope I'm not wrong about you."

I pull back a little so I can look at him.

"That's why you mentioned the goddesses back then."

He knew that when I saw one I'd know what she really was and what she inflicted on humanity. And now, I realize he knew about my gift back then, or at least had a hunch. He wanted me to learn the truth about my ability.

His eyes fix on mine. They're so bright and clear, an open book, so long as I'm willing to read it.

He nods. "The goddesses of destiny were once powerful and good. Sadly, they're no longer what they once were."

He caresses my hair. His touch conveys pure solace, reassurance, and support. My heart races as I lose myself in Noah's eyes and find in them the thing I so desperately need.

"I can understand how you must feel right now. It never feels good to extinguish a life."

His words are scarcely more than a whisper, and I can see in his face the pain he carries around with him. It's not easy for him either, being forced to take a life. Even if it saves humanity from immense suffering, his soul is burdened with guilt every time. He must have already endured so much. What price has he been forced to pay for his life as a Noctu? He's seen and done things that plague him to this day, things he'll never forget. It's clear to me now that he's not the heartless murderer I once thought. He's a person just like me, who carries around this terrible anguish. And he's done horrible things – just like I have. Neither of us will ever forget them. We're more similar than I realized, and I feel closer to him than I ever expected.

I run my fingers through his hair without taking my eyes off him. Warm eyes, as open and honest as a tranquil sea. I want to sink into them and for us to share our pain.

I lean forward slightly, feel his intoxicating breath on my lips and a tingling sensation deep inside me. One last look in those eyes, then I seal his wonderful lips with a kiss. Everything in me begins to spin as I press myself harder against him and run my fingers tenderly over his chest. In this moment, we're just two wounded souls who have found one another.

- End of book 2 -

Continued in volume 3:
Rise of the Phoenix

Printed in Dunstable, United Kingdom